Maria 1"

Deseré

A Love Story of the American South

Maria McKenzie

July 28, 2019

Mary,
I hope you enjoy
my story!

Love,
Maria

Cover Art by Teresa "Terry" Hull Tolentino

Edited by Lisa McKenzie

ISBN: 1979663785
ISBN-13: 978-1979663786

For Richard, Matthew and James

ALSO BY MARIA MCKENZIE

The Governor's Sons
"Realistic, multifaceted characters make for an especially engaging novel."
Kirkus Reviews

Escape: Book One of the Unchained Trilogy
"...the book is a joy to read... A very simple, compelling and historically authentic read."
Maria Mohan, *Maria's Book Blog*

Masquerade: Book Two of the Unchained Trilogy
"If, like me, you are a fan of historical fiction -- especially when it's done with a real feel for previous eras -- then you'll love *Masquerade*..."
Robert Masello, author of *The Romanov Cross* and *Robert's Rules of Writing*

Revelation: Book Three of the Unchained Trilogy
"This book was enthralling from page one..." **Cynthia West,** *Amazon Review*

From Cad to Cadaver
"...Overall, this is a fun story and is definitely worth a read."
Paolo's Blog

Visit or contact Maria at
www.mariamckenziewrites.com

ACKNOWLEDGMENTS

Again, many thanks to the amazing Lisa McKenzie who continues to stretch me as a writer, and forces me to see beyond the surface and peel back many layers as I venture along the way. She's the the greatest writing coach ever!

Thank you to all of my incredibly talented writer friends: Andrea Rotterman, Barbara Timmins and Janet Allen. Your feedback, insight and story ideas are invaluable!

Thanks to my wonderful husband, Richard, for all of his illuminating feedback and his beautiful poetry!

Thank you to Dr. Alpen Razi of California Polytechnic State University and his 2015-2016 African Survey Class for their enthralling story ideas that enriched the plot of this story. It was my pleasure to work with Dr. Razi and write this novel as part of a project for his class.

Thank you to artist Terry Tolentino for painting such beautiful cover art!

Thanks again to Paula McKenzie Nahm, my amazing mother-in-law, for a final sharp-eyed proofreading!

Thank you to Frédéric Favray for his help and patience in assuring the accuracy of the French dialogue included in this story.

Thank you to Dr. Philip Diller for his patience and medical expertise in answering all of my medical questions.

Thanks to Patrick Bragg, my awesome brother-in-law, who led me to overcome my writer's block by suggesting a scene quite pivotal to the story.

Thank you to Dr. Cristy Robinson for her creative input and medical knowledge.

Thanks to my fantastic boys, Matthew and James, who helped me create the storyline in the underground tunnels.

"Human behavior flows from three main sources: desire, emotion and knowledge."

Plato

Prologue
1835
Beaufort, South Carolina

"Why does he insist on bringing *her* in here?" the woman hissed in a loud whisper meant to be heard.

"Whatever *she* touches, I won't buy!" the other woman said, not even attempting to whisper. "The Hinkleys ought not even allow her inside, or him either with his peculiar self!"

Jeremy Albright ignored the conversation directed at him and the little girl who held his hand, as they walked into the white frame building known as Hinkley's General Store.

While taking in the aroma of molasses and kerosene, Jeremy removed his top hat and readied himself to comfort the child. Yet he noticed she was smiling, observing her surroundings, oblivious to the rude dialogue that had come from the two ladies who looked at bolts of fabric near the front of the store where there was also an array of thread, buttons, ribbon, lace and an assortment of girls' and ladies' hats. The two women, bedecked in large bonnets and puffy-sleeved dresses, sneered as Jeremy walked by them with the dusky colored child wearing a blue cotton dress and white pantalettes.

Outfitted in a beige cutaway coat, gray waistcoat and beige trousers, Jeremy was a tall stately man in his forties who'd been considered dashing in his youth, but now merely handsome. He squeezed seven-year-old Deseré's tiny hand, signaling her to keep up with him, because her pace had slowed. But in moments she tore from his grasp, skittering toward the two ladies to get a closer look at a bonnet. The women gasped in distaste, backing away from the child, but Deseré, too distracted by the hat, seemed not to notice. Lavishly trimmed with large purple flowers and thick pink ribbons, the hat was quite a sight to behold for a little girl. "It's beautiful!" Deseré exclaimed.

The ladies grimaced as Jeremy approached his charge. He ignored them, focusing only on Deseré. The child was exuberant and a rare beauty who reminded Jeremy of his little sister Amanda, who'd died at the age of six. To Jeremy, the girl seemed to bring Amanda back to life. Taking hold of Deseré's hand he said, "Come along now, we mustn't tarry."

Deseré fell in stride next to him, but kept her glistening head of blond curls turned in the direction of the hat.

Jeremy walked to the back of the store. The heels of his short boots clicked against the hardwood as he passed by barrels filled with lamp oil, molasses and vinegar. Floor to ceiling shelves stocked with glass jars, tins, soap, candles and dishes were on all sides of the store, with long counters in front of them and a walkway in between. The counter fronts were closed, but the backs were open with space for drawers and bins that stored flour, beans, rice, tea, sugar and salt. On top of the counters were glassed-in showcases containing candy, pins and needles, and tobacco. Iron pots and pans, lanterns, buckets and shovels hung from hooks in the ceiling.

Once at the back of the store, Deseré sat with Jeremy on a wooden bench as he fitted himself with a new pair of leather boots from Charleston that came up to his knees. But she continued to gaze longingly at the bonnet toward the front of the store.

"Alright, Miss Deseré," he said playfully, "let's pay for these boots, and perhaps buy you some candy." Once back at the front of the store, Jeremy placed the boots on the counter.

"Masta Jeremy," Deseré said, "may I *please* have that bonnet?"

Bertha Hinkley, the shop owner's wife, stood at the cash drawer. "She's not worth that much!" the woman said, looking at Deseré. Mrs. Hinkley was a flat-faced woman with a small pug nose. "Bringin' that little yellow darkie in here, I'm disgusted to see her even askin' for anything! If I was you I wouldn't buy it for her, it's worth more than she'll ever amount to."

Jeremy looked down to see tears in Deseré's large blue eyes. He stooped next to her and said softly, "You're worth the world to me." Then, standing up, he said loudly to Mrs. Hinkley, and for all those in the store to hear, "We'll take that bonnet and whatever else she wants, because she's worth that and more!"

On the way home to St. Helena, Deseré proudly wore her new bonnet. The drive would be long, three hours by carriage. As Jeremy's servant George drove, Jeremy sat with Deseré on cushioned black leather seats.

With dust flying as the carriage wheels trounced over the bumpy terrain, Jeremy said, "We have lots of time for a story."

"May I read you one?" Deseré asked brightly.

"Of course." Jeremy pulled a copy of *The Hunchback of Notre Dame* from beneath his seat. "This story takes place far away in Paris, France, across the ocean. Perhaps I'll take you there one day." He opened the book. "I'll help you with all the big words."

"Masta Jeremy, you said I'm good with big words."

"So you are," Jeremy smiled, "but you don't know them

all yet."

****

That evening after supper, Deseré sat at a small table in the basement room she shared with her mother, Patsy. After admiring the prized bonnet Masta Jeremy had given her, and then giving it a thorough examination, Deseré took a pair of scissors to it and gently removed every piece of ribbon and every flower, carefully placing them in the order she'd removed them. After the bonnet was completely bare and its accouterments neatly assembled, Deseré grabbed her tiny sewing kit. In addition to needles and spools of thread, it was filled with pieces of ribbon, patches of fabric, and an assortment of buttons. With her nimble fingers, she would reassemble the bonnet and make it even more beautiful than before by using some of the baubles from her sewing kit. For a moment, Deseré thought about calling on the seamstress Addie for help, but then decided she could re-create the bonnet on her own. Smiling, she threaded a needle.

Chapter 1
Ten Years Later
Spring, 1845
St. Helena Island, South Carolina
Pleasant Wood Plantation

"William," Deseré slipped her hand through the crook of his arm, "after we get married, then what?" William was a tall man, the color of copper. He and Deseré, who was now seventeen, walked along the road near the edge of the murky blue water of Station Creek.

"Then what?" William snorted. "What do you expect?"

"I'm not sure," Deseré said.

Towering live oaks shrouded by clumps of billowy Spanish moss stood around the creek. Their branches, appearing as if sheathed by long gray hair, swayed gently in the wind. As Deseré and William strolled over a sandy road covered with bits of broken oyster shells, the dank smell of creek water filled the air. Deseré gazed adoringly at her beloved, then gripped his arm tighter, relishing the feel of him. His reddish brown skin glistened in the sun. His frame was firm and muscled and his chest broad.

"Life won't be any different." William grimaced, creasing

the features of his handsome face. His nose was long and keen like an Indian's, and his lips full. With gray-black eyes, cheekbones high and sharp, and thick black curls of hair, he was beautiful for a man, Deseré thought. He could build anything, and he was smart. He could read *and* figure. Deseré sighed dreamily, musing that William was perfect in every way.

Feeling a cool breeze brush against her cheek, she beamed, looking up at him. "But we'll be together," she said. A blue heron squawked in the distance.

"Yup."

Crestfallen by his response, Deseré gazed down for a moment. "Doesn't that make you happy?"

William stopped walking, then looked down at her and smiled. "'Course it does. You know you're the prettiest girl around."

Deseré *was* pretty, and she'd been told that countless times because of her delicate features, ocean blue eyes, sand-colored skin and flowing blond hair that resembled waves of brass intertwined with strands of spun gold. But a slave girl's beauty was more of a curse than a blessing. Thankfully, however, she'd been spared what her mother had had to endure.

"But..." William continued, then trailed off.

"But what?"

He started walking again, leading Deseré with him. She still held tight to the crook of his arm. "We could have our own lives...belong to ourselves...if..."

"If we ran away." Deseré rolled her eyes. "You gonna start that crazy talk again?"

"It ain't crazy!"

"You can't escape livin' on an island. Folks have tried but they always get caught."

"Not always," William said. "It ain't impossible, 'cause where there's a will there's a way."

"But why would you even want to escape? You got a

good masta."

William was silent for a moment as he trudged forward with her. "First off, I don't wanna belong to nobody, and second," he kicked a rock, "I don't belong here."

"What do you mean you don't belong here?"

William gazed up into the deep blue sky, watching seagulls fly freely above. "I lived in a lot a places before my last masta sold me South, and the thing is...I don't fit with these folks...and I don't want to. Bein' cut off from everything out here in these islands, black folks 'round here act like they don't know much uh nuthin' besides what's on they own plantations."

"Is that so bad?" Deseré asked.

He shoved his hands deeply into his pockets. "Guess what I'm sayin' is...I ain't never been no place where the nigguhs are as ass-backwards as they are here!"

Deseré's eyes widened. "Are you sayin' I'm—"

"No, Deseré, and you know I'm not. You live in the big house. You're sophisticated, as the white folks say. And to me...you're 'bout the onliest thing that makes life tolerable."

Deseré smiled, yet she understood his frustration. St. Helena was her home, but she'd heard Masta Jeremy explain to a visitor from Virginia who'd accused the field hands here of speaking with an inarticulate jabber, that they'd learned the ways of the whites very slowly. There weren't as many whites as negroes on the island, and because of this, the slaves' ability to speak English here were less advanced compared to slaves in the other parts of the state. They'd learned to speak from their parents and grandparents who'd been taken from Africa. So their speech sometimes seemed garbled to those from the outside.

"But don't you wanna be free?" William asked.

"I guess, but..." Deseré's eyes dropped to the ground.

"Uh-huh," William said. "Masta Albright treats you kindly. You don't have to do much of nothin' besides sit around lookin' pretty."

"That's not true! I'm a house servant, and I do plenty of work. I set the table, I clear the table, I dust, I sweep, I help with the soap makin', candle dippin', *and* I sew. I'm the best seamstress around — or, at least I will be one day."

"Uh-huh."

"I made this," she swept a hand down her pink muslin dress.

"Yup, and it don't look like servants' clothes."

"Masta Jeremy bought me the fabric. And when he buys you, we'll be at the same place, and he'll be just as nice to you as he is to me."

"Yup," William agreed, noncommittally.

"You ought to be happy knowin' you'll live here!" Deseré smiled. "Pleasant Wood lives up to its name."

And in Deseré's mind, it did. Surrounded by marshes, rivers and creeks, Pleasant Wood Plantation was located on the Sea Islands in the South Carolina Lowcountry on St. Helena Island. Although several other plantations were on the island, none were as special as Pleasant Wood, and that was because of Jeremy Albright.

"Masta Jeremy wants all his people to marry, and he never separates families. So we'll be here together as man and wife forever," Deseré said, gazing toward the big house.

It faced Station Creek and sat comfortably surrounded by a stately stand of live oaks. A three-story dwelling, the big house was T-shaped, and sheathed in white clapboard with red brick chimneys at each end. A single-story portico with four majestic columns was at the front of the house, while at the rear was a two-story balustraded porch with six square columns aligned on each floor.

Jeremy Albright's father, Elias Albright, was from Camden, South Carolina. He'd married Isabelle Finch whose family owned several plantations on the Sea Islands. Pleasant Wood on St. Helena, had been given to Isabelle when she married.

Her husband, Elias, hadn't been too particular about

owning a plantation, especially since he'd been influenced by the Quakers in his hometown who opposed slavery. However, Elias had shouldered the responsibility of Pleasant Wood to please his bride. He did his best to be a planter as well as a benevolent slaveholder, and Jeremy carried on that tradition when he inherited the plantation after his parents' deaths some twenty years earlier.

Once the three-hundred and sixty-five acre plantation with over fifty slaves became his, Jeremy continued to allocate his people large portions of land on the estate that they could work themselves for their own families.

"Masta Jeremy will give us land," Deseré said, "and he'll let you build us a fine cabin. He promised."

"A white man's promise ain't worth piss."

Deseré smacked his arm. "Masta Jeremy's promise is gold!"

"Umph. That so?"

"Yes!" Then Deseré lowered her voice. "He'll even want me to teach our youngins to read, long as we don't tell anybody off the place what we're doin'."

Long before, lots of masters had encouraged their people to attend Sunday schools that taught them to read and write. Early statutes against teaching slaves to read had been ignored when the Sunday schools began instruction. However, this practice had been abandoned about a decade earlier because of Abolitionist agitation. Now planters feared the consequences of their slaves gaining too much knowledge.

This, however, was not a concern to Jeremy Albright, and now that the Sunday schools no longer existed, he encouraged the older generations that had learned to read to teach their children. And he took it upon himself to ensure that all of his house servants were literate. Yet he cautioned his people to keep their literacy a secret for their own protection.

Although the other planters on the island were unaware

that Masta Jeremy allowed his slaves to learn their letters, they did disapprove of his leniency toward them. Deseré had once overheard a visitor warn him that, "You can't control your niggers if you make yourself too familiar with them and treat them as equals."

"Masta Jeremy lets me help with teachin' all the youngins on the place to read," Deseré said, "and figure, but I can't wait to teach my own—I mean our own."

"Deseré!"

She heard young voices calling her name and turned to see two little dark-skinned slave girls, sisters of about six and seven-years-old running toward her. Barefoot, they wore calico dresses falling just above their ankles. Dark curls framed their happy faces.

Smiling, Deseré stooped down to greet them, "Mae and Jenny! Ya'll know William?"

The little girls said a hasty hello to William, then quickly turned their large brown eyes back to Deseré.

"You come listen to us read tonight?" Jenny said in a loud whisper. "We learn de book you taught us."

"Mama said it be perfect," Mae said, her voice slightly louder in its excitement, "but you read better than she do."

"I'll come by after supper," Deseré said.

Jumping up and down, the little girls squealed with delight. Deseré hugged them, then watched as they ran off toward the quarters.

"Good thing both of us can read." Deseré stood up, once again sliding her hand through the crook of William's arm.

"I ain't no teacher," he said, as they began to walk again.

"You never know," Deseré smiled. "And with all the building you do, I bet you can teach figurin' better than me."

William shrugged his shoulders. "Guess I could teach... Maybe help the youngins feel like they more than just chattel." Silence lingered between them for a few moments. "Sounds like you got our whole lives planned out. Even got me roped into teachin'.'"

"Well," Deseré started, "I don't have our *whole* lives planned out. Least not yet."

William stopped walking again. "Look at my hands." He held them out for Deseré to see.

She took them in hers. They were rough to touch; the strong hands of a skilled carpenter, bulging with veins and sinew. She turned them over to look at palms well-etched with lines and an array calluses. Out of all the slave craftsmen, carpenters were the elite, and William performed lots of work at his plantation, as well as many others his master rented him to. He'd come to Pleasant Wood last year to work with Jeremy Albright's carpenter Shamus, to rebuild one of the outbuildings that had been damaged in a fire. Using hand tools like a saw, plane, axe, hatchet, auger, adze, chisel and drawing knife, William could build anything.

He pulled his hands from Deseré's, then dropped them to his sides. He began walking quickly and Deseré hurried to catch up.

"I work with my hands and I get little to nothin' for it."

"Your masta gives you food, clothes, a place to sleep," Deseré said, latching onto his arm.

"And when Masta Norris rents me out, he takes a share of the money. I get twelve dollars a month—six for me and six for Masta Norris. If I wanna buy our freedom one day, how am I gonna do that? Masta Norris paid seven-hundred dollars for me. He didn't want to sell me, but Masta Albright offered him nine-hundred. Your master's willin' to pay that much so I can be here with you."

Deseré smiled. "I know, and if he owns us both, we'll be guaranteed a good life and—"

"And we'll still be slaves! It ain't right! If I had my freedom, I could make a good livin, for *us*, Deseré, but if I'm stuck here, I'll never have nothin'!"

Deseré paused for a moment. "But you'll always have me. Ain't I worth more to you than your freedom?"

"Deseré," William said, almost in disgust, "ain't nothin' worth more than freedom!"

Tears welled in her eyes as she looked at him. "Not even love?"

William frowned shaking his head. "Love is some woman's notion," he grumbled. "Even when we are married, you won't be completely satisfied with bein' a well-treated house nigguh *slave*!"

"That's not true," Deseré said, trying to hold back her tears. "I'll have you."

William put a consoling arm around her. "That won't be enough. You'll want your freedom. You just don't see it that way yet. But one day you will."

Chapter 2

With hands clasped behind his back, Jeremy Albright paced the hardwood floor of his morning room. The hearty yellow pine creaked with every stride. Large open windows lined deep blue walls, filling the room with refreshing spring air. Blue velvet draperies, tied back with shiny gold tassels, hung over sheer white curtains that swelled like mist in the subtle breeze. Jeremy mopped his furrowed brow with a handkerchief, reflecting on what he'd just seen from those very windows only moments earlier.

Deseré had walked arm in arm with William, appearing even more enamored of him than the last time she'd seen him. During the week, the young man managed to visit once or twice after he'd completed his work for the day. Quite the strapping young buck, muscular and well-formed, he'd stay for about an hour, then return back home to Wesley Ridge Plantation, a little over a mile away.

William seemed a nice young man; there was none more industrious. Jeremy, however, had doubts about his upcoming union with Deseré. When William was with Deseré, Jeremy noticed that she was the one who was all smiles and giggles. William smiled, but not the smile of a man in love. He was older than Deseré, but shouldn't true love reduce even the most rigid man to a puddle of folly?

"Masta Jeremy?"

Jeremy's thoughts were interrupted upon hearing Deseré's voice. He stopped pacing in front of an ornately carved fireplace, and turned toward the doorway where Deseré stood.

"You wanted to see me, sir?" she asked.

"Yes, Deseré, my dear." Jeremy gazed at her beauty and the innocence she reflected like an angel. "Come in."

Smiling, the girl strolled into the room. Her pink muslin dress covered her petticoats. He'd purchased the fabric for her in Charleston and enjoyed watching it now, seeing how Deseré's hands had crafted it to life. The dress lightly swished across the hardwood, then quietly brushed over the blue and gold Oriental carpet that covered the center of the room.

Jeremy sat down on a blue velvet settee, gazing up at the girl's sunlit blond curls. Patting the cushion next to him, he said, "Please, sit down." Inviting a servant to sit with him was inappropriate, but Jeremy didn't care, it was his house and he'd do as he pleased. Deseré hesitated, then slowly sat next to him spreading her skirts, and then primly laced her fingers in her lap.

Jeremy ran a hand through the graying waves of his hair. "Did you enjoy your visit with William?"

"Yes," Deseré nodded, "I always do."

A tall man who'd accumulated a bit of girth around the middle, Jeremy stood. Looking down at Deseré, he pursed his lips. "You say you want to marry him...but are you absolutely sure?"

"Yes, Masta Jeremy. Why are you askin'? He's worth his weight in gold." She paused, then wringing her hands said, "I know he's costin' you a lot, but...but you're not havin' second thoughts...'bout buyin' him, are you, sir?"

"No, no," Jeremy assured her, "I have no doubt about his

ability. I'm sure he'll be worth every penny; especially to you," he smiled. "And besides, Shamus is getting up in years and I do need another carpenter."

The average price of a field hand was about five-hundred and fifty dollars, but a tradesman cost more. Nine-hundred dollars was a rather high price even for one as skilled as William, but it was the price that William's owner had agreed to, and Jeremy would pay it for Deseré's sake.

Jeremy didn't consider himself the most prosperous of planters, nor did he use his land to its fullest potential. Part of this was out of consideration to his people. However, he wasn't particularly motivated to plant with extreme enthusiasm since he'd received a good bit of money from his mother's estate. His grandparents had sold three plantations before they died, leaving Jeremy's mother, their only child, Isabelle, a fortune of seventy-five thousand dollars, which Jeremy had inherited along with Pleasant Wood twenty years ago.

He still possessed a good cushion of money, yet with yearly plantation expenses, such as taxes, food and clothing for the servants, tools and seed, it wouldn't last forever.

Jeremy said, "It's just that you seem overly eager to marry him, and I don't believe William shares the same—shall we say—enthusiasm that you do. When did he ask you?"

"When did he ask me what?" Deseré feigned innocence.

Jeremy cocked his head at this. She knew what he meant. "To marry him," he said.

"Oh." Deseré's eyes dropped to her lap, then moved to the marble top table in front of her. "Well…" she began, appearing to study the swirls of gray in the polished white stone as if she were reading a map, "…he didn't ask me exactly… I just suggested it a few times…"

Jeremy removed his round spectacles. While cleaning them with his handkerchief, he said, "So, did you suggest it enough to make him *think* it was his idea?"

Forgetting the marble, Deseré's gaze met his. Her blue

eyes sparkled and with a little smile, she said, "Maybe."

Despite himself, Jeremy smiled back. She had that affect on him. At fifty-one years of age, he was old enough to be her father. He'd never married and had no children of his own. Deseré, who so reminded him of his deceased sister, was the closest thing he had to a daughter. She wasn't his, but he had no wife to embarrass, so if people chose to think that he'd fathered such a splendid creature, he wouldn't dare stop them. Perhaps that was better than the truth he hid about himself.

Jeremy sighed, a bit exasperated by the girl's forwardness, as well as her young man's past, which Deseré knew little about. Over five years earlier, William had attempted an escape. That was before he'd been purchased in Charleston by Norris Wesley, his current owner.

Who William had tried to escape with, was what Deseré needed to know. The only information Jeremy had was based on rumor from Wesley. Yet Jeremy hoped that one day soon, William would tell Deseré the complete story of his unfortunate exploit, and more importantly, of his traveling companion. Jeremy believed it wasn't his place to tell Deseré. If William didn't, however, Jeremy would have no choice. He would inform Deseré's mother, Patsy. He doubted she knew the whole truth, and he assumed she wouldn't want Deseré to walk into a marriage completely blindfolded.

"He loves me, Masta Jeremy," Deseré said. "That's the important thing. That's what you said."

"Yes, that is the most important thing, and I'd see that the two of you were never parted." Jeremy was silent for a few seconds. "William is a talented fellow...and worldly. Before coming here, he lived in Virginia and Kentucky. And Mr. Wesley has hired out his services as far away as Charleston."

"I know all that, Masta Jeremy."

"And he's twenty-eight," Jeremy went on. "You're only seventeen and not nearly as experienced in the ways of the world."

"With love, that don't matter."

"Doesn't matter," Jeremy prodded with a slight frown. He preferred his house servants to speak properly.

Deseré laughed. "Yes, Masta Jeremy."

She hardly sounded like a Gullah, Jeremy thought, but, nonetheless, she'd picked up bad habits of speech from William. "Being around him makes your speech disintegrate."

"No it *doesn't*." Deseré laughed coquettishly. "I just wanted to get a rise out of you."

Jeremy heard footsteps, and in seconds he and Deseré looked toward the doorway to see Deseré's mother, Patsy. The woman wore a simple blue homespun dress with a white apron.

"Pardon me, Masta Jeremy," Patsy said.

"Quite alright, Patsy. I assume you're looking for Deseré."

"Yes, sir," Patsy said. With her straight black hair pulled tightly in a bun at the crown of her head, her widow's peak glistened keenly like a claw.

As far as women go, Jeremy mused, she was beautiful, with gracefully sculpted cheekbones and skin the color of cinnamon.

Raising a brow, Patsy regarded her daughter sharply with large eyes as glassy black as obsidian. "Deseré, time for you to set the table and stop lollygagging with Masta Jeremy."

Deseré stood quickly from the sofa. "Yes, Mama, but Masta Jeremy just wanted to have a word with me."

Jeremy smiled. "I think we're finished for now, Deseré."

As Deseré started for the dining room, Patsy stopped her. "Before you set the table, go to the kitchen house and tell April not to let Lily cook the biscuits until she has more practice."

"Didn't you tell her that already, Mama?"

"Just do as I say," Patsy snapped, wanting the girl out of

earshot.

"Yes, Mama," Deseré quickly left the room.

Chapter 3

When Deseré left the morning room, Patsy still stood in the doorway. She inhaled deeply, pursing her lips. At thirty-two-years old, Patsy, although a mere servant, assumed the role of plantation mistress, overseeing the day-to-day operations of the household.

After hearing the backdoor shut behind her daughter, Patsy said, "I beg your pardon, Masta Jeremy, but I fear my daughter has developed a rather high opinion of herself."

"Is that so?" Jeremy tipped his head slightly, then walked to his plantation desk. Large and made of black walnut, it sat against a wall in the morning room. Now Jeremy stood directly to Patsy's right, but she could barely see him from the hall.

Patsy took two steps inside the room, just as Jeremy let down the drop front of the desk, revealing a series of large and small compartments for letters, ledgers and journals.

"Deseré mustn't think she's better than anyone else," Patsy said. "You've mentioned more than once that she reminds you of your dead kin, but she's only a servant. And inviting her to sit on the settee with you causes jealousy among the *other* servants."

Patsy took a large step back and leaned from the room.

She peeked down the hallway, hoping no one would overhear them. Yet she caught a glimpse of Emmett, the butler, at the other end, walking from the dining room toward the basement steps. A tall, yellow man of middle-age with short curly hair, he looked toward Patsy with a disapproving sneer, then disappeared down the stairs to the above ground basement. Emmett had told Patsy where Deseré was earlier.

Patsy stepped back into the morning room. "And besides, it isn't proper," she said.

Jeremy fingered through some letters placed neatly in one of the small square compartments. "I consider Deseré something more than just a servant," he said. Finding the correspondence he sought, Jeremy pulled it from the desk and perused its contents. "To me, she's a special child, beautiful, intelligent, sharp-minded." He glanced at Patsy, "None too different from her mother."

Patsy smiled. "I appreciate your sentiment toward her. I appreciate that *you* yourself, taught her to read and write... But the way you dote on her, sir...some folks think the unspeakable!"

A glimmer of hope sparkled in Jeremy's eyes. "That I'm her father?"

Patsy clucked her tongue. "Or worse!" Jeremy only laughed at her exasperation, as if pleased that others might think that she, or *Deseré,* were his concubine—indeed!

"The important thing is that we know neither of those scenarios is true," Jeremy said, "but I'll see to it that she's always protected."

"I thank you for that, sir."

Jeremy gently touched Patsy's shoulder for a moment.

"And you've done more than enough for me," she said. "You were an answer to prayer when...when you...took me in..." From the bowels of hell, she thought.

Patsy had been purchased at fourteen by a Mrs. Matilda Creech. The Creech's owned a plantation two miles north, called The Hollows. Mrs. Creech wanted her eighteen-year-old son to marry the wealthy heiress of a plantation on Edisto Island. Trouble was, the girl was only twelve at the time. So Patsy was bought to keep the young man "occupied" until the heiress would be deemed old enough to marry four years later.

The young man was a timid soul who felt sorry for Patsy and never laid a hand on her. His father, Mr. Laird Augustus Creech, however, was a different story. His disposition was despicable, especially after imbibing spirits. Overcome by lechery, Masta Creech couldn't keep himself from Patsy and for one year persecuted her. His licentious behavior ceased only after Mrs. Creech unexpectedly walked into the parlor one day to find him on the sofa on top of Patsy.

A drunken Creech tried to explain away the situation, by slurring, "This isn't what you think. She—she's a devil woman! I was forced by her hand into this unfortunate predicament! I—I had no choice!"

Mrs. Creech wasted no time dragging Patsy out to the smokehouse for a whipping, which Mrs. Creech herself administered. Afterwards, she made it known that once Patsy recuperated from her thrashing she'd be put up for sale.

Patsy had been put up for sale once before. Since the age of four, she'd lived with a kindly Christian mistress in Beaufort who'd taught her to read and write. Patsy had been fourteen when her mistress died, then she'd been sold as property from the estate, which is how she'd ended up being purchased by Mrs. Creech. Patsy would have gladly run into the snare of death than be forced into the evil clutches of another vile beast. So a few days later, after Patsy had regained her strength, she ran away from The Hollows and hid in the woods for two days, until she made it to Pleasant Wood.

She'd heard about Pleasant Wood at a praise house

meeting. Two or three times a week Baptist slaves met at praise houses on different plantations where they sang and prayed. It was at one of these meetings that she'd learned of Jeremy Albright. Any who knew him swore there was no man more righteous than he.

Patsy arrived at Pleasant Wood looking like a feral animal. With her wavy hair wild and untamed, she was covered with cuts and scratches from the woods, and her back still seeped with blood from the lash. She begged Jeremy Albright to intervene on her behalf and purchase her from the Creeches. It was only after the transaction was successfully completed that Patsy realized she was carrying Creech's child...Deseré.

"I hope to always do what's best for Deseré," Jeremy said, breaking Patsy's train of thought. He looked back at the letter he held. "Wesley has agreed to sell William to me at the end of three months."

"So he and Deseré can marry then?"

"Yes," Jeremy said, still eyeing the letter. "Mr. Wesley says that by then William should be finished with the mill he's building at one of the O'Malley places." Albright folded the letter then put it back in its place. "But in my opinion," he looked at Patsy, "I don't believe this marriage is in Deseré's best interest."

Patsy's eyes grew wide. "But she loves him, sir, and he loves her."

Jeremy nodded saying nothing. His narrowed eyes and tightened lips revealed that he was unconvinced.

"He wants to marry her!" Patsy insisted. "And he's a good man."

"Does Deseré know of his failed escape?"

Patsy's breath caught, surprised that Masta Albright would bring this up. "William told her, but it was a long time ago—he was a much younger man, then—young and foolish."

Albright crossed his arms. "Is there anything else you

know about that caper of his — anything else he's told Deseré concerning it?"

"No, Masta Jeremy, only that he tried to run, and that he was caught and punished — sold South. But being here at Pleasant Wood should make him forget about ever wanting to run again. You give us a degree of freedom he's never known."

Jeremy Albright did his best to treat his slaves as practically free in everything but name. He would have set them free if it weren't for the rigid code of laws restricting emancipation, and the difficulty negroes faced living as free people in South Carolina. Manumission laws had become extremely stringent because some freed slaves, such as the sickly, elderly and those known as trouble-makers, were a burden on the community. Now slaves could only be freed by an act of the legislature.

"That'll calm down his thinking," Patsy went on, "that is, if he's thinking about running again. Besides, I've never had what Deseré has — and I want her to have that — the love of a man she wants."

"Patsy," Jeremy smiled, "I would welcome any man you fancied into my estate."

"I realize that, sir. Perhaps one day... But right now, I'm content to live through Deseré. And I know you'll always keep her safe."

"Of course, and the safest place for her is Pleasant Wood." Jeremy sighed. "I'll see to it that William has a good life here. I certainly can't have him running away with your daughter."

Chapter 4

It was three o'clock in the afternoon. Jeremy rode home on horseback from the Lodge Hall of the St. Helena Island Agricultural Society where the Agricultural Planters Meeting had just taken place. The lodge was located less than two miles north of Pleasant Wood.

While heading home, Jeremy traveled a dirt road surrounded by gigantic oaks and lofty evergreens. The sky was a dreary gray, yet it darkened quickly as angry black clouds rolled across the horizon. The earthy smell of rain filled the air. A strong wind kicked up, whistling noisily through the tall trees. Branches swayed and leaves crackled amidst the forceful gusts. Within seconds a shower began to fall. Jeremy saw a flash of lightening, then heard a rumble of thunder. The rain became heavier, pelting him with the pressure of tiny fingertips. With his riding crop, Jeremy swatted his horse on the rump. Boaz, a red gelding, was swift. He galloped more rapidly now, his silky black mane flying. Only half mile to go until they reached home.

The black sky flashed silver. Boaz turned from red to an eerie shade of gray for a moment. From the sky, a walloping crack of thunder exploded, startling both horse and rider.

Boaz reared, whinnying in fright. He pranced furiously, front legs airborne, as if trying to take off in flight. Jeremy held fast, but was thrown from the animal's back, losing his broad brimmed hat in the process. Boaz, relieved of his burden, made a hasty retreat home, but Jeremy lay injured, unconscious, his head against a rock.

Jeremy opened his eyes. The rain continued to beat down on him. Unsure of how much time had passed, he struggled to stand from a thick layer of mud that nearly sucked him back to the ground. Slowly, Jeremy pulled himself to his feet, then began to stumble toward the house, lucky to be alive, he thought. How much unfinished business did he have to address before his death? His will was in order, his taxes paid, so to the best of Jeremy's knowledge, all things regarding Pleasant Wood were in fine fettle. Yet there was that one little issue about William. One he could easily tend to today. He'd at least tell Patsy. No time like the present to—

"Masta Jeremy!" Jeremy heard male voices shouting at him in unison. Straining to look through the storm, he saw George, the stableman, and Tom his helper running toward him. Both were tall and dark, though George was thickly built, and Tom was as thin as a fence post.

Once they'd reached him, Jeremy noticed that George carried a thick wool blanket, large enough to shield the three of them from the pounding rain.

"Good, God Almighty!" exclaimed George, once the blanket covered them. "Blood spewin' from yo' head like water from a pump."

As they walked, Jeremy touched his temple and brought back bloody fingers. "Goodness, me," he said, then reached beneath his cloak in search of a handkerchief.

George and Tom stood on either side of their master, securely grasping his arms in an attempt to steady his stride.

"Oh, hash!" Jeremy said, pressing the handkerchief to his head, "I'm fine." He tried to pull away from his faithful servants but almost lost his balance.

"Let us he'p you, suh," Tom said, once again firmly gripping his arm. "You ain't awright yet. Boaz come run back wit'out you like a scalded haint. We worry you struck by light'nin'."

"Nothing happened as serious as that!" Jeremy scoffed. "I've fallen off a horse a few times in my life." He laughed a little, trying to lighten the mood. "And I've certainly hit my head more than once."

****

Patsy gasped. "Masta Jeremy, what happened to you?" she asked, alarmed upon seeing Jeremy walk through the front door, assisted by George and Tom.

"I'm fine," Jeremy said, finally pulling himself free from the stable hands. "I appreciate your assistance," he said to them, as George hastily folded the wet blanket and slung it over his shoulder, "but now, I assure you, I am fully recovered." Tom and George glanced at each other, then at Patsy. "Tom, if you wouldn't mind," Albright said, "my boots." He sank onto an ornately carved high-back foyer bench made of dark wood. Tom stooped down and pulled off his master's muddy boots. Albright thanked him and smiled. Then he stood and walked a few paces away from the stable hands in his stocking feet. Turning to face them he said, "See, good as new. Now, you two needn't worry about me any longer."

Patsy nodded to the men. "I'll see to it that he's alright," she said, as she saw them out. Panes of leaded glass rattled as she closed the door behind them, blocking out the sound of still hard falling rain.

"My, my..." Patsy sighed, as she walked to her master. Water streamed down Jeremy's face in rivulets and he held a bloody handkerchief to the side of his head. He was covered in mud and his clothes smelled like wet dog. Patsy helped him remove his soaking frock-coat but noticed that his suit was saturated as well.

"What's all the ruckus?" Deseré asked, as she traipsed from the back of the house to the foyer.

"I'm no worse for wear," Jeremy smiled at her. "The thunder startled Boaz and I was thrown."

Deseré's eyes widened. "Masta Jeremy, you look like ten miles of bad road!"

"Deseré!" Patsy exclaimed.

Jeremy only laughed. "I imagine so."

Patsy handed the girl Albright's frockcoat. "Take this to the wash house." Deseré frowned, trying to keep her fingers from touching the mud caked on it in several spots. "You're slow as molasses in January," Patsy said. "Take it now, girl!"

"Yes, Mama." Deseré ran off down the hall toward the backdoor, holding the dripping coat by her fingertips a good distance away from her dress.

"Let me tend your wound," Patsy said, reaching to take Albright's handkerchief.

He put up a hand to stop her. "In a moment, Patsy. First, I must get out of these clothes."

"Then I'll send for Jax to help you."

"No, don't bother the old soul," Jeremy said calmly. Ajax was his body servant, but he'd also been Albright's father's body servant. Now the old man was past seventy and moved rather slowly, especially up the stairs. "I don't want to trouble him; I can manage on my own."

"Well then, after you've changed, you must allow me to dress—"

"Yes, yes," he sighed, "you may then tend to this...this inconvenience. I suffered quite a nasty bump on the head, and I was surprised I could stand without feeling any ill effects, other than a bit of dizziness."

"You're sure you're alright, sir?"

"Yes, Patsy, I fine... But I've realized that life can be snuffed out in an instant. As I walked back to the house, I had a bit of time to reflect. While you dress my wound, we need to talk about something...something I've been putting off, but no longer." He turned away from her and reached for the hand carved stair railing, then began his ascent.

Patsy felt her heart drop as she watched him climb the black walnut steps, water dripping from his clothes onto the red floral patterned stair-runner. Her mind raced through every devastating scenario. Were his taxes paid? Had he lost money somehow? Would he have to sell his people to pay off a debt of some kind? Patsy tried to remain calm as she asked, "Something...serious, Masta Jeremy?"

Jeremy stopped, turning to face her. "It's about William."

"Oh." Patsy felt a slight bit of relief, but at the same time a sense of trouble.

"I believe it's something you should know," Albright said, resuming his climb. "I'll leave it up to you to tell Deseré or not, since William hasn't mentioned it."

"I see," Patsy said quietly.

"I shan't be more than a few minutes, then I'll call you up."

****

An hour later the sun was shining, yet Patsy still waited for her master to ring for her. She sat in the basement on a bench near the foot of the steps, waiting and at the ready, with a wash pan of hot water, bandages, and a needle and thread in case his injury required stitching. Although Masta Jeremy didn't drink, she'd poured a small glass of brandy to numb the pain. In addition, she'd gathered yarrow leaf and yarrow flower powder to assist with healing his wound.

Prior to sitting down, Patsy had busied herself with some other household chores, but now enough time had passed for her to be worried. She stood, taking a deep breath, and walked up the basement steps. Then Patsy went outside through the back door and climbed the gray servants' steps to the second floor. From the sloping balcony, she re-entered the house, then walked down the hall toward her master's bedroom.

She knocked lightly at his door. "Masta Jeremy?" No answer. Patsy rapped harder a second time. "Masta Jeremy?" She paused for a moment, thinking she should go in to check on him. However, without his permission to enter, she might catch him in a state of undress. She shuddered at the thought.

Masta Creech wore a male corset over his protruding belly. He'd tried to keep it covered because it had embarrassed him, but Patsy had seen the silly undergarment beneath his shirt while he'd... had his way with her.

Masta Jeremy was a bit thick in the middle, but hardly in need of a corset. Nevertheless, she'd hate to see him indecently exposed in any way. Besides, she wouldn't dare put herself in a compromising position. Masta Jeremy was a kind man, but he was a man, and a white man at that. Emmett, the butler, was in the sick house suffering from a stomach ailment, so Patsy had no choice but to trouble Jax.

She hurried from the house, then back down the outside steps to the kitchen house, about thirty feet away. Jax's daughter April was the cook at Pleasant Wood. When Patsy burst through the kitchen house door, April and her daughter Lily, a newly assigned kitchen maid, were preparing supper. Jax, dressed impeccably in one of his master's cast off suits, sat at a simple wooden table sipping from a steaming cup of tea.

"Jax, you must come quickly!" Patsy said. "It's Masta Jeremy."

"Masta Jeremy?" Jax said, rising slowly.

Patsy had learned that in Homer's *Iliad* the mythological character Ajax was described as one of great stature and colossal frame. He was fearless, strong, powerful, and possessed a high level of combat intelligence. Patsy had no knowledge of what Jax had been like as a young man, he'd been rather advanced in years when she'd arrived here, but now there was no doubt that he couldn't possibly live up to his namesake.

A shade lighter than nutmeg, Jax was balding and what sparse hair remained on his gleaming pate was gray. For a thin man, his face was a bit jowly. His chin receded and his eyes were slightly bugged. Patsy chided herself for thinking that as the man aged, his resemblance to a turtle continued to increase. Masta Jeremy had said that he and Jax had once been the same height, but Jax had been shrinking steadily over the past several years due to stooped posture caused by a hunched back.

The old man shuffled his feet slowly, then grabbed the cane he'd placed near the door.

"What happened," April, a round-faced woman asked. She was a bit darker than her father, and stirred a large cast iron pot hanging over the fire in the red brick fireplace.

"Is he hurt?" Lily, a thin copper colored girl of about fifteen asked.

As the girl poured yellow cornbread batter into a skillet, with a good bit of the mixture missing the pan, Patsy explained the situation in great detail, hoping that would increase Jax's pace. It did, but only from the likes of sorghum flowing in the dead of winter to honey flowing in the cool of springtime.

Once at the house, Jax carefully navigated each outside step, one at a time, with both feet. "Rheumatism's worse today 'cause of the rain," he said on his painstakingly slow ascent.

"Well," Patsy walked behind him, feigning patience, "it's cleared up now, and I don't suppose Masta Jeremy's going anywhere."

"Could be he jes' took a nap on account uh his head. Mebe he didn't realize he needed a rest. You'll see you frettin' over nothin'."

Once they reached the top of the stairs, Patsy quickly moved past Jax, then waited for what seemed at least a quarter of an hour for the old man to walk the few yards down the hall to Masta Jeremy's room.

"Now, don't you worry none, Patsy," Jax kindly assured her, as he approached his master's bedroom. "He'll be alright." Upon reaching the door, Jax strained to pull himself straighter, then knocked with the authority of a trusted and faithful servant who'd served two generations of Albright men as body servant. "Masta Jeremy," he said loudly, and with the same authority, "we want to assure your well-being; make sure you don't need us to call for the doctor."

No answer.

"Jax, please!" Patsy begged. "Just open the door!"

"Now, Patsy, I've served Masta Jeremy since his daddy died. We'd best follow protocol and wait for his—"

"Jax! I knocked twice before I ran to fetch you!"

The old man sighed. "Alright, Patsy." Raising his voice, he shouted, "Masta Jeremy, I'm coming in without your permission, and I mean no offense." The old man slowly turned the knob, then pushed open the squeaking door. As he walked inside, Patsy followed closely at his heels. Peering over his shoulder, she saw her master's feet first, and then the rest of him.

Jeremy was in a dry shirt and trousers. Now that the clouds had lifted, he was bathed in rainbows streaming in through a stained glass window. But with open eyes, staring aimlessly, he lay sprawled on the floor in front of his dresser, dead.

CHAPTER 5

"So there was no way possible that Masta Jeremy could have freed us upon his death?" Patsy asked Josiah Simmons, Albright's business manager.

Masta Jeremy had preferred the term business manager, to the term overseer. She stood with Simmons in his parlor, aware that yesterday he'd traveled to Beaufort to meet with Masta Jeremy's lawyer.

Simmons only shook his head, appearing unable to speak for a moment. After several seconds he finally said, "Not with the current law, Patsy. All of you can only be freed by an act of the legislature. Besides, the lawyer said that Mr. Albright believed you'd be best off here, and that his heir would see to that. Unfortunately, however," Simmons looked down, "that's not in writing."

"I see," Patsy said. So there was no guarantee that the new heir *would* see to that.

Two days earlier, the household had become discombobulated upon hearing of Masta Jeremy's death. None of his slave family would think of escaping. Getting from the island to the mainland seemed as difficult as getting to Africa. The patrollers would surely catch them, so they'd await their fate, which now lay in the hands of a new master. So far, that was the only information Patsy had been able to glean from the business manager.

Simmons lived in a small house on Albright's property that was fit for a man with a family. A parlor and dining room were downstairs, and two bedrooms upstairs. But Simmons, a man of about thirty, was unmarried and lived alone.

He was a Yankee from Pennsylvania that Masta Jeremy had met during a business trip. Impressed by his business acumen and knowledge of farming, Albright had offered him a job. That had been nearly ten years ago.

Masta Jeremy had never fancied the business end of running a plantation, so he was more than happy to provide Simmons with the opportunity to handle his business affairs and oversee the planting. Patsy handled the day-to-day operation of the household, and she knew that if she'd been a white woman married to Masta Jeremy, she would have handled the finances as well.

Simmons was a kind man of pleasant disposition, who treated the servants of Pleasant Wood with as much respect as Masta Jeremy had. Simmons was a dark-haired man, slight of build and very handsome. Yet now his warm brown eyes were red-rimmed and watery, with puffy red circles beneath them. Although Patsy had never seen alcohol in Simmons's house, today she wondered if he'd been drinking. She glanced around quickly looking for bottles but saw none.

"Mr. Simmons," Patsy said, "what can you tell me about this new master? As you understand, we'd like to know what the future holds for us," aside from terror, consternation and fear of the auction block, she thought.

Raising his gaze to hers, he said, "His name is...Anthony Sinclair. He's Jeremy's nephew. Mr. Albright had no brothers and only one surviving sister. Her first-born son is to whom he bequeathed his property. Mr. Albright's lawyer will be sending him the correspondence regarding the estate in the next day or so." Simmons then proceeded to pull a handkerchief from his pocket and wipe his eyes. Astonished, Patsy realized he'd been crying. "I'm sorry," he said.

"We're all sorry," Patsy said softly. She'd already shed an abundance of tears over her master's death, as had Deseré and the other servants who'd sobbed and shrieked in despair, as well. With the death of a kind master, Patsy reflected, a slave is left unprotected and alone because the law regards him as devoid of rights and no more than another bale of merchandise.

Simmons began to weep softly into his handkerchief. This horrified Patsy. She'd never seen a white man cry, and today she had little patience for it. Patsy pursed her lips, thinking that her life, and foremost, her daughter's life, were at stake. Right now, Deseré's protection was the most important thing to her. Patsy would rather die a thousand deaths than see Deseré subjected to a demoralizing existence such as the one she'd experienced at the hands of Masta Creech!

Simmons sniffed, breaking Patsy's train of thought. "He was like a father to me," the young man said through his tears, "...and more..."

Patsy began wringing her hands. Simmons was a modest man, almost delicate. He and Masta Jeremy had met early each day in the morning room along with Eulee, the hand considered the head man, to discuss the business of the day. But in the afternoons, Simmons and Masta Jeremy had had private business meetings at Simmons's house nearly every day — including weekends!

Patsy supposed Simmons would miss him quite a bit, especially since he'd been like a father...and more. She frowned, unsure of what to think, so only said, "Yes — he was kind to all of us... But now we must make provisions...and be prepared for what's to come."

"Yes." Simmons blew his nose. "Forgive me."

"Expressing one's grief is nothing to forgive."

Simmons smiled, appearing appreciative of her sympathy and then proceeded to tell Patsy what little he knew about Anthony Sinclair, mainly regarding his upbringing and occupation.

Patsy nodded. "But what of his character? Is he a kind man, cut from the same mold as Masta Jeremy?"

Simmons hesitated. "Patsy, I know nothing more than what I've told you. I'm sorry I can't tell you more."

Patsy strained to sound gracious. "I appreciate what you have told me. We'll make the best of things."

"I fear," Simmons began, "that it's time for me to...take my leave."

"Take your leave?"

He hesitated, then once more wiped his eyes. "There's no point in me staying here. I'm going back home to help my father work the family farm."

Patsy's mouth dropped open. "You mean you're leaving us," she exclaimed, "for good?"

Simmons smiled sadly. "Not right away, of course. I'll— I'll stay until after Mr. Sinclair is situated. Eulee knows more about cotton than I do. He can educate Mr. Sinclair about its cultivation, as well as the cultivation of all the other crops."

Patsy nodded, blankly, still processing the fact that Simmons was leaving. Eulee was the most capable hand on the plantation, perhaps the equivalent of a driver, but Masta Jeremy didn't call him that. To him, Eulee was the head man.

"Eulee and the other hands can carry on in the fields," Simmons continued, "but when I'm gone, if Mr. Sinclair should have questions regarding the finances...perhaps you can guide him."

"Me?" Patsy's eyes widened as she placed a hand on her chest.

"Mr. Albright told me that you're a very capable woman

and quite sharp with figures. I'll go over the books with you."

"But—"

"And I'd like Deseré to be present as well. Mr. Albright said she's just as keen with figures as you are, and—"

"Mr. Simmons," Patsy interrupted him, "what you're suggesting is preposterous. The new master of this estate will *not* listen to his newly acquired *negro* servants about— about the management of this estate!"

Simmons folded his handkerchief and put it in his pocket. "I will do my best to educate Mr. Sinclair before I leave. Then I will simply inform him that you and Deseré may prove of assistance if necessary, while he searches for a new business manager."

Scrambling for another explanation as to why his suggestion was implausible, Patsy took a deep breath. "Mr. Simmons, we're women."

Simmons shrugged. "Perhaps Mr. Sinclair will catch on quickly and choose to handle the finances himself. Or perhaps he'll marry a *woman* proficient in running the business end of things."

Of course he was right, women could be just as adept in business matters as men, but pushing that thought aside she pleaded, "Or perhaps you'll just consider staying on?"

Simmons said, "There's no point," then added softly, "not without Jeremy." His eyes misted over for a moment. Then appearing to take hold of his senses he remarked, "What I teach you will enhance your value to Mr. Sinclair."

Patsy considered this for a long moment, then said, "Though you mentioned that he's a Yankee, you said he was born in the South, and that he spent his early years on a plantation. So since he's no stranger to owning people, he mustn't know we can read—or rather that any of us here at Pleasant Wood can. He could punish us—separate us—or even sell us all!"

"I understand, Patsy," Simmons assured her. "Yet let's

think about this...the law says it's illegal for a slave to be taught to read, but there's no law against one knowing how to figure."

Patsy pursed her lips, nodding.

"And to be honest," Simmons continued, "there's at least one servant on every plantation that can read. Wouldn't you agree?"

Patsy nodded again.

"Well," Simmons smiled, "this plantation can have two literate servants, you and Deseré."

"Not Deseré," Patsy said quickly. "She will learn whatever you deem fit to teach her, but I'd prefer the new master not know she possesses any...*important* knowledge. I believe the more ignorant he believes she is, the safer she'll be. As long as he's aware that Deseré is adept at many chores, assists the seamstress and is efficient in running the household in my absence, I believe he'll value her for that. I'll help him with the books—if he should ask. However, I seriously doubt that he will. And please, Mr. Simmons, promise that you'll tell him my reading is only rudimentary."

"From what Jeremy said, you're a voracious reader."

Patsy frowned. "Mr. Sinclair may not appreciate that."

Simmons nodded thoughtfully. "Then I'll tell him you can only read a little, but that you're quite skilled with numbers."

Patsy sighed. "I suppose that'll be alright. Numbers are certainly less of a threat than words."

Chapter 6

"I don't know, Addie," Deseré said to the seamstress. The woman was of a golden brown hue. She stood outside the doorway of Deseré's room in the basement of the big house. "Mama doesn't know anything else."

Slightly plump and middle aged, Addie sighed, distraught. "I just thought Patsy might have found out somethin' else."

"I haven't." Patsy said, as she walked down the stairs from the first floor. "Now," she said, stopping next to Addie, "I suggest you go to your room and destroy anything you have that will prove you can read, as I told you earlier."

"Alright, Patsy," Addie said, "Goodnight."

"Goodnight." Patsy walked into the room she shared with Deseré, then closed the door behind her.

Deseré said, "She just wanted to know what's gonna happen to us." Patsy remained silent as she walked to the little pine nightstand by their bed. "Mama, do you know at all?" Deseré's tone was fretting. The time for tears was behind them, now full-fledged worry had set in. It was near bedtime, but the women weren't close to turning in.

"I don't know," Patsy said, removing a Bible and a copy of James Fennimore Cooper's novel *The Pathfinder* from the drawer of the nightstand. She then took a quick look from the back window nearby. About sixty yards beyond the kitchen house was a long row of wooden negro cottages. These were much nicer than the cabins found on other plantations. Whitewashed, with porches, windows, chimneys and wood floors, each had an apartment called a hall with two sleeping rooms and a loft for the children.

Patsy had explained the situation to as many of the servants as possible, including Jax and Emmett, who stayed in closet sized rooms near the pantry behind the dining room, as well as the others who stayed in the basement. April and Lily shared a room down here, along with Addie and Sophia, the women who were seamstress and weaver, respectively. Patsy hoped all were destroying anything that would expose learning from their rooms or cottages.

"You think the new masta will treat us just like Masta Jeremy?"

Turning away from the window, Patsy said, "His name is Mr. Sinclair, and everything boils down to money, Deseré, so Masta. Jeremy's good intentions about us staying here because we're better off may go unheeded."

"You think we'll be sold?"

"I don't know, Deseré."

"If he does sell everything, he could sell me to William's place, and you, too, Mama. I think Masta Wesley would buy us."

"Deseré, if the new masta were to sell us, it would be to the highest bidder!"

"But—"

"Oh, hush, child, and give me that book!" She snatched Edgar A. Poe's *Tales of the Grotesque and Arabesque* from Deseré's hands. "We're fortunate enough to know our letters and you read this trash!" Patsy placed the books on the pinewood dresser near the door of the room. "Take these upstairs and put them back on the shelves in the morning room first thing tomorrow. On second thought, take them now!"

"Why? The new master ain't comin' for weeks."

"*Isn't* coming," she corrected her daughter, then muttered, "If he does come at all." Sinclair lived up North. He could have the lawyer here disperse of the property and be done with it. "Just do as I say, Deseré! With Masta Jeremy gone, you never know who could come along and see something—or say something!"

"Yes, Mama."

As Deseré took the books from the dresser, Patsy motioned toward a stack of diaries by the fireplace, where inside a fire burned. "Have you put all your diaries there to be burned?" Over the past few years, Masta Jeremy had indulged Patsy and Deseré with new diaries so they could record their thoughts.

"Yes, Mama," Deseré replied. "All my diaries are there."

"Good," Patsy sighed, "I'll burn them now." She threw the diaries into the fire, one by one, and in moments, the flesh-like stench of burning leather infused the room. As the fire began to crackle, Patsy looked on sadly as the leather covers of the diaries turned black and the papers in them disintegrated amidst slashing orange flames into brittle flakes of ash.

"Didn't Mr. Simmons say Masta Jeremy's heir was from Ohio?"

Patsy turned to look at Deseré, surprised to see that she was still standing there holding the books. Patsy bit back a scolding for the girl not taking them upstairs yet. "Yes, Deseré, but the young man was raised in Georgia until he was nine or so. That's when his mother remarried a Yankee and they moved up North."

"You said that was a long time ago. So that—Mr. Sinclair—he's grown now. Livin' up North, he won't want to deal with no plantation."

"With *any* plantation! Sakes alive, Deseré! You have excellent command of good English, so stop speaking like a field hand! I imagine slave-holding is ingrained in the young man, despite his living in a free state for twenty years. So we don't know if he'll keep this place or sell it and all of us along with it!" Exasperation muddled her voice. "But we must be prepared, and depend on the Lord for strength. Philippians chapter four, verse thirteen says, 'I can do all things through Christ which strengtheneth me.'"

Deseré nodded, not giving the scripture much thought.

"And," Patsy continued, "we must be strong and courageous. Joshua chapter one, verse nine says, 'Be strong and of good courage, be not afraid, neither be thou dismayed: for the Lord thy God *is* with thee whithersoever thou goest.'"

"Mama, we're slaves," Deseré smirked. "If the new masta's a mean man and we go 'round actin' too strong and courageous, we'll end up gettin' beat to death."

Patsy raised a brow. "*Beaten* to death. And if that should happen, at least we'll be with the Lord in a better place."

"You think he'll be cruel?"

"I don't know, Deseré, but he mustn't know we can read. If the new masta is a cruel man, no telling what he'll do if he discovers our literacy... And beating us to death isn't outside that realm of possibility. Yet, even if he's kind, with our knowledge of letters being against the law, it'll only make things more difficult for us. I'm hoping, that if, God forbid, he does sell the place, perhaps he'd be willing to keep us as servants. But Deseré, you must wear your hair back or keep it covered to look unenticing so he won't... Well, at any rate, he could take us back to Ohio. We'd be free there and he could pay us for our service, so we must make a good impression. Speaking of which, Mr. Sinclair wants to teach us about the books."

"What books?"

"The books — the ledgers — the finances."

"Why?"

"Mr. Simmons will no longer be working here." Patsy

explained his offer to Deseré. "It certainly won't hurt for you to have the knowledge Mr. Simmons will share. It could help you in life at some point, but if Mr. Sinclair should need help with business matters, I'll be the one to provide it. I don't know what to expect, Deseré, but we must ready ourselves and hope for the best."

"What about me and William?"

Patsy sighed. "What about the two of you?"

"Will we still be able to marry?"

Patsy slowly walked to their bed, a corn husk mattress on a simple wooden frame. As Patsy sat down on it, she said, "I wish I could say yes, Deseré, but you know as well as I that that decision will be up to the new masta."

"What if he says no?"

"We'll pray he says yes. It's in God's hands now... He knows what's best."

"And I know it's best for me to marry William."

"Deseré...we can't always know God's plan for us."

"But it all seems so perfect with me and William, and I—"

"Masta's last words were about William," Patsy interrupted.

With the books still in her hands, Deseré quickly sat next to her mother. "What did he say?"

After a deep breath Patsy spoke. "Masta Jeremy had something to tell me about him...something he thought I should know... But he went to change before explaining himself...then he died."

Deseré cocked her head, frowning. "Probably didn't matter none."

"But now," Patsy said sadly, "we'll never know..."

.

Chapter 7

The sun shone through the cascading live oaks, casting a lacy shadow on a sea of black crepe in the Pleasant Wood graveyard, a quarter mile beyond the big house. A pleasant breeze blew gently, combining the sweet scents of magnolia and honeysuckle, with the musty scent of hay and the stench of manure.

"...for out of it wast thou taken: for dust thou art, and unto dust shalt thou return..." Patsy heard the bearded Reverend Perkins say as the funeral service came to a close.

From within the community, over a hundred white folks were there arrayed in black, and behind them, just as many negroes dressed in their Sunday best. Addie was next to Patsy, who stood on tiptoe trying to see over black clothed shoulders and bonnets. Deseré, on her mother's opposite side, clutched William's arm so tightly, Patsy heard him tell the girl to loosen her grasp. Deseré, uncertain of life without Masta Jeremy, paid more attention to her beau than the funeral ceremony. Patsy had nudged her several times to stop her from whispering in William's ear about pleading with Masta Wesley to purchase her along with her mother.

"The Lord is nigh unto them that are of a broken heart,"

Reverend Perkins continued, "and saveth such as be of a contrite spirit..."

A gentleman in front of Patsy bent down to retrieve his wife's handkerchief, giving Patsy a clear view for a few moments. Wearing a black suit, Jax slowly walked toward the coffin, his body bent from old age and sadness, then he turned to face those in attendance. Now Patsy saw the sheen of tears upon the old man's face. Masta Jeremy's will stated that Jax sing at his funeral.

The gentleman in front of her stood up again, blocking Patsy's view, but hearing Jax's sad, soulful voice, wavering with years of age was enough. Patsy closed her eyes and listened as he sang.

Jesus, lover of my soul,
let me to thy bosom fly,
while the nearer waters roll,
while the tempest still is high.
Hide me, O my Savior, hide,
till the storm of life is past;
safe into the haven guide;
O receive my soul at last.

Other refuge have I none,
hangs my helpless soul on thee;
leave, ah! leave me not alone,
still support and comfort me.
All my trust on thee is stayed,
all my help from thee I bring;
cover my defenseless head
with the shadow of thy wing.

Patsy concentrated on the words and said a silent prayer... Hide me oh my Savior 'til the storm of life is past... Not knowing what fate lay ahead, praying was the only thing she could do. Patsy gazed around, seeing that the colored men and women were teary eyed and downcast. The white ladies appeared this way as well, acting appropriately enough to show feelings expected at a funeral. Yet Patsy noticed that the only white man to be visibly distraught was Josiah Simmons.

Although the other white men didn't appear to smile, they did reflect a sense of relief, or perhaps even triumph, in their carefree manner as they left the burial ground to approach the big house where the repast was laid out on the rear porch and the brick-laid garden below. Was this because Jeremy Albright was dead? Patsy knew that, due to the kindness he expressed toward his slaves, he possessed a reputation as a trouble-maker.

Patsy saw Angus O'Malley walk toward Simmons. O'Malley's several plantations were some of the most prosperous on the island, and his slaves, because of maltreatment and overwork, were the most likely to try to run, though none had ever been successful. O'Malley owned the old Creech place. He'd acquired it after Mr. Creech died years earlier from the effects of his love for liquor. The Widow Creech had been eager to sell. Her son did marry that plantation heiress on Edisto Island, so Mrs. Creech moved there — or so Patsy had heard through the slave grapevine.

O'Malley had four grown sons that were married. Each lived at and managed one of their father's other plantations. His youngest child was a girl named Careen, who was eighteen and unmarried. Patsy had seen earlier that all the O'Malleys were in attendance. Fortunately for them, they favored their mother.

Loud and crude, Angus O'Malley was an ugly man in his late fifties. His round head was plastered with thinning black hair. His small black eyes, deep-set within wrinkled folds of skin, sharply darted about the Pleasant Wood land as though assessing it. His smile, reminiscent of a railroad track, was inhabited by widely spaced, tobacco stained teeth.

A flat nose, perhaps broken in youth, spanned from one mutton chop covered cheek to the other. In addition, he was a large man, more wide than tall, and in need of a corset. His belly protruded beneath the straining buttons of his black vest as if he were carrying a child! Patsy shuddered.

She saw O'Mallley clap Simmons on the shoulder. He looked as if he were offering words of condolence, yet as they walked by Patsy, she heard something disturbing.

"...Simmons," O'Malley said in deep, gravelly voice, "I need to talk to you about how to make this place a heap more profitable. Ya see, once that new heir takes over, things might be run around here the way they oughtta be. Albright could've earned more if he'd been willin' to work his niggers harder to harvest more of his land."

Patsy grabbed her skirts and followed them, keeping a few paces behind so she could keep listening.

"I'm not sure —" Simmons began, but O'Malley cut him off.

"A lot more cotton can be grown here, but Albright wasn't willing to use his darkies for the God ordained purpose they're made for! Now, as soon as that heir arrives, I'll be the first to welcome him. I can teach him all he needs to know 'bout runnin' a plantation. Main problem 'round here's that the darkies don't know their place. A lot goes into making a successful plantation, and a good wife who knows her way around one certainly can't hurt. That boy's single, and so is my Careen, but with him comin' from up North, no tellin' if he'll want to keep the place or not. Now if he don't, I'll be happy to buy it."

Chapter 8
Four Weeks Later

Self-assured, that's what Anthony Sinclair told himself. He must not only *be* self-assured, but he must *appear* self-assured. He wasn't, but he could at least pretend and *act* the part. His journey had started several days earlier. He'd traveled by steamer from Cincinnati to Charleston, and then taken another steamer from Charleston to Beaufort. That's where he'd been met by Josiah Simmons, and now they rode by open carriage to the Pleasant Wood Plantation big house. They'd almost reached their destination. It had been a three hour ride, and George, the stableman and coachman, drove them while attired in a top hat, black jacket and boots to his knees, while a pair of bay horses pulled the carriage through the forest over a sandy dirt road scattered with broken oyster shells.

Anthony sat across from Simmons who explained the surrounding community. Anthony, however, was too busy taking in the densely wooded southern atmosphere to listen that closely. The spring air was cool. He could smell the sea salt, but also the sweet fragrance of lily of the valley, and the intoxicatingly bold scent of magnolia. He inhaled, trying to absorb that intoxicating boldness, but instead only breathed in a whiff of Simmons's peppermint hair oil.

Anthony smoothed his own pomaded dark hair. Then he undid one large button on his double breasted cutaway jacket and slightly loosened his large bow tie. As the carriage trounced along the road near what he'd learned was Station Creek, Anthony could see the big house ahead, and all the negroes belonging to the estate assembled to meet him.

"There are the servants, as you can see," Simmons said. "I'll introduce each one and you'll find that there are none more loyal..."

Anthony paid little attention to what Simmons said. He was too busy wondering who was more nervous, the servants or himself. Yes, he held their fates in his hands, but did he really want to? And if not, what would become of them? Owning human beings... As a young boy growing up on a plantation, that had seemed only natural, at least in a way. But could it seem so again?

When the chance of owning a plantation had presented itself, Anthony had realized he had two options: to sell the place or keep it. Keeping it had somewhat of an appeal, since held pleasant memories from his southern childhood. Yet he pushed that consideration aside, thinking that he'd have to see the place first in order to make a decision. Then he began weighing his options. If he sold the place, he could put the money he earned into building his new law practice. But then he'd reflected that he was being given an opportunity to help, *and* he could earn money, possibly more as a planter than a lawyer. So, he'd finally decided that instead of selling off the place along with its servants, he would help the enslaved by being a benevolent owner to them. That had seemed the most magnanimous decision, even though he still struggled a bit with the idea of owning people.

Anthony possessed a desire to help, although he'd made some poor decisions by assuming he could win battles that were already lost causes. He'd become a lawyer in order to help, but had made a dreadful decision in his law career by trying to help a risky client. Even in matters of love he'd made an unfortunate mistake, thinking he could save the woman he'd fallen in love with from her own impulsiveness.

Simmons said, "I'm sure you'll find the house to your liking."

Taking his mind from his past and his eyes from his newly acquired people, Anthony studied the stately white house. It sat surrounded by oaks, while on the front grounds chickens and guinea hens pecked busily in the dirt. As the carriage slowed, ducks and geese emerged from the creek and squawked loudly, as if in greeting.

"It's not palatial," Simmons went on, "but it is beautiful, and you'll see..."

Ignoring Simmons, Anthony's mind wandered to the past. He vaguely remembered this place. His mother had been born and reared on this plantation, but she'd fallen in love with Robert Sinclair, a man from Georgia whose family owned a large rice plantation called Willow Haven. That's where Anthony had spent his childhood. His memories of Pleasant Wood were sparse; he only remembered visiting a handful of times as a child. Then, after his father died and his mother remarried and moved to Ohio, they hadn't come back.

When the carriage came to a complete stop, Anthony stepped from it and looked toward the field hands. They stood on one side, neatly lined in rows of ten. They numbered about forty. On the opposite side stood a smaller group of about a dozen of what he assumed to be the tradesmen and house servants. The hands and their children were dressed neatly in work clothes, the men in long sleeved cotton shirts and pants and the women in long sleeved cotton shifts and brightly colored head wraps. Though the clothing was well-worn, it was a far cry from ragged. The house servants and tradesmen also appeared well-attired.

The tradesmen wore vests and jackets, the maids blue homespun dresses with white aprons and white turbans. There was an old man-servant who wore a well tailored suit, and a butler uniformed in livery.

Simmons introduced Anthony to the tradesmen and house servants first, starting with a fellow named Eulee. "Eulee is the head man around here, and a born leader. He's quite knowledgeable about cotton, as well as all the other crops. He's one you can depend on for most anything."

The man was tall, heavy set and muscular. He looked to be about forty. His features of a broad nose and full lips were clearly African. Eulee's skin was as dark as coffee, and his teeth gleamed white as ivory. He seemed to swell with pride during Simmons's introduction.

"I'm sure we'll become well acquainted," Anthony said.

"Yes, suh," the man smiled.

Simmons then introduced him to the carpenter, Shamus, an older light-skinned fellow in his sixties and Hew, the blacksmith, a dark-skinned man who appeared to be about fifty.

The old man in the suit was introduced next. "This is Ajax," Simmons said. The elderly man bowed slightly to his new master, allowing the sun to reflect from his balding scalp for a moment. "Ajax served as body servant to Mr. Albright's father, then to Mr. Albright, and now you," Simmons said.

"I do recall meeting you when I was a boy." Anthony smiled.

"Yes, sir, Masta Sinclair, long ago when your mama came from Georgia with you to visit."

Simmons steered Sinclair by the elbow to the next servant, Emmett, the butler. The slim yellow man wore a grim expression. He said nothing, only lowering his head in greeting.

Simmons moved on, still guiding Anthony. "This is Patsy, the housekeeper." Patsy dropped a quick curtsy as

Sinclair repeated her name. She was a nice looking woman with intelligent eyes. She appeared knowledgeable, and much more self-assured than he felt. "She runs the household," Simmons went on, "and can tell you whatever you need to know about Pleasant Wood."

April the cook was introduced next, and then her daughter Lily, the kitchen maid. Anthony then met the weaver, Sophia, and the seamstress, Addie. Both were handsome women, plump and of medium height, in their mid-forties. Sophia's skin was brown like cinnamon, while Addie's appeared a deep yellow gold.

The last house girl he met stood next to Addie. The girl kept her turbaned head down. "This is Patsy's daughter, Deseré," Simmons said. "In addition to being a housemaid, she assists the seamstress."

Deseré, Anthony thought...pretty name. Desiré... Desired one in French.

The girl curtsied, as all the other women had upon meeting him. But when she lifted her eyes to his, Anthony was immediately taken aback by her beauty. Her eyes were large and as blue as the Mediterranean. Feeling his heart pound, he studied her face. Her skin was smooth and fair. It shimmered under the sun, glistening like burnished gold, and her lips, like rose petals, appeared soft, pink and plump. Silky blond ringlets escaped from her turban, lightly caressing the graceful curve of her neck.

She...Deseré...was the most beautiful thing Anthony had ever seen, and her name the most beautiful he'd ever heard. The turban she wore did nothing to detract from her comeliness, and the simple dress could hardly hide the shapeliness of her full breasts and tiny waist.

"She's young," Simmons said, "but Patsy assures me she's just as capable of running the household as her mother."

Simmons led Anthony in the direction of the field hands next, yet by the time Simmons finished introductions, the only name Anthony could remember was Deseré...

Chapter 9

"I appreciate you coming to call," Anthony said to Angus O'Malley, as they entered the pale green parlor. The pocket doors to the adjoining back parlor, a less formal room for family, were closed. From what Simmons had told Anthony about O'Malley, Anthony was convinced he wouldn't like the man.

"I had to see how you were doing after your first week here!" O'Malley exclaimed jovially. He then perused the room, setting his sights on a handsome Rococo Revival armchair covered in gold velvet upholstery. O'Malley trudged toward it over the red and gold Oriental carpet. With a wide seat and expansive peanut-shaped back, the chair appeared a sturdy piece of furniture, but as O'Malley settled his hefty frame into it, Anthony had his doubts.

Across from O'Malley, Anthony lowered himself into the matching gold velvet sofa. Its back was low in the middle and high on both ends, surrounded by an intricately carved wood frame of scrolls, shells, flowers and grapes. From the sofa, Anthony watched O'Malley's girth mold itself into every inch of the armchair's enveloping upholstery. Its ornately carved front legs and knees appeared to give a bit under the older man's weight. Anthony held his breath, hoping it wouldn't break.

"So what d'ya think of the plantation so far?" O'Malley asked, now seated on what appeared to be his throne. Although too large to casually sprawl back in the chair and cross a leg over his knee, he managed to hold court just the same, with his substantial trunk securely, and rather snugly, embedded in the cushioned back, his massive arms planted over the chair's scrolled arms, and his enormous feet, sprouted from mammoth legs, rooted to the Oriental carpet.

Anthony smiled in response to O'Malley's question. Hoping not to appear as ignorant as he felt, he tried to look confident. Placing an ankle over his knee, he said with nonchalance, "I still have a lot to learn." And not only about planting, Anthony thought.

O'Malley dressed the part of a successful planter and Anthony studied his clothes. The cut was a little different, but that wasn't surprising. Cincinnati always seemed to be a bit behind the times. O'Malley's suit was patterned in a fabric of small brown and white checks. However, it wasn't just cotton, like Anthony's black suit. O'Malley's ensemble had a slight shine to it. It must be a blend of cotton and linen. Anthony decided to have a couple of suits made of cotton and linen, with one being in that same brown and white checked pattern.

"It's a lengthy education process," O'Malley said. Anthony moved his gaze from the man's clothes to his eyes. "...and with you bein' a Yank and all, it wouldn't have surprised me if you'd said you plan on sellin'."

The windows, covered with red velvet drapes, were open, allowing a cool breeze to fill the room, carrying with it the scent of leather and O'Malley's sweat, covered by cologne that smelled of spiced liqueur. Despite the cool air, O'Malley sopped a sheen of perspiration from his balding head with a handkerchief. Anthony, sweating due to anxiety, pulled a handkerchief from his own pocket. After swiping his forehead and feeling the resulting moisture,

Anthony realized he was sweating just as much, if not more, than O'Malley.

The older man's massive bulk hunched forward. "So do you?" O'Malley prodded hopefully.

"Plan on selling?" Anthony asked.

"Yes, or are you gonna keep the place?"

Seeing Deseré appear in the doorway, Anthony's heart-rate increased slightly. He said without hesitation, "I plan on keeping it."

Deseré walked in carrying a tray with iced-tea and pound cake. The girl was lovely, Anthony thought, even wearing that simple blue homespun dress and white turban. He hadn't seen much of Deseré since his arrival. Over the past week she'd kept out of his way for the most part.

Moving his focus back to O'Malley, Anthony added, "I've been reading all the agricultural journals I can find to bring myself up to snuff."

"So you have." O'Malley's eyes roved over Deseré as she served his tea. "Let's see what you've learned so far. If I was to ask you how much cotton a healthy male hand could pick in a day, would you know?"

While O'Malley took a long sip of tea, Deseré placed a tall glass in front of Anthony. With her back to O'Malley, she mouthed a figure. Entranced, Anthony studied her rose petal lips as they formed a number.

"Two-hundred pounds," Anthony replied to O'Malley.

"Very good," the older man said. Deseré turned from Anthony and placed a piece of cake on the center table for O'Malley. Like a giant at a doll's table, he immediately grabbed the dainty china plate. Digging into the sweet with a delicate sterling fork, he asked, "And if I was to query you as to how much it cost to produce one bale of cotton, would you know that?"

As Deseré circled to Anthony to serve his cake, she silently spoke another answer. This time while he watched her beautiful mouth, he wanted to kiss it. Unnerved by his thoughts, he chastised himself for thinking so inappropriately about a servant.

Anthony cleared his throat, then repeated Deseré's silent response. "Between seventy-five and one-hundred and fifty dollars."

As Deseré turned from them to leave the room, O'Malley laughed. He eyed the girl's backside as she sashayed away. Not removing his gaze from her, he said, "You've learned a little, along with inheritin' a fine lookin' wench."

Anthony noticed Deseré's shoulders stiffen and her gait quicken as she exited the parlor.

O'Malley looked at Anthony. "Prostitution ain't as rampant in the South like it is up North," he said, while casually waving his fork through the air. "No need for it, if you get my drift. Not with girls at your disposal that look like that. And if they resist, it ain't for long...not with the power of the lash."

Appalled, Anthony felt his face blanch and the hair prickle on the back of his neck.

"When it's your property," O'Malley grunted, "you can do anything with it ya please."

Whatever slight dislike Anthony had felt for O'Malley to begin with, had immediately turned to extreme disgust. Aside from his wardrobe, Angus O'Malley was not one Anthony would emulate. He struggled enough with the issue of owning human beings, and Anthony would never tolerate such vile behavior towards them.

O'Malley took another bite of cake, as if talk of violating helpless women was the most natural thing in the world. "Now back to your test," he said, with a mouthful. "How many pounds of cotton during a normal season could one hand pick?"

Anthony took in a quick breath. He'd read that, but he'd read so much he couldn't remember exactly. So waving a hand through the air, he said something safe. "Several thousand pounds."

O'Malley's eyes narrowed. "You wanna be more specific...or do you need help from that fancy lookin' wench of yours?"

Anthony looked down for a moment, feeling his face burn. "Touché," he said, embarrassed, then met the man's hard black eyes.

"Touché, indeed. It'd be about seventeen thousand pounds. You're green yet, you are. Now," O'Malley wagged a stubby finger in Anthony's face, "if you're gonna hold onto the place, you have two choices. You can keep it small and unimpressive, like your uncle did. Or, if you wanna be successful like me, I can teach you all you need to know."

By the time O'Malley had lectured him on the cultivation of more land, crop rotation, seed selection, compost, the purchase of additional slaves, the use of a negro driver and the hiring of a "real" overseer to replace the soon to be departed Simmons—who in O'Malley's opinion was somewhat of a Nancy—Anthony's head was spinning.

"Perhaps we can discuss this more at length at a later time," Anthony said. "What you've described is rather staggering at this point. Perhaps the place is enough for me as it is, but I won't know until after I've been here a while."

"Fair enough," O'Malley said, "but you don't know what you can do. You don't know what you're capable of! Great success awaits those who are keen to grab it. And if things don't work out, I'll be ready to grab this place right out from under ya!" O'Malley laughed heartily, "At a fair price of course."

"Of course."

****

After O'Malley left, Anthony set off to find Deseré. He wanted to thank her for her help. Anthony walked to the rear of the house, just in time to see the girl from the back door helping the old man, Jax, down the steps. The elderly man had a cane, and once at the foot of the steps, he tried to shoo Deseré away, but she only laughed, continuing to hold onto to the crook of his arm and slowly accompany him to the kitchen house. Once Deseré saw Jax safely to his destination, she swiftly returned to the big house and dashed up the steps. As she rushed through the back door, Anthony was waiting for her.

He smiled. "I wanted to thank you for your assistance."

"You're welcome, Masta Anthony." Slightly out of breath from her rapid run up the steps, Deseré said nothing more, but appeared eager to ask something.

"Is there something you need?"

"Yes, sir," she said quickly. "I wanted to ask permission to see someone who'll be comin' to call on me directly. It won't be any longer than half an hour and I'll be back in plenty of time to help with supper chores."

"Of course, Deseré, I see—"

"Thank you, Masta."

Before Anthony could say anything else, the girl hurried off. The next time he saw her, it was from the window of the morning room. He'd been looking off into the distance, wondering just how much cotton the place was capable of producing, then his breath caught at the sight of her.

She'd taken off the blue homespun frock and now wore a yellow dress with short puffed sleeves. The bodice enhanced her tiny waist and revealed the curves of her breasts, which were earlier concealed by the trappings of the plain blue fabric. Her hair, once confined by the nondescript white turban, now tumbled freely in golden waves beneath her shoulders.

He'd never seen her out of the homespun and turban. Now, he thought, astonished by her beauty, she hardly appeared a slave. Feeling his heart become liquid warmth, he watched as she laughed playfully while walking backwards, talking to someone. *C'mon,* he heard her say through the glass. She held out her hand. Then Anthony's mood changed from astonished to incensed. A large negro appeared. Smiling, he clasped Deseré's hand. Then the two walked on arm in arm. Anthony's heart ceased its melting and instead began racing.

Before he realized what he was doing, Anthony had left the house by the front door. He marched to the edge of the porch and leaned slightly over the railing. He heard them approach beyond the azalea bushes that lined the side of the house.

"He's a Yankee," the negro said, "so you can't expect much. 'Less he's an abolitionist fixin' to free you. What I wouldn't give for that."

"Far's I can tell, he ain't," Deseré said. "He's a lawyer, and that ain't no use since he wants to be a planter. But he don't know much uh nothin'. Mr. O'Malley sat there with his big fat self askin' him questions 'bout cotton, but I had to sneak him the answers so he wouldn't look like a blame fool!" she laughed.

Anthony felt his fury rise. The nerve of her, laughing at him, and gossiping about his shortcomings to some strange negro! Once they were visible to him from the porch, Anthony's nostrils flared, as he snapped, "Deseré!"

Both of them stopped, startled by his appearance at the railing a few feet above them.

"Yes, Masta," Deseré said, her blue eyes wide with shock and surprise. She knew he'd overheard them. The buck was taller than Anthony and bigger through the chest. He was solidly built like an oak and stood by silently, waiting to be addressed, yet he didn't look down. With his head held high, he stared straight ahead. When he did look down, it was only to pull out a gold pocket watch and check the time.

Feeling slightly intimidated by the negro's size and bearing, Anthony chose to stay above them on the porch. "Who's this?" he asked Deseré sharply.

"William, sir," she replied.

"Boy," Anthony said with authority.

William's gaze met his. "Yes, sir." His brown eyes held fast to Anthony's. They were determined, as if they demanded respect.

Anthony didn't like that. "Where did you get that watch?"

The negro's determined eyes flashed. "I didn't steal it, sir." His voice was calm, not allowing a trace of the temper evident in his eyes. "It was a gift from my masta."

"From which plantation do you hail?" Anthony demanded.

"The Wesley Place, Masta."

"I see." From the porch, Anthony studied the buck. He was handsome, perhaps in his late twenties, and to Anthony's dismay, appeared to be more than just a field hand. Although his hands appeared rough, he wore cotton breeches and a long sleeved white cotton shirt and dark vest. The way the shirt and vest adhered to his body displayed his muscular physique.

Anthony puffed out his chest, and with slim comfort, glanced at his hands for a moment. They were smooth, free of calluses, and white. Then Anthony thought of the gentlemanly qualities he possessed, qualities this negro would never hold. He frowned at the way Deseré clutched William's arm possessively. "So the person you wished to meet is your beau," he said to Deseré. It was more of an accusation than a question.

"Yes, Masta," she said. "We plan to marry, with your permission, of course, but your uncle gave it already, before he passed on," she rambled quickly. "His intent was to buy William so he could be here, with me." Then she added hastily, "Sir."

Marry? This news displeased Anthony. "So," he looked harshly at William, "just what do you do at the Wesley place?"

"I'm a carpenter, sir, the best around, but I can do anything required, sir," William said confidently, standing taller. "I'd make a fine addition to your place, sir."

"*I'll* make that decision," Anthony said. Then he glanced

at Deseré. She clung to William's arm more tightly now. "I need you back inside."

"But, Masta—"

"Now!" Anthony turned on his heel, leaving them alone, yet once back in the house he felt his heart sink because of his cruelty.

Chapter 10

Several moments later, Deseré hesitantly approached the entrance of the morning room. She watched Masta Anthony for a moment. He stood at the window with his back toward her. With one hand on his hip, and the other perched against the window frame, he didn't realize she was there.

Deseré took a moment to study him. For a white man, she mused, he wasn't bad looking, although his looks couldn't compare with William's. Masta Anthony was taller than his uncle had been, and broad through the shoulders. His black hair was thick and slightly wavy, and recalling his square jawed handsome face and chiseled features, she thought of his dark brown eyes, which seconds later turned to face her.

"Come in," he summoned.

Deseré still wore the yellow dress, but wished she'd changed back into the blue homespun. She felt exposed and didn't like the way he looked at her, like a dog drooling from his chops while watching a child eat fried chicken. Mama warned her about not looking enticing in front of the new master. Well, Mama wouldn't see her now. She'd been sent to Saint Helenaville with Emmett to pick up some dry goods and hadn't yet returned. But when her mama did get back, Deseré knew she'd get a tongue lashing.

"So," Masta Anthony said, "with your knowledge of the fields, perhaps that's where you belong." His tone was angry. Deseré realized she'd hurt his pride, but it wasn't her fault he was stupid—at least where planting was concerned. Now he'd threatened her and she'd have to mend the damage by putting salve on his wounds.

"I'm sorry, sir," Deseré began. "I don't know much...just a little more than you." As her mother had advised, she wouldn't let him know that Simmons had instructed her on planting and finances during the four weeks prior to the new master's arrival.

"I spent my early years on a rice plantation. I know nothing about cotton."

"But it seems you remember how to treat your slaves," she said smartly. Deseré knew she shouldn't have said that; mustn't be fresh to the white folks. Mama had admonished her more than once for not holding her tongue, but sometimes she just couldn't help it.

For a long moment, Masta Anthony said nothing. He only glared at her, then, "Tell me this, why didn't my uncle ever have an overseer or a driver?"

Deseré said, "He had Mr. Simmons as business manager, and Eulee as head man. I reckon he thought they did well enough." Masta Anthony kept quiet for a moment, but she knew his wheels were turning.

"The day after I arrived," Anthony said, "Simmons rode me around the place. It seems like a blur when I think about it now. I'd like to look at the cotton fields, but I don't want to wander around for an hour trying to find them. So I'd like *you* to walk me there."

"I'll fetch one of the hands," Deseré said quickly, trying her best not to let it look like she was disobeying him. Instead she hoped he'd see her suggestion as a better idea.

"Did you misunderstand me, Deseré? I said *you*."

Feeling her jaw tense, Deseré hesitated, but she couldn't say no. "I'll change."

"Keep that on."

Upon hearing his words, she trembled.

****

Anthony looked up at the clear, cloudless sky, blue as a robin's egg. The sun still shone brightly and a soft wind blew around them as he and Deseré walked down the steps from the back of the big house and then over the intricate brickwork of the flower garden. Once they'd reached the end of a brick pathway, they walked on grass toward the cotton fields. Two brown and white hounds, Jasper and Darcy, his Uncle Jeremy's hunting dogs, ran ahead of them, chasing each other and occasionally stopping to tussle. Once the dogs were out of sight, he noticed that Deseré had fallen in step a few paces behind him. He stopped turning to face her. "Why don't you walk up here with me?" he asked. "Am I moving too fast?"

"I'm your servant, sir," Deseré said. "I'll direct your path, but it's my place to walk behind you."

Anthony pursed his lips. "Of course." He hesitated, then said, "I don't mind...breaking the rules." Deseré kept her eyes on his remaining quiet. "Walk with me," Anthony said, "I insist. It'll be our secret."

Hesitantly, Deseré walked beside him saying, "Guess you are a little like your uncle."

"Is that a compliment?" he asked.

"Take it any way you please, sir," Deseré replied, but Anthony didn't appreciate the smartness of her tone.

As they strode beyond the big house, several outbuildings appeared. The kitchen house was closest to the mansion and built with a chimney the width of a wall. The smell of ham and cloves wafted from it. Deseré pointed out three nearby brick cottages, the spinning house, the weaving house and the sewing house.

They walked by the negro cabins next, and Anthony slowed his pace while looking at how nice they were. Rather than cabins, they appeared as cottages with windows and porches. Over a dozen children, who appeared anywhere from four to ten years of age, ran squealing happily, chasing one another, unaware, Anthony thought, of what the future held for them as enslaved individuals.

"Masta Anthony!" a little boy yelled. He was one of the older children. With teeth white and even, and the boy's dark skin gleamed. Soon the other children, seeing their new master, called to him as well, waving happily. Anthony felt a tinge of nostalgia, thinking of his own childhood friends who'd been the slave children long ago on his father's plantation. But then the nostalgia was replaced by awkwardness as Anthony waved back, thankful that his future children would never be owned by anyone else.

****

By the time they reached the cotton fields, it was almost five o'clock. And that, Anthony had learned, was the end of the day for the field hands. The ground they stood on was dark gray with charcoal dust and shell fragments resembling sand. They were on the northeast side of the property and it smelled of freshly turned soil and manure. The fields stretched before them with earth hoed into high oval beds spread about five feet apart from center to center. Anthony counted twenty one slaves in the field working in teams of three.

"So they're planting," Anthony said, trying to make this sound more like a statement than a question.

"Yes, sir," Deseré said, her tone cool.

Anthony watched as one hand drilled a hole in the soil, then a second sprinkled seed into it, and a third covered the hole with a hoe.

"Simmons told me this is eighteen acres," Anthony said.

"Yes, sir," Deseré replied.

By now several of the hands had noticed them watching.

Some waved and others nodded in Anthony's direction. None smiled. Anthony sensed their civility contained no warmth, only wariness.

Seeing Deseré beside him, some eyed her longer than necessary in what looked like distress, as if Anthony were about to devour her. As they gazed upon the girl, some whispered to each other. They didn't trust him, Anthony thought. But he supposed that's how it should be, to get the most work out of them.

Then a large black man approached them. It was Eulee, the head man. He appeared to wear a genuine smile and his dark skin glistened with sweat. He removed his wide brimmed straw hat, revealing his shortly cropped black hair.

"Good afternoon." Anthony smiled stiffly.

"Aftanoon, Masta." Eulee's brown eyes, bright and discerning, moved to Deseré's. "Dezray." He pronounced her name with a lazy drawl. She didn't respond right away. Instead, she looked down. And when she did, Anthony caught a flicker of concern cross Eulee's countenance. But in less than a second, the jovial smile returned when his eyes met Anthony's.

"Eulee," Deseré said quietly. Her gaze remained on the ground, as if she were embarrassed to be seen with her new master. Served the girl right, Anthony thought. If she could parade around in that dress with William, she could parade around in it with him, as well.

"Plantin' here ought be finished tomorrow, suh. The hoein'll begin when the cotton puts out 'bout the fifth leaf. Then it'll need to be hoed again 'bout five to eight mo' times."

"I see," Anthony said.

"Yes, suh. I'd like to show you the potato land. Some of the hands plowed it today so I'd like to show you what they done."

"I appreciate your desire to familiarize me with the land, but perhaps you can show me tomorrow."

Eulee glanced at Deseré. "It won't take long."

"Surely it can wait," Anthony said. "Deseré was just showing me the fields." A bell started to ring, signaling the end of the work day. "And besides, now your day is over. I'm sure you're eager to get back to the quarters."

Kneading the rim of the hat he held, Eulee said nothing, but for a moment glimpsed Deseré again. She continued to gaze downward, clutching her skirts.

"I insist you go to the quarters," Anthony said firmly, wielding his power, surprised by how much he enjoyed it. He felt a tinge of guilt. But the man *had* worked all day.

"Yes, suh." Eulee slowly walked away, joining the other hands who now trudged from the fields. Yet he gazed over his shoulder one last time to look at Deseré, whose face remained downcast.

With Eulee and the hands leaving, Anthony soon had Deseré to himself. He studied the acreage. "Eighteen acres isn't that much. I suppose my uncle could have grown more, couldn't he?"

****

Deseré peered down at the hem of her skirt, and then her shoes. Ignoring Masta Anthony, she paid more attention to the far away sounds of the cows mooing, horses neighing and chickens clucking. Exasperated, she wondered why he'd dragged her to the cotton fields. She hadn't been around him much since his arrival, but in what little time she'd been in his presence, he'd put on the airs of a gentleman. But Mama said all men are the same, savage beasts, regardless of their airs. Of course she couldn't have meant Masta Jeremy or William.

If Masta Anthony were to show his beastly side, wouldn't she have seen it by now? Deseré wondered. He did look at her in the yellow dress like he thought she was pretty, though at the time he'd reminded her of a drooling mongrel. But he hadn't touched her, and he hadn't said anything ungentlemanly, like that pig-faced Mr. O'Malley. The worst

Masta Anthony had done was insist she show him to the cotton fields. Now she could only hope that she kept her shoes and dress clean.

She wore flat-heeled Moroccan slippers. Cream colored with gold stitching, they'd been a gift from Masta Jeremy that he'd bought her in Charleston, and she only wore them on Sundays or with William. Same with her dresses, made from fabric Masta Jeremy purchased for her. She held up the skirts of her yellow dress, despising her new master and not paying him any mind when he spoke.

"Deseré," he said sharply, "I asked you something."

She sighed. "Oh, I thought it was rhetorical." His eyes widened, in what she assumed was surprise at her knowledge of that word.

"Rhetorical?"

"You do know what that means?" She tried to control her sarcasm, but just barely.

"Of course I do," he said exasperatedly, "but how do you?"

"Your uncle taught me a thing or two," Deseré said. "But to answer your question, I suppose Masta Jeremy could have grown more, but he was satisfied with the eighteen bales his land produced. He'd sell it to a factor in Charleston." Anthony knew a factor was an agent who'd take about a four percent commission. "And," Deseré went on, "Masta Jeremy sold some of the other crops, like the potatoes and corn, to the local markets, and a lot of the grapes he shipped up to the Northern markets."

"Grapes?" Anthony asked. When Deseré nodded he said, "How many acres of those?"

"'Bout ten, I think."

"So it's a small vineyard."

"Yes, sir. And the income from them is quite considerable." Deseré chided herself for showing off with the knowledge Simmons had taught her. She wouldn't provide any further details. Mama warned her not to sound as if she knew too much.

"Oh? Seems like my uncle taught you more than a thing or two."

Deseré only smiled. "Most of the crops grown here are used to keep us self-sufficient," she said. "That's what Masta Jeremy called this place, self-sufficient."

There was additional land beyond the fields overgrown with trees that seemed endless. Anthony pointed toward it. "That land could be cleared and cultivated too. I want to produce more than eighteen bales of cotton. In addition to being self-sufficient, I'd like this place to earn a good amount of money. O'Malley thinks it could."

Deseré nodded, feeling a knot in her stomach at the mention of the fat man's name, and the horror stories of overwork, starvation and flogging she'd heard about at his numerous plantations.

"So, Deseré, tell me..."

She waited, looking at him, but he didn't finish his sentence. "You mean tell you 'bout cotton? Like I said, I don't know much, but Eulee, he can tell you anything you wanna know." She gazed over Anthony's shoulder in the direction Eulee had walked off earlier. Deseré could no longer see him, but she shouted his name. Before she could call again, Anthony stopped her.

"Quiet, Deseré. You needn't call Eulee, because I wasn't asking you to tell me—'bout cotton," he smiled, imitating her, "I want you to tell me—'bout you."

"Me?"

"Yes."

This conversation caught Deseré off guard. Was it the start of something beastly? Now looking at Masta Anthony, she felt frightened, like a squirrel just snatched from the ground by the talons of an owl. "Wh—what do you want to know?" she stammered.

"The dress you're wearing...it hardly looks like the dress of a servant. How did it come to be yours?"

"Masta Jeremy was fond of Mama, so he was fond of me..." She went on to explain his generosity and how he'd treated her almost like a daughter.

"Did he...care for your mother?" Anthony asked.

"Yes — but not in the way you're implying. He's not my papa. *He* was a gentleman. And about my dresses, Masta Jeremy bought me the fabric; I sewed them. He even told me that one day he'd take me to Paris and let me pick out lots and lots of fabrics myself. 'Course that was before..."

Anthony nodded. "I understand... So not only are you a seamstress, you're one of great talent."

She felt herself blush slightly. "If Mama heard me agree to that, she'd say I was bragging."

This made Anthony smile.

"I'd be happy to do some of my handiwork for you," she said. "Masta Jeremy had two fine suits made in Charelston, not long before he died, and I reckon they'd fit you with some slight alterations."

Anthony nodded, appearing pleased. "I'd like that very much."

"Good," Deseré smiled. "Addie and I will begin the alterations tomorrow, if that meets your approval, sir."

"Tomorrow is fine," Anthony said. "Now, what else you can tell me about you?"

Deseré hesitated for a moment. "I've told you all there is to know about me," she said, "aside from the fact that I *love* William..."

****

Her voice seemed to melt at the mention of his name, and the smile left Anthony's face as he looked into hers. Although his mood had darkened upon hearing her say *William*, his heart pounded. Deseré's wide blue eyes were clear and innocent, her soft cheeks like milk and roses, and her pink lips, lilacs in bloom. Golden hair blew about her delicately sculpted shoulders in soft silken waves. What would it feel like to kiss her, to touch her...? Anthony shook those thoughts from his mind.

"So...I'd like your permission to marry him...soon as possible."

Why had he insisted on Deseré walking him to the fields? Was it an excuse to spend time with her? That was ridiculous. She was a mere servant girl and nothing more. Regardless of why he'd asked her to accompany him, the last thing he wanted to hear about was her love for another man. But why was that a concern...when she was only a slave?

"Masta Anthony?"

He was staring at her, although she'd stopped talking a moment ago. Feeling awkward, Anthony started, "You — want to marry," then regaining his footing from the earlier encounter at the porch, he went on, "and you wish me to buy him, as my uncle would have, so he can live here."

"Yes," she smiled, a hopeful glimmer in her eye.

Anthony's heart dropped as he mumbled, "I'll talk to his owner regarding his price."

"Thank you, Masta!" Deseré's smile widened and she clasped her hands over her heart. They pressed against the smooth softness welling above the lace trimmed bodice of her dress. "Does this mean you're giving your permission?"

"No." Anthony watched her face fall. "Only that I'm considering it." He stepped closer to her. She stepped back. "Deseré, you needn't be afraid of me," Anthony began, but he was then interrupted by someone shouting.

"Masta Anthony!" It was Eulee. Anthony turned to see the hand running toward them. "Pardon me, sir," he said, as he approached from a several yards away. "I heard Dezray call. Thought maybe she convinced you to let me show you the potato land."

"I appreciate your willingness to show me, Eulee, but —"

"Pardon, sir, but I forgot to mention something important," he said, slowing his pace as he reached them.

"Some of the seed is rotted, so we might not have enough to plant."

"Masta Anthony, sir," Deseré said, "My chores are with supper. I need to get back to the house, with your permission." She curtsied quickly.

Anthony sighed, shoving his hands into his pockets. He looked from Deseré to Eulee, then back to Deseré. "Very well, you may go, and Eulee can show me the potato fields," he said, feeling his lips turn downward as he spoke, "and explain in detail the uh...rotted seed situation."

Deseré swirled to go in a flurry of yellow, then ran as rapidly as her skirts allowed. Anthony watched her for a long moment, trance-like studying the graceful way she moved, as if being carried by the cloud of yellow dress. Catching himself, Anthony's gaze quickly shot to Eulee's. Their eyes held for an instant, until Eulee looked away.

****

The next morning, Anthony stood in the back parlor attired in one of Jeremy's suits with Deseré and Addie standing behind him, tailoring the jacket to fit. Each woman had a large sewing basket woven from sweet-grass, filled with spools of thread, needles and an assortment of buttons, and each of the ladies had a satin pin cushion close by, bulging with straight pins.

Addie said, "He's broader up top than Masta Jeremy, so the shoulders need to be let out."

"If I cut open the fabric," Deseré said, "I should have about three-quarters of an inch to work with."

Addie agreed, then, adjusted Anthony's sleeves, noting that they needed to be let down just shy of an inch.

While Addie slipped the jacket from Anthony's shoulders and placed it over a chair, Deseré moved to stand in front of him. He was several inches taller and attempted to disregard her closeness. Yet when Deseré ran her hands around the vest covering his torso to make various adjustments, he found he couldn't.

"Raise your arms, sir," Deseré said. "This needs to be taken in just a tad. It's loose through the middle." After she and Addie pinned the side seams of the vest, Anthony removed it.

While Addie placed the vest with the jacket, Deseré moved her hands to his trousers, tugging at both sides of the waist-band. Anthony tried to ignore the feel of her fingers, but again found this rather difficult to do.

Deseré reached for her pin cushion. "They need to be taken in a little too." After she and Addie pinned the waist-band appropriately. Deseré knelt in front of him, pulling at the hem of his trousers. "And they need to be let down 'bout half an inch," she said. Then, running a hand mid-way up his leg for a moment, Deseré remarked, "This is some very fine wool."

"Just stick to the hem, honey," Addie said, as if reading Anthony's mind.

Although Deseré's touch was merely meant to feel the fabric, to Anthony it created a titillating sensation. He prayed to suppress the physical change occurring upon his person.

Deseré stood up, oblivious to the effect she had on him. "Alright, Masta Anthony, I'll have this suit altered for you in the next few days. You feel like tryin' on the other one?" she asked innocently.

Anthony hesitated, deciding it best to avoid any further embarrassing predicaments he might not be able to control. "Uh, this will do for today," he said.

Chapter 11

My Dearest Friend,

I will forego the amenities and proceed to the heart of the matter. I take it as the keenest of insults that I have not received a response to my first letter delivered to you in the land of Dixie. Although we do not see eye to eye on the "peculiar institution" in which you are now immersed, as your friend, I do deserve to know what your future plans entail. Ridding yourself of the place, I hope! Is that not what you said at one time? I will be in a state of sheer discombobulation if you have indeed decided to become a slave owner! Good God, man! Is that why you have neglected to correspond with me?

Over a month had passed since Anthony's arrival. Since then, Simmons had resigned and the weight of the plantation now rested firmly on Anthony's shoulders. It was Saturday and he sat at the plantation desk in the morning room. The ledgers, papers and agricultural journals that his uncle and Simmons had used were now in his possession and stored here.

Reading an issue of *The Southern Agriculturalist* yet again, he tried to absorb as much as possible to become a successful planter. Yet he could only take in so much information at a time. He'd put aside the journal to re-read a letter from an old friend in Cincinnati, Henry Braithwaite.

A boy had picked up the mail from St. Helenaville yesterday and two letters had arrived from Cincinnati. The letter Anthony read now was Henry's second letter to him. Anthony had failed to respond to his friend's first letter, partly out of shame; nor would he respond to this one, purely out of guilt.

Have you completely given up on your law career? At one time you said you'd sell the place and use the funds in building your new practice. God allows things to happen for a reason. Your partner made a poor choice that hindered your success. God, however, provided an opportunity that could be a great financial blessing for you, as well as a blessing to the enslaved souls you could emancipate. I, on behalf of the Ohio Anti-Slavery Society, would be happy to welcome them to Cincinnati and see that they are provided the means and resources to begin anew here in Ohio or Canada. There is, however, another option of which I am sure you would prefer: that I place them in the hands of American Colonization Society and have them shipped to Liberia.

Henry and his sarcasm, Anthony mused. Putting down the letter, he thought about his predicament and hoped success in this venture wouldn't elude him as it had in his law career. Although uncomfortable with the institution, he *needed* slavery in running the plantation to succeed, and his people certainly needed him for his benevolence as a slave owner. Because of state law, he couldn't free his human chattel, nor could he afford to pay them. The money his uncle had inherited twenty years earlier was now his. It was far from depleted, yet paying the people would slowly drain it away over time since it was used to keep the place afloat. In addition, some of the hands had recently been afflicted with cholera. He'd already lost two to the disease, and the loss of more would be a significant blow to his manpower, as cotton was a demanding crop. Purchasing new people would be expensive. A thought that hypocritically disgusted him.

Anthony stood to stretch his legs and walked to one of the windows only to see Deseré talking and laughing with William. Anthony's lip twitched. He loosened his cravat, then turned toward the doorway upon hearing footsteps. It was the somber-faced Emmet. On a tray, the butler carried a crystal brandy decanter with two matching snifters.

"Your brandy, sir," Emmett said, bowing slightly.

"Thank you, Emmett," Anthony said. "Just place it on top of the desk."

"Yes, sir."

As Emmett set the decanter down, Anthony asked, "Will more brandy need to be ordered any time soon?"

"No, sir," Emmett said dourly, "there are several bottles in the basement. As I'm sure you know," he added with a touch of disdain, "aside from medicinal purposes, your uncle abstained from alcohol. He did, however, keep a generous supply on hand to serve his guests."

"I see," Anthony said.

"Will there be anything else, sir?"

"No, Emmett, you may go."

As soon as Emmett was gone, Anthony poured himself a drink. He wouldn't drink more than he could hold. He was a gentleman; besides, he knew first-hand the ravages of alcohol. While in his teens, he'd seen one of the men who worked at his stepfather's meat-packing plant stumble into work drunk, unable to stand and blathering nonsense. Anthony had sworn he'd never touch spirits, but that changed with the downturn of his law career. Since then he'd found comfort in a swig or two to calm himself in situations of extreme distress. He took the first swig a little too fast, coughing at the heat and intensity of the brandy, then he picked up the letter again, bracing for Henry's continued admonishment.

My sincerest apologies if your intention is indeed to sell the place and liberate its slaves. I can only hope that it is, for do you not remember the riots here in our Queen City, the last a mere four years ago? Must I remind you that I was in the thick of it? With my dear friend and fellow abolitionist Cornelius Burnett, I was there in his candy shop when that angry mob, armed with clubs and stones, stormed the streets and demolished the doors and windows of his store before marching off to Bucktown to do more of the same!

Do you not remember the other riots in our city's past? The burning of negro tenements? The sight of negroes being assaulted wherever they were found in the streets, being subjected to such violence as to cause death? Having lived here and seen that to which the colored are subjected, how could you in good conscience be a slave owner?

Anthony recalled those riots, caused by pro-slavery sentiment and the abolitionist propaganda that angered Cincinnati businessmen eager to do business and maintain good relationships with the slave-owning southern states.

Violence and destruction... Anthony sighed. At least in the South, the negroes were contained and controlled. As slaves, they knew their place, and no chaos or wild riots would ensue. And if one treated one's people well, he rationalized, there wasn't really anything wrong with the institution. Besides, it was the law of the land and freeing negroes here was a complicated process that would have to involve their relocation, if indeed their freedom were granted by the legislature. Anthony reminded himself that he was no stranger to slavery, since he'd lived on a plantation in his youth.

He took another sip of the amber-colored liquid, this time feeling a smooth burn as it trickled down his throat.

Anthony wondered if he'd made the right decision in taking on this place. He'd given up the idea of selling it, and now felt too debased to admit this to his friend, even though his keeping the place was for the good of the people here, though making money and boosting his reputation wouldn't hurt either.

Anthony had never assumed a career as a planter would be in his future. He'd attended the Cincinnati Law School with every intention of becoming a practicing lawyer in his adopted city, which was exactly what he'd done, but things had happened, causing a turn for the worse.

Is success what you seek most above all else? Are you trying to impress your stepfather? Only strive to please your Heavenly Father. I can assure you, He does not approve of the "peculiar institution" you have possibly chosen to embrace! Also, my friend, seek solace in prayer, not spirits. That said, I hope that by now you can put your experience with Edith behind you. I will mention her no further.

Anthony's heart constricted upon reading the woman's name. How he'd loved her... Another sip of alcohol eased the pain. He'd confided only to Henry about what had happened between him and Edith.

I do not wish to offend you, my dear Anthony, my only hope is to inspire you in making the right choices in the one life you have been given by your Creator.

Yours in Christ,
Henry

Anthony put Henry's letter down, letting its words sear his mind again as they had yesterday. He hadn't always made the right choices, but sometimes circumstances had been beyond his control and had influenced poor decision making.

Upon graduating from law school, Anthony had been asked to become a partner with Raymond Pohl, a friend he'd attended law school with who'd inherited his elderly uncle's law practice. They'd done well as jack-of-all-trades lawyers by accepting criminal as well as civil cases, until Raymond had disgraced himself by having an affair with a dance hall girl. The ill-fated publicity had severely limited business.

During that time, Anthony had taken on the case of an accused murderer. He'd had his reservations, but because of a slump in business, and the fact that the man could have been innocent—and needed help—he took the case anyway. If only he hadn't... Anthony took a longer sip, feeling the heat in his belly burn like hot coals. His client had been proven innocent, but tried to kill someone a week later. The victim of the attempted murder survived, leaving no question of the identity of his assailant. In addition, there had been a witness to the attack. That led to more bad press for the law office, since Anthony had defended the now second-time attempted murderer.

Shortly following that debacle, the dance hall girl went to the papers with Pohl's bastard child in tow. Then, a humiliated Pohl committed suicide, and that was the end of the practice. Anthony had sought employment with other law offices, but found no one to employ him. He'd been in the midst of building a solo practice when he'd received news of his inheritance.

After another toss of brandy, Anthony reached next for the letter from his mother, Leona. He'd tried to read it yesterday when it first arrived, but couldn't stomach the contents. After briefly perusing the newspaper clipping that had fallen from it, he'd put it away. Now emboldened by spirits, he thought he'd give reading it another try. He unfolded the stationary and was again confronted by the dastardly clipping. This time he read it slowly.

Mr. Abraham Weld of Clifton and Miss Edith Emory of this city were united in marriage at the residence of the bride's parents Tuesday evening at 7:30 o'clock, Reverend Bernard James of this city officiating. The groom is an industrious architect and the bride is the daughter of Gerald Emory of this city, and an estimable young lady. Their many friends extend congratulations.

Anthony put the clipping face down on his desk, seething. Another taste was in order and he took one, grimacing as he swallowed. Yes, the groom was an industrious architect *and* the son of a wealthy beer brewer, and the "estimable" Edith married for money! At one time she'd declared her love to Anthony but upon learning that he was the stepson of a wealthy man, rather than a blood son, and that an inheritance wasn't necessarily guaranteed, Edith had set her sights on greener pastures — the she-devil! She'd been an impulsive girl, one to leap before looking, yet Anthony was convinced that with his calmer demeanor, they'd be a perfect match. He could help her by taming her spontaneity and foolhardiness. In the end, however, he'd been the fool.

Anthony took a deep breath and read his mother's letter:

Dearest Anthony,

I hope this letter finds you well. I do miss you immensely and pray that you are not overwhelmed by your Uncle Jeremy's plantation. I have nothing but fond memories of Pleasant Wood as I think of growing up there with my brother. Have you made a final decision regarding the place, to sell it or keep it? As you well know, managing a plantation is an enormous responsibility.

Pausing from the letter, Anthony thought back to first receiving the news of the inheritance from his uncle. He'd originally thought that the only way he could make a decision to keep the place or sell it was to see it. His mother had told him it was completely up to him. Henry, however, had said that there must have been some form of derangement in his mental capabilities for even considering the idea of owning a plantation.

Henry was an outspoken abolitionist, and Anthony suspected his fervor in abolitionism stemmed from that of his housekeeper, Marissa Brown. She was as brown as her name implied, and young and beautiful. Henry wasn't married nor looking to marry; however, he did look at Marissa with unmistakable affection. If Henry's feelings for her were indeed as Anthony suspicioned, then *he, Henry,* was the one with questionable mental capabilities! The woman was a *negro* — his *housekeeper* — for Heaven's sake!

Although Anthony didn't agree with Henry on every point, through his influence, Anthony had become slightly opposed to slavery. Yet in Cincinnati, Anthony had been alarmed by the social consequences of abolitionism because of the numerous runaway blacks, newly escaped from Kentucky, via the Ohio River, that sauntered through the streets at all hours of the day and night. He found himself instead favoring colonization schemes that would ship free blacks to Liberia. Henry thought that a drastic solution, but Anthony believed there was nothing wrong with it, and viewed it as beneficial to negroes, as well as whites. He glanced at his mother's letter, then picked up where he'd left off.

May I be frank with you, my darling? My father was kind to his people, as was Jeremy when he inherited the place after Father's death. Your father, however, God rest his soul, instituted, shall we say, a firmer hand at our beautiful rice plantation, Willow Haven. I realize that as a child you were oblivious to his treatment of our people. Needless to say, Willow Haven was much more profitable than Pleasant Wood ever was, but I was happy to wash my hands of it after I married your stepfather.

Anthony looked away from the letter angrily. Wash her

hands? Willow Haven had been near and dear to Anthony's heart. Although he realized the difficulty his mother would've faced in managing the place without Father, to speak of it so callously seemed a personal affront.

Mother had gone from plantation mistress to the wife of a glorified Catholic butcher, or should he say pork baron? Anthony felt himself scowl so sourly his expression could curdle milk. His stepfather's meat packing plant, though profitable, was hardly pretty. The canals ran red with animal carnage, the German immigrant workers left at the end of the day soaked in blood, and swine roamed the sidewalks in the Packing House District eating all the debris left over from the day's slaughtering. Wash her hands, indeed!

After Anthony's father had died, his mother had met Elton Miller through a mutual acquaintance. Eventually, she'd married him and moved up North to Cincinnati with nine-year-old Anthony in tow. Not only had she become a Yankee, she'd become a Catholic, and she'd sold the plantation where Anthony had spent his childhood years — the happiest of his life. And what had broken his heart the most was leaving his mammy behind. Mammy Lucy, he'd called her. She'd been more of a mother to him than his real mother, so in essence Anthony felt he'd lost both parents, as well as his home.

A year later, Anthony's mother had given birth to Anthony's half-brother, Luke. Since his mother's re-marriage to Elton, Anthony had felt displaced in his mother's life, and once she'd borne Elton's son, Anthony felt like an outsider in his family, and always second-best to Luke.

He inhaled slowly, then turned his attention back to the letter and continued reading.

...Though not an abolitionist, Elton finds slavery absolutely repulsive. He used to say in jest that he married me to take me

away from the horrors of it. Speaking of marriage, I enclosed Edith's wedding announcement. I heard that she and her new husband plan to take a tour of Europe sometime in the near future. Edith is such a lovely girl. I suppose I will never understand why you allowed her to slip through your fingers. If you had married her, perhaps she could have helped you in making a decision about Pleasant Wood. I assume she does not approve of slavery and would have urged you to sell, but I could be wrong. As I mentioned, owning a plantation is not an easy task, especially without a good wife to assist you in managing its day-to-day operation. I pray that you will find the perfect wife, as there are surely several southern belles from which to choose. Be cautious, however, in your choice. As Proverbs says, "Who can find a virtuous woman? for her price is far above rubies."

Now, I must share news about your brother Luke. After he graduates from college in May, your stepfather is appointing him to a position of management in the company! I am sure that Luke will write to you and tell of all the details, of which I cannot begin to explain.

Anthony smirked, looking away from the letter for a moment. He wouldn't wait with bated breath to receive correspondence from Luke. Anthony then reflected further that Elton had never offered him a job. He drained the snifter. Elton had paid for Anthony's education, but he'd claimed his meat packing plant already had a lawyer and there was no need for another one.

Do take care of yourself, my darling. I hope to visit you soon.

All my love,
Mother

Anthony put the letter aside. Once more he stood and walked to the window. Deseré was still with William, appearing awestruck at his every word. The mention of

Edith's wedding, and now the sight of a coquettish Deseré flirting with William, called for another drink. He trudged back to the desk and poured one.

Following a short swallow, Anthony asked himself whom he was trying to deceive. The thought of living in the South on a plantation had somewhat appealed to him from the start. Happy childhood memories returned of his father, who'd taught him how to hunt, shoot, and fish. Then there was Mammy Lucy, who'd always kissed away his tears. Her husband, Uncle Jack, had sat Anthony upon his knee many a time and told him stories. Anthony remembered lots of happy times in their simple cabin. Compared to the opulent big house where Anthony lived, Mammy Lucy and Uncle Jack seemed richer in the simplicity of their lives. They had each other, plus enough love to lavish on him.

Swirling the brandy in his glass, Anthony again approached the window thinking of how he missed that and how carefree and happy he'd been back then. With all the negro children to play with, he'd never been lonely. He remembered the lively music of his father's people and their melodic singing. Even the food of the South was special.

Elton hired only white servants and Anthony hadn't had a decent biscuit in years. Elton's cook, Eunice, made a superb dinner roll, but her attempt at biscuits resembled tree bark. And who'd ever heard of putting milk on grits? Anthony relished April's biscuits and gravy here at Pleasant Wood, as well as her creamy grits with butter, and whatever else she prepared. Each dish served up remembrances of a more pleasant time.

Aside from his nostalgia toward the South, his vow to be a benevolent slaveholder, and the possibility of earning a great deal of money as a planter, there was something else, something more dangerous that would have compelled him to stay here regardless...

Deseré.

His feelings for her overwhelmed him more than the

management of the plantation itself. Anthony had stopped denying that he wanted her. She was his slave. She belonged to him. He had every right to take her by force, as O'Malley had bluntly implied. But Anthony wouldn't do that. He wanted more than just her flesh... He loved her... The admission almost startled him, but it was true. He desired that Deseré look at him with longing, the same way she looked at William. If he could, he'd sell his soul for that. Anthony was determined that one day she would love him back, and want him as badly as he wanted her. Had he loved Edith as much as he now loved Deseré? In retrospect, Anthony thought not.

His emotions swirled in torment. Deseré was a human being, just as he was, and he owned her. That wasn't right; but was it right to own any of these people? Anthony forced those thoughts away. He was a kindly master. Then his flawed introspection brought him full-circle. He owned Deseré, yet could he ever possess her heart?

With fury and the feel of a knife wound to his heart he watched Deseré kiss William. Anthony imbibed a generous gulp of alcohol, feeling his chest burn like lightening. He coughed again, but didn't remove his eyes from Deseré and William, still locked in an embrace. Yet in seconds, he watched William pull from her arms. The buck looked around quickly, as though making sure no one had seen them, and then casually waved goodbye. William had neglected, however, to glance up at the window where Anthony stood. Then Deseré ran after William for another kiss. Again, the buck cautiously gazed around to make sure they were alone, then obliged, and hurried off. William didn't deserve her. Anthony glowered, finishing off the remains in his second snifter, scorching his insides. On the occasions he'd watched them, it was always the same. Deseré appeared the more enamored.

Anthony thought that if he were Deseré's young man, he would never leave her side. And if her heart were his, he'd take her to New Orleans and have her declared as white. He knew that could be done. He'd been in a saloon over the Rhine in Cincinnati once, with of all people, Henry Braithwaite, another teetotaler, and a mutual friend from New Orleans who'd been in town to escape the summer heat of the South. The man knew of someone who'd fallen in love with his mulatto concubine and chose to take matters into his own hands.

At the time, Anthony thought the situation appalling. Whereas Henry had asked several questions, which had furthered Anthony's suspicion regarding Henry and Marissa, who could hardly pass as white. Now, recalling that conversation, Anthony reflected that all the man had had to do was vouch to the courts that he knew the girl's family as white.

With Deseré, Anthony could do that, too. It was a lie, of course, but at least then he could marry her. Marry her? What was he thinking? Perhaps the alcohol was thinking for him, because Anthony was hardly Henry Braithwaite! And besides, Deseré had asked Anthony's permission to marry William. As of yet, he hadn't given it. He turned rather unsteadily from the window, then called Emmett to send for her.

MARIA MCKENZIE

Chapter 12

Anthony glanced at his pocket watch. Nearly half an hour had passed. Deseré appeared at the entrance of the morning room. Anthony stood from his desk and began to approach her, but nearly stumbled over his feet. Deseré's eyes widened at his clumsiness. Abashed, Anthony steadied himself by holding onto the edge of the desk.

"Come in, De-shary," he said, realizing his words were slightly slurred.

As she took two timid steps inside the room, Anthony looked her up and down. She'd changed from the peach colored dress she wore with William to a plain blue homespun frock, and she'd turbaned her hair.

"If you hadn't changed," he said sternly, trying to sound in control of her, as well as his senses, "you would've arrived sooner...not kept me waiting."

Deseré looked down, her face flushed. "Sorry, Masta Anthony."

Concentrating on his enunciation, he said, "I realize it is Saturday...only a few light chores are expected of you, but...with your mother nursing the sick servants with cholera in the quarters, she assured me...you'd assume some of her responsibilities."

"Yes, sir."

"Have you?" Anthony stepped forward, but almost fell. He clutched the desk more firmly, "Or has *William* taken up too much of your time?"

"Masta Anthony, I told you I'd do everything before William came to see me, including distributing the rations, and I did."

He wanted to keep Deseré longer, just to gaze at her beauty. Yet the guise of a reprimand was wearing thin. He wanted to tell her he loved her more than William ever would. "Deseré, I—"

Anthony looked away, catching himself just in time. The alcohol had loosened his tongue. He restrained himself from saying anything further. Not only would he raise a topic that was taboo, he'd make a puzzle-headed fool out of himself in the process. He'd think of something else to prolong his time in her presence. However, the last thing Anthony wanted to do was bring up the subject of her impending marriage.

"You what, Masta?"

"Nothing," he snapped, still looking away.

"Well, I have something I need to discuss with you."

He glared at her for addressing him so forthrightly, but she seemed undeterred.

"You still haven't given your consent to me and William." Had she read his mind? Anthony said nothing. "To get married," Deseré continued, as if he were unaware of to which matter she was referring.

"No, I haven't," he said slowly. "The next time William is here...I'll speak to him. *Then* I'll make a decision."

"Why?"

She was a fresh girl. "You needn't concern yourself with why."

Deseré's eyes dropped, then she raised them and looked

past him toward the desk, surely noticing one more open agricultural journal upon a pile of many.

Embarrassed by his slight inebriation, as well as still not having mastered the art and knowledge of planting, Anthony quickly blurted, "You may go now."

****

Although Masta Anthony had dismissed her, Deseré didn't move immediately. Her eyes scanned the stack of journals on the desk, as well as the letters he'd been reading that had arrived from up North. He was Yankeefied. Talked liked a Yankee and still didn't know the first thing about being a planter! He was a lawyer, and he should have stayed in Ohio and practiced that despicable profession!

Every time Masta Jeremy had dealings with his lawyer, he'd come home and joke, "The first thing we do, let's kill all the lawyers." He said that was from Shakespeare, so Deseré guessed they'd had a bad reputation for a very long time. And Masta Anthony appeared sloppy at times. More than once she'd noticed his loosened cravat. Masta Jeremy would never have allowed his clothes to look that way. And Masta Anthony wasn't as nice as Masta Jeremy. His disposition was cool. Or maybe he just hid behind that cool disposition because of his stupidity in managing a plantation.

And he *drank*! Right now, wobbling around, he was acting drunk as a boiled owl. Deseré smelled the alcohol on his breath and her eyes traveled to the decanter sitting atop his desk. Raising her chin high, Deseré thought of Masta Jeremy who didn't drink. *He* was a good man. But after one month, Deseré had determined that his nephew was apparently a no-account.

Anthony followed her gaze to the decanter, then a sly smile curled his lips. "A drink?"

Deseré gasped, feeling the blood rush to her face.

He laughed. "I'm only jesting."

Deseré suppressed a smirk, trying to hide her contempt and repugnance. "Yes, Masta," she said, and then quickly turned to leave.

"Deseré," he called before she'd left the room.

She circled to face him.

"I—I would appreciate your help."

"My help?" Did he sense her contempt?

"Your...moral support, shall we say."

"Oh?" Deseré studied him, wondering what type of game he was playing.

"It's no secret that—this life—it's new to me. I experienced it as a child, but now—being responsible for all of this—it's...daunting. I've come to depend on your mother for running the household. I'd like to know I can depend upon you too."

Deseré pursed her lips. "Yes, sir."

"Thank you, Deseré."

"You're welcome, Masta Anthony. But it won't be long 'fore you find a wife. I 'spect Miss Careen O'Malley will have her sights set on you once she meets you today."

His eyes widened, as if surprised by her remark. He didn't smile, but only mumbled, "Perhaps."

****

Anthony wondered how he could have forgotten. The O'Malleys were coming for dinner at two—one hour from now—and he'd drunk a rather ample quantity. At least it was after noon. Nevertheless, Anthony would need to sober up and change. Now, feeling a bit queasy, he'd need to repair to his bedroom to repair himself.

Releasing the desk, Anthony said, "Since I've given Emmett the afternoon off—"

"I remember, Masta Anthony, you told me yesterday that you want me to serve."

"Yes," Anthony said. "Now, I must attend to my appearance before the company arrives." He walked slowly from the room, forcing himself to keep his balance. "Send Jax to help me," he said to Deseré.

"Yes, sir," she replied.

****

Deseré watched as Masta Anthony left the room and started a slow ascent up the stairs. When she could no longer hear his footsteps, she took a quick peek in the hall from the morning room to make sure she was alone. Before setting off to find Jax, she went to Masta Anthony's desk. It wasn't the journals she was interested in, but the letters. Perhaps they'd shed more light on her new master and his former life in Ohio. She didn't feel the least bit guilty about prying into his business. Knowing as much as possible about the white folks was a part of slave survival.

Before Deseré picked the up the letters, she saw a newspaper clipping. The middle of a story appeared to be about a telescope, its top and bottom sentences cut. This had no meaning, so Deseré turned the clipping over to find the wedding announcement of an Edith Emory.

Picking up the letter closest to it, she perused it quickly, learning that it was from Masta Anthony's mother. She mentioned Edith as "a lovely girl," and that she couldn't understand how Anthony had let her get away.

The other letter was from a friend. Deseré rapidly scanned it, noting that this friend sounded like an abolitionist. He scolded Masta Anthony for becoming a slave owner. Deseré sighed. She was fine with Masta Anthony as the new masta. Not knowing anything about a plantation, he was easy to manipulate. So as long as he let her marry William—and why wouldn't he—she'd be happy. Deseré didn't read the entire letter, but instead skipped to the end. Then she saw that this man, Henry Braithwaite, mentioned Edith too. *Also, my friend, seek solace in prayer, not spirits,* she read. *That said I hope that by now you can put your experience with Edith behind you. I will mention her no further.*

Was that what was causing Masta Anthony to drink? Deseré wondered. Had he run away from Ohio and decided to stay here on account of a love gone wrong? Feeling pity for him, and shame that she'd thought so disparagingly of him, Deseré hoped that perhaps Miss Careen could mend his broken heart.

Chapter 13

"I won't lie," Deseré heard Mr. Angus O'Malley declare at the dining room table. She refilled his wine goblet as he continued, "I wanted this place as soon as I heard your uncle died!" To emphasize this, O'Malley banged a beefy fist on the table, making the china and crystal rattle.

The company had arrived promptly at two, and Deseré, watching out for her master, had kept a keen eye on him ever since he'd appeared to greet them. At the time, Masta Anthony had looked sober and smelled heavily of spices. The scent of alcohol he'd imbibed earlier was masked by stick cinnamon and whole cloves. Jax told her he'd provided the masta those spices to chew soon after he'd given him two cups of strong black coffee.

Now in the dining room, Masta Anthony, still exhibiting a temperate disposition, was seated at the head of the table. Mr. O'Malley was at the foot, and the two ladies sat on either side, facing each other.

"Angus!" Mistress O'Malley admonished her husband, "you mustn't be so brash. For you to carry on so is disgraceful." As Deseré poured more wine into Mistress O'Malley's goblet, she thought the woman quite handsome, too handsome for the likes of Mr. O'Malley.

Dignified, the lady sat straight and tall, her floral patterned dress buttoned high at the neck. Mistress O'Malley wore her dark brown hair rolled on the sides with the back arranged in a chignon. Her deep brown eyes were sharp, her cheek bones high, and her thin lips a rigid line. Although more aesthetically pleasing than her husband, it was well-known through the negro grapevine that she was a strict plantation mistress. While she'd never administered the lash, she was quick to order her overseer or her driver to perform the dreadful deed.

"You must forgive my husband's frankness regarding business," Mistress O'Malley said to Masta Anthony.

He smiled at the lady. "I believe Thomas Jefferson said that honesty is the first chapter in the book of wisdom."

Deseré had only given Masta Anthony a quarter of a glass of wine to begin with, mindful to keep him self-possessed. It had already disappeared. Now she only replenished his goblet with a thimbleful. He downed the swallow immediately, giving Deseré a sly, yet discreet smile. Deseré blushed and turned away.

As Deseré approached Miss Careen with the wine, the young lady placed a hand to her cheek. Demurring to Masta Anthony, she said, "My father seems to express himself a bit too honestly at times."

"And where money's concerned, it's always the best policy," O'Malley laughed.

Both ladies gasped.

"Now Angus," Mistress O'Malley smiled, though her eyes remained steely, "you stop with that talk."

As Deseré replaced the empty basket on the table with a new one full of fresh cornbread, Miss Careen attempted to smooth the situation by complimenting the food.

Deseré caught Masta Anthony's eyes upon her. Then she observed Miss Careen and Mistress O'Malley looking at Masta Anthony. They'd seen him gazing at Deseré and now they peered at each other. Miss Careen looked down, as though embarrassed, while Mistress O'Malley's brows rose in disapproval.

****

Careen knew what her mother was thinking... She was thinking about Wildrey...

****

Deseré lowered her head as she walked to the sideboard against the back wall. She placed the empty bread-basket there, then uncovered a silver platter of fried chicken to start a round of second servings. She began with Mr. O'Malley. With two glasses of wine under his belt, he leered lasciviously at Deseré. Inwardly, she cringed.

"Angus," Mistress O'Malley said sharply, "help yourself to the *food*." Her thin lips tightened.

Then Mr. O'Malley looked Deseré in the eye. "And what fine food it is." Deseré remained straight-faced. Her insides convulsed.

Using silver tongs, O'Malley grabbed a thigh from the platter, then spouted off, "No denying Jeremy was well fed! As a matter of fact, he was the picture of health! Who woulda thought a bump on the head would kill him?"

Miss Careen's complexion deepened to red. She dropped her gaze and busied her hands with the linen napkin in her lap, as if trying to escape the current conversation.

****

Careen had loved Wildrey, and she always would. Wishing she could have had a life with him, Careen still reminisced about his handsome face, lush auburn hair and misty green eyes. The disgrace, which her parents had tried to hide, still caused them great shame, especially since Careen felt not in the least contrite. Getting her married off had been a top priority to her mother and father, and marrying her to an outsider was even better, since no hint of the indiscretion would have stirred near his unsuspecting ears.

Trying to be polite and rejoin the discussion, Careen said softly, "It was a shock to us all to hear of Mr. Albright's unfortunate demise." She then refused more chicken as the astonishingly beautiful servant girl, Deseré, approached.

"Indeed it was," her mother said, as the servant moved on to Mr. Sinclair. "His departure was a reminder that only the Great Almighty knows the number of our days."

Careen noticed Mr. Sinclair looking at her. He was quite a handsome man, but while Careen held his eye and smiled shyly, Mr. Sinclair allowed his gaze to stray from hers, and instead focus on Deseré.

Careen realized Mr. Sinclair would never have room in his heart for her, or anyone else, because he was already in love and made no attempt to hide it. Careen had loved too, that way, once...

****

As Deseré offered Masta Anthony the platter of chicken, she heard a slight sigh escape from Miss Careen. Then it took Masta Anthony two tries to grab a drumstick with the tongs because he paid more attention to Deseré than the poultry. Miss Careen's eyes dropped to her lap again. Masta Anthony was being rude to the young lady, Deseré thought, or perhaps he was still a little pickled.

Miss Careen was surely a fine lady. She ate like a bird, merely appearing to pick at the small portions of greens, sweet potatoes and black-eyed peas on her plate. And in addition to her lady-like appetite, Miss Careen was quite lovely. Here eyes were light brown and matched her thick golden brown hair. Her face was soft and gentle, her pink lips a perfect crescent, and her nose though long, was slender and perfectly shaped. She was pretty, Deseré thought, except for her ears.

Miss Careen wore her golden brown hair parted in the middle. A large braid was twirled in a bun at the crown of her head, but the side tresses, curled in an array of ringlets, only partially covered her ears, which were large and

100

pudgy, slapped on the side of her head like biscuit dough. Unfortunately, they resembled her father's ears, but at least they were the only feature she seemed to have inherited from him. Her ears were somewhat hidden, so Masta Anthony was sure to be enthralled by her. The well-formed young lady wore an ivory silk dress patterned with pink roses and red cherries.

Deseré didn't know Miss Careen that well, but the young lady had been to Pleasant Wood on several occasions when Masta Jeremy had entertained. She'd never been cruel to the servants and seemed a gentle soul with a pleasant disposition. Miss Careen would be a perfect plantation mistress, Deseré thought. She was kind and quiet, not at all like Mistress O'Malley. Perhaps under her, Deseré and her mama could keep running things and keep the "pleasant" in Pleasant Wood.

What Deseré did know about Miss Careen was that she'd spent two years at some female college in North Carolina. Talk was she was supposed to have been there for four. No one knew why she'd come back after only two. She was such a shy thing, Deseré reckoned, maybe she just missed home.

****

How unfortunate, Careen mused, that her feelings for Wildrey had caused such a scandal. She'd met him at a social event hosted by her school. He'd worked as a clerk in a local bank and seemed to be an upstanding young man. He'd thought Careen beautiful, and told her so many times. Even when she'd admitted to hating her ears, he'd said what they looked like didn't matter because he loved every inch of her. Wildrey had come to visit almost daily after their initial meeting. It was her fault for suggesting they leave the school's parlor and walk outside. But they'd been caught, unchaperoned, holding hands. That in itself was enough cause for her expulsion. But then, something even worse had come to light...

"May Jeremy rest in peace," Careen heard her mother say, "and may you, Angus, stop niggling Mr. Sinclair!"

"Now Gertie, me wantin' this land don't come as no surprise!" Angus laughed.

"Mr. Sinclair," Gertie said, "again I ask that you excuse my husband's lack of tactfulness."

Anthony smiled. "I have no objections to a man who speaks his mind."

"Good fellow!" Angus exclaimed. "And I'd have no objections to having you as a son-in-law."

Careen gasped, feeling her face burn. She placed a hand to her cheek. "Father, please!"

"You marry her," Angus pointed to his daughter with a fork dangling collard greens and a strip of fat-back, "you get fifty niggers along with her."

Careen stiffened, feeling as if she wanted to die. Her father was so crude, so crass. And when the truth about Wildrey had been exposed, he'd nearly disowned her. It turned out that Wildrey, himself, was a mulatto and escaped slave, passing as white. At first Careen had felt angry at his deception, but then she'd realized Wildrey's desperation to better his life by making a difficult choice that put his very being at risk. Then she'd loved him all the more for his bravery. News about the scandal alerted his master of his whereabouts, and he'd been captured and taken back into bondage. Careen had wanted to die after that, the expulsion from school no longer mattering. After crying for a month and not eating, she'd been forced to endure a "normal" existence under her parents' roof. But because of Wildrey, she'd never look at negroes as chattel again.

Deseré offered Careen more black-eyed peas, but she refused, while her mother scolded, "Angus, you've said quite enough!"

"Miss O'Malley may not find me to her liking," Anthony said, rather off-handedly to Careen. Then he turned his complete attention to Deseré as she offered him the peas.

Careen felt slightly crest-fallen, though not surprised, when Mr. Sinclair gazed intently at Deseré, rather than the food, while attempting to scoop up the peas with a large spoon. Careen looked at Deseré, then after several seconds, when Anthony's eyes finally met hers again, she said, "I'm rather uncertain of our compatibility."

Silence lingered for a long moment until her father finally bellowed, "Now, now, we can't be too hasty in matters of love. Only time will tell!"

MARIA MCKENZIE

Chapter 14

It was past eight o'clock in the evening, and by a dimly burning kerosene lamp, Anthony sat in the back parlor dozing in a burgundy velvet arm chair. Upon hearing footsteps, he awakened to see Deseré, still attired in blue homespun and white turban, peeking in at him from the hall.

"Deseré." He smiled, happy to see her. "You caught me napping." Despite the simple frock, she was still the most beautiful thing he'd ever seen. "I suppose I should retire."

"The O'Malleys wore you out, sir?" she asked.

"They did indeed. Come in." He gestured for her to enter the room. As Deseré came toward him, he smelled a hint of rose water. "After dinner," Anthony said, "Mr. O'Malley insisted I go to his place. He gave me an extensive tour of *his* cotton fields—I can't recall how many acres—then we played billiards for a good while, and then enjoyed some of *his* brandy."

"Oh." Deseré stood before him, her golden skin aglow in the dim light. He sensed a hint of disapproval in her voice.

"Don't worry," Anthony said, "I didn't indulge beyond my capacity. And lastly, Mr. O'Malley invited me to go hunting with him and his sons tomorrow."

"You takin' Jasper and Darcy?" Deseré asked. "They haven't been huntin' since your uncle died."

"Oh, yes," Anthony nodded, "I plan on taking the dogs. I'm sure they'll enjoy themselves, and hopefully I'll be fully recuperated by morning so I can too. Right now I'm feeling fine, aside from being a little tired and having aching feet. I wore new boots that aren't quite broken in. Now I'm dealing with the consequences." Though fully dressed, Anthony wore a pair of black cloth slippers embroidered with gold stitching. He slipped them off and then began rubbing one of his stockinged feet.

"If you'd like," Deseré smiled warmly, "I could do that for you."

Anthony hesitated. He hadn't asked her, nor had he considered doing so, but since she'd offered, he wouldn't refuse. Settling back in his chair, he said, "Alright, then."

Deseré knelt down. She lifted one of his feet, then gently began kneading it with her fingers. "I used to do this for Masta Jeremy when his feet were sore."

"Oh," Anthony moaned, rolling his eyes, "that feels...quite nice..." Then he watched her hands delicately squeeze his foot, but his eyes didn't remain there for long. Instead, they traveled to the neckline of her dress then downward where her breasts welled beneath the blue fabric. He imagined what they'd look like bare.

"He especially liked it when I did this." Deseré proceeded to caress the ball of his foot and the soft flesh beneath his toes.

"Oh..." Anthony closed his eyes, then leaned his head back for a moment and exhaled deeply, luxuriating in the softness of her touch. He felt his heart beat quicken.

"I knew you'd like that," Deseré said, as though pleased with her work. Anthony could hear the smile in her voice.

"So...what did you think of Miss Careen?" she asked.

"What?" Anthony raised his head and gazed down at Deseré. Her head remained lowered as she continued to work on his foot. Anthony took in the golden softness of her velvety skin as he studied her hands and neck. His eyes moved to her chest again and remained there. He squirmed a little, feeling a slight discomfort beneath his waist.

"Miss Careen, what did you —"

"Oh, yes, Miss Careen," Anthony said. "She's quite lovely, though I think she's hiding something."

"Like what?"

"I couldn't say...I suppose we all have our secrets. But despite that, she seems very nice... Even though she has ears like a leprechaun."

Deseré gasped, looking up at her master. When he began laughing softly, so did she. "Shame on you, Masta Anthony." Gazing down again, she said, "Well, despite her ears, she'd make a good wife; born and raised on a plantation, you know. But don't you worry about the household and the fields. Eulee can run things with his eyes closed and Mama and I can help you with the house."

"I can't tell you how much I appreciate that."

"And Mr. Simmons, he taught me and Mama — well — I mean — I suppose he taught you as much as you need to know." Deseré began working on his other foot. "But back to Miss Careen, I think she likes you."

Amused, Anthony said, "How could you tell?"

"Just the way she looked at you — and the way she smiled when she looked at you. You know what I'm talking about, Masta Anthony."

"Do I?"

"You should. She's a woman, you're a man."

"So I am..." The two remained silent for a few moments, as Deseré carried on softly squeezing and rubbing his foot. Then Anthony said, "What I do know, Deseré...is that you're quite beautiful."

Deseré released his foot, as if it had become leprous. With terror in her eyes and a mouth slightly agape as if poised to scream, she appeared horrified.

Fright wasn't the reaction Anthony had expected. He was hoping she'd at least be flattered. "Perhaps I've spoken out of turn," Anthony said, "but I won't apologize, because it's true." Deseré stood quickly, the warmth gone from her face. "And I've told you before," he continued, "that you needn't be afraid of me."

"May I go, sir?"

Anthony slouched sighing. "Yes."

"But before I do go, Masta Anthony, William will be in Beaufort all next week..."

Anthony's back stiffened with resentment. Always William, he thought.

"...but he'll come here next Saturday. And you said next time he's here, you'd talk to him about us gettin' married. So will you please do it then?"

Anthony hesitated for several moments, then tightly replied, "Yes."

The warmth returned to her face. "Thank you, Masta Anthony. And your uncle gave us permission to have our ceremony right over there," she gestured with her hand to the adjoining receiving room, "in the front parlor." She smiled, gazing toward the elegant room closed off by the pocket doors. It was only used for entertaining and special occasions, and what could be more special than her wedding? Anthony mused bitterly. Meeting Anthony's eyes once more, she said, "Will that be alright with you?"

Anthony took a deep breath. "I'll consider it."

"Thank you, sir." Deseré swirled away from him, and Anthony, feeling his heart sink, watched her rush from the room.

Chapter 15

The weekend had rolled around once again and it was Saturday. Patsy had finished distributing the rations from the doorway of the storage barn, and now slowly made her way back to the big house. Yet by the time she reached the kitchen house, she began feeling weak. Sickened by the smell of cinnamon, Patsy became dizzy and slowly wandered to the back of the kitchen near a stand of oak trees. Hot fluid welled in her gut like a torrent, constricting her insides as she vomited on the ground.

Swaying slightly, Patsy placed her hand on a tree to regain her balance. Standing still, the putrid taste of what she'd just disgorged still fresh, Patsy tried to push a dreaded thought from her mind. Two hands had died from cholera. The others who'd suffered from the malady had recovered. However, Patsy now believed she'd been afflicted. The dysentery had started last night, and now the vomiting had begun. According to the doctors it wasn't a catching disease and couldn't be passed from person to person. Instead, they claimed it was caused by breathing in bad air. What kind of bad air, Patsy wasn't sure, but whatever caused cholera,

Patsy feared she had it. Unfortunately, she'd used the last of the laudanum while nursing the sick hands, so she'd have to talk to Masta Anthony about procuring more. Meanwhile, she'd make do.

"Mama!"

Patsy heard Deseré calling from the direction of the big house and quickly wiped her mouth with a handkerchief. She stood tall, trying to regain her composure, and then walked away from the trees and the pool of vomit toward Deseré's voice.

"Mama!"

Patsy emerged from behind the kitchen house. "Yes, Deseré."

"There you are!" With a broad smile, Deseré ran to her mother and embraced her playfully. "William's here!"

Patsy forced a smile as Deseré released her. "Good." She gazed at her daughter's sky blue dress. It enhanced the blueness of her eyes. "So now he and Masta Anthony can have that talk."

"Finally!" Deseré exclaimed brightly. But then the smile left her as if she appeared to see her mother for the first time. "Mama, you look a mite pale. You alright? And I...smell something. Did you vomit?"

"I'm fine," Patsy lied, "and I'm happy for you. Before you know it, Deseré, you'll be married."

"And free to live a happy life with William," Deseré smiled, "just like Masta Jeremy promised."

"Yes... I see no reason for Masta Anthony to deny you that." Patsy stood silently for a moment and then dropped her eyes to the ground.

"Mama, you look ill."

Patsy met Deseré's gaze. "Dear, I'm fine. But remember, your life as a slave may not always be as you wish. There may be unspeakable hardship ahead."

"Masta Anthony seems as nice as Masta Jeremy, Mama. I can't see us ever bein' any worse off."

"Masta Anthony may seem nice, but...happiness in this life isn't always guaranteed. Just know that Jesus learned obedience from what He suffered..."

"Mama, what are you talking about?"

"And once made perfect...Jesus became our salvation..."

"What?"

"Remember, eternal hope is offered by Jesus to those who put their faith in Him."

"Mama, I know. But why are you telling me this now?"

Patsy shook her head. "I don't know. I just feel the Lord placed those words in my heart for you." She smiled. "Now, I'm feeling tired. I'm going to lie down. After William leaves, come tell me about his meeting with Masta Anthony."

****

It was early afternoon when William, dressed in a suit passed on to him by his owner's son, approached the back entrance of the Pleasant Wood big house.

Emmett, the drab-faced butler, opened the door. "He's waiting for you," the man said. Then leading William down the hall to the morning room, he mumbled, "And he's helped himself to a little liquid fortification in your honor."

In moments, William stood at the entrance of the morning room. "Come in, come in," Sinclair beckoned jovially to William. Emmett bowed slightly and disappeared.

Now both men were alone and stood near the fireplace. "Brandy?" Sinclair offered.

William was surprised by this. Other than being given spirits as a gift by some of his masters, he'd never been invited to drink with them, which he supposed was a good thing. He didn't drink. Instead he'd sell the alcohol he'd been given, using it as a source of income.

William declined Masta Sinclair's brandy, wondering why this meeting was even necessary. Masta Albright had given his permission for William to marry Deseré a while back. So Sinclair, being the new masta of Pleasant Wood,

111

surely by now could've said yes or no to their impending union without this formality. But what white folks want, white folks get. William tried not to smirk as he and Masta Sinclair exchanged pleasantries.

"All's well at Wesley Ridge, I assume?" Sinclair asked.

William held his head high, catching a glimpse of the brass chandelier above them, suspended from a large sunflower medallion. "All's well, sir."

"Well, that's good, very good indeed." Sinclair clasped his hands behind his back. "Now...I suppose we should discuss you and Deseré." He began pacing. "I realize it is your intention to marry her."

"That's right, sir." William looked down at the hardwood floor for a moment, restraining himself from rolling his eyes since Sinclair had known they'd wanted to marry practically since his arrival.

Sinclair stopped pacing near the window a few yards away from William that faced Station Creek. The white man gazed out toward the blue-gray water as he spoke these words, "But I also know it's your desire to be a free man."

William's eyes widened as Sinclair turned from the window to face him. "I want that more than anything, sir," William said.

"Well," Sinclair walked directly in front of William and stood still. With a smile and a whiff of brandy wafting from his breath, he said, "that's why I wanted to see you. I'm prepared to give you a choice."

"Alright, sir." William could barely contain the eagerness in his voice.

"I already purchased you from Master Wesley for the agreed upon price my uncle offered. However, I asked Master Wesley not to tell you, because I wanted to share the news with you myself today. I officially own you now and you have my permission to marry Deseré. Then the two of you can remain here at Pleasant Wood and you can spend the remainder of your days working as a master carpenter. I believe that's the life my uncle offered you, is it not?"

"It is, sir," William said unenthusiastically, wondering where his freedom fit into this equation.

"That offer is your first choice," Sinclair said. "Here's your second. I will give you your freedom and you may leave Pleasant Wood, but—"

"I'll take that, sir."

As if pleased, Sinclair's brows rose. "I see you're quite keen on that idea."

"Yes, sir."

"And," Sinclair went on, "I have a friend in Ohio who's an abolitionist. He can help you make a fresh start as a free man."

"That sounds mighty fine to me, sir."

"Good. I thought it would. And I'm sure my friend can make some contacts for you in the carpentry world. But regarding this choice, there is one caveat."

"Caveat?" William asked, unsure of the word.

"Condition," Anthony clarified.

"Oh." There was always a catch with the white folks, William thought. He shouldn't have been surprised. "That condition bein', sir?"

"That you...not...marry...Deseré." He spoke each word slowly to make his declaration clear.

Yet William seemed confused. "Sir?"

"It's simple, William, your freedom or Deseré. The choice is yours."

"So," William began, "if I don't marry Deseré, I can have my freedom...but if I do marry her, I stay here."

"Yes," Sinclair confirmed, "and lead what I should think would be a fulfilling life...with the woman you love."

William said nothing. He only looked down at the dark wood floor planks, pondering his options.

"I realize a bit of effort goes into freeing a man in this state," Anthony said, "but as a lawyer, I've looked into that situation..."

To be his own man, William thought. Freedom was what he'd sought for as long as he could remember. Now the chance not to belong to any white man was being dangled in front of him like fresh meat before a hungry bobcat.

"...I've already sent the appropriate correspondence and placed the wheels in motion to seek permission for your manumission by both houses of the legislature..."

As Sinclair continued speaking, William stood speechless, still looking down, lost in his thoughts...especially thoughts of Celia.

"However," Sinclair said, "if you choose to remain here, I will cease and desist with that effort."

Why would he want to remain here? William thought. Although St. Helena was better than most places for negroes, it was a no man's land filled with the most ignorant, puddin' headed negroes he'd ever seen. And leaving the island to go to a sophisticated place like Charleston didn't happen near enough.

"It's also important to know, that as a free man, you will not be allowed to ever enter South Carolina again."

A free man... That's what William wanted to be. He could give less than a half a pail of compost to ever set foot back in South Carolina, or anywhere in the entire South for that matter. He bitterly mulled over the life he'd lived in bondage. At age twelve, he'd been sold away from his mother. The sound of her heart-wrenching cries that day had never left him. Since then, he'd been owned by several masters and lived on several different plantations, and on each one he'd seen frightful things too horrific to speak of, like that little girl.

The child was only seven, William remembered, and she'd been beaten by the overseer 'cause she couldn't work fast enough. Then being delirious and cut up, she'd wandered off to find her mother. When the little thing walked over a bridge, being disoriented, she must have fallen off into the pond below.

It wasn't until days later that William found her body and pulled it from the water. Her face had been mostly eaten away, and her dress was the only clue to knowing who she was. When the child's mother saw her, she screamed just like an animal. Her cries were high pitched and sharp. They cut through the air like a blade had sliced her heart in two.

"Take as long as you need to think about this," Sinclair said.

Freedom now stared William in the face. Did he really need to think about it? He'd never had any say in his life. From the age of fourteen to seventeen, he'd been rented out as a field hand. And rented hands weren't treated nearly as well as the ones owned by the plantations. As a rented hand, he was temporary, and overseers weren't all that interested in the long term well-being of a rented hand and his ability to work. So being more hungry than usual wasn't uncommon in William's life during those times.

Someone else had always been in charge of him. Now, William thought, it was time for him to be in charge of himself. He was thankful for his skill in carpentry. That's about the only thing he could be grateful to a white man for. William's third master had purchased him when William was about eighteen. He'd noticed William's ability to whittle and seen that he was an expert at carving anything with a knife, so that master apprenticed him to one of his carpenters. But then, after William had become a master carpenter, he'd been rented out more times than he could remember, earning that master a tidy sum of money in the process.

Since carpenters were considered the cream of the crop among the slave craftsmen, William was treated with a bit more care, especially when working on the white folks' houses, churches and municipal buildings. But he'd still felt like he was only a tool, rented at his master's whim. He wanted to possess his own life, his own time and his own money. Could he really have that now?

Masta Albright had been a nice man. Masta Sinclair seemed to be as well, but William didn't trust any white man. He had once, but where had that gotten him? His fourth master had promised to sell him his freedom. But when William had earned the agreed upon sum of money, his master had reneged on the bargain. He'd lost William in a bet, like he was just a chiffereaux or a head of cattle. But the master didn't tell that to William until after he'd taken William's money. So William did the only thing he could at that point — for him and Celia — but it had been a mistake.

William had been sold South and ended up at Masta Wesley's place. Wesley was a decent man, but again, as his property, William was rented out from place to place. He couldn't see this man, Sinclair, not doing the same thing. He raised his eyes to meet the white man's before him. "So the only condition to me having my freedom is not marrying Deseré?" he asked, warily, although he already knew the answer.

"That's right. I know this is a difficult choice," Sinclair said, "so why don't you sleep on it and — "

"Pardon, sir, but where 'bouts in Ohio does your friend live?"

"Cincinnati."

"Close to Kentucky?"

"That's right. You have...loved ones there?"

William didn't answer. Thoughts of Deseré clouded his mind. She was pretty alright, and William was fond of her, mighty fond...but if given the choice between her and freedom...with Celia... "I'll take my freedom, sir."

Sinclair smiled. "I thought so. I'll keep you apprised of your status with the legislature."

"And how long will all this...rigmarole with the legislature take?"

"I should say...a matter of weeks. But I assure you, William, I will do everything in my power to expedite, or rather, hurry along the process. Now, Mr. Wesley said that if you chose your freedom, he'd allow you to stay at Wesley Ridge until the legalities are complete and I've made arrangements for you up North. And as a token of my word," Anthony pulled a small pouch from his pocket, "I want to give you this."

William took the pouch and looked inside. To his astonishment, he saw five gold pieces.

"That can go towards your new life. I'll provide more later."

"I—I thank you, sir," William said, "but why are you doing this?"

Sinclair lowered his head, then took a step forward. Just as he raised his head to meet William's eyes, Sinclair reminded William of a stag brandishing his rack, ready to battle. Now, mere inches from William, Sinclair said, "That's none of your concern. However, I realize I've placed you in a difficult situation... When you see Deseré...you needn't tell her anything, if you wish. Just tell her she can speak to me about what we've discussed. And in the meantime, I suggest you don't come here again—for Deseré's sake."

Chapter 16

Deseré sat on the bottom step of the back porch eagerly waiting for William. She couldn't wait to hear what had transpired between him and Masta Anthony. Perhaps Masta Anthony wanted to provide an extra special ceremony. Maybe that's why he felt it important to meet with William. Whatever the reason, Deseré didn't care. She finally had permission to marry him!

Upon hearing the door open, her heart leapt. She looked back only to see Emmett. Turning away, she said, "Oh, it's just you."

"Girl," he said walking down the dozen wooden steps, "you ain't gonna like what you gonna hear."

When Emmett reached the bottom step, Deseré looked up at him dismayed. "What you talkin' 'bout?"

Before Emmett could respond, the back door opened again. Deseré's head shot back to see William. Feeling her face brighten, she stood quickly, grabbed her skirts and rushed up the steps to meet him. Once on the porch she clutched William's arm, then for a brief moment watched Emmett walk toward the kitchen house. William didn't appear as elated as she'd hoped, and instead of looking at her, he gazed straight ahead.

"William," Deseré said, as they slowly descended the steps together, "what's wrong?"

"Your masta...he bought me already."

"Already?" Deseré squeezed his arm more tightly, grasping it closer to her side. "He didn't even tell me! He must've meant to surprise me—so that means we can marry right away!"

"But..." William hesitated. "He's...he's givin' me my freedom."

"Your freedom?" Deseré's eyes grew large. "I'll be free! We'll both be free! Oh, William—that's what you wanted!" No wonder he seemed so distant. He'd wanted his freedom. Now he had it and wasn't quite so sure how to handle it, especially with a new wife in tow. "We'll be fine," she said, once they reached the bottom step. "Masta Anthony will make sure of that. You just wait and see! We'll have—"

"No, Deseré," William interrupted, as their feet touched the brickwork.

"No?"

William finally turned his face to hers. Looking deeply into her eyes, he said, "I'll be free... but you won't."

At this, Deseré saw a hint of tears in his eyes. "I won't be free," she said, "but you will be? So we'll be married and—"

"No, Deseré," William said firmly, the tears gone. "Talk to your masta. He'll explain everything. But after he does...you won't want to see me again."

"William!" She embraced him tightly. "That can't be true! You're everything to me!"

"Deseré," William disentangled himself from her arms, "don't." He started to walk away, but she ran after him.

"William," she called as he kept walking. Catching up to him she said, "No matter what, I'll want to see you again—I love you!" William stopped and looked down at her, his eyes filled with what she assumed to be compassion. She grasped him around the neck, and tried to pull his face to hers, yet he resisted. "I love you!" she declared, although it sounded more like a plea.

"Deseré..." As he spoke her name, she looked longingly into his eyes. Then she realized she'd been mistaken. His eyes didn't reflect compassion, but pity. "...you go talk to Masta Sinclair. Do it now, then you'll understand."

As William walked away, Deseré saw Emmett's unsmiling countenance from the kitchen house window, tinged with sympathy. When the butler's face disappeared an instant later, Deseré, certain she'd tie a knot in his tail, wondered what he knew. Then she ran up the back steps to confront Masta Anthony.

Deseré flung open the back door only to find her master standing there, as if he'd been waiting for her. Forgetting her place, she cried, "You're freeing him?!"

Masta Anthony stood straighter. "Deseré, calm yourself."

"Calm myself?! But you're freeing him and not me! Why? What did you say to him?"

Grabbing her arm, he said, "Come with me." He led her down the hall to the morning room and released his grasp. Then he said quietly, "I gave William a choice."

"What kind of a choice?"

"Keep your voice down," Anthony admonished. "I told him he could stay here and marry you, or he could have his freedom and a fresh start in Ohio...without you. He chose his freedom."

Deseré burst into tears. "You didn't give him a choice at all! Not when you offered him the world!"

"If he'd loved you he would've stayed!"

Wiping her eyes with backs of her hands she wailed, "You think I don't know he doesn't love me?!"

Anthony looked at her, surprised.

"He could've *grown* to love me and he would have if you hadn't—"

"You're wrong, Deseré. *I* care for you more than he could

ever love you."

This shocked Deseré.

"What I did, I did for your own good," he said. "You shouldn't have to beg for a man's love—not when I could give you..."

Masta Anthony trailed off before finishing his sentence, but he'd said enough to unnerve Deseré. She didn't ask to be dismissed, but merely fled the room, feeling in need of her mother. Masta Anthony didn't stop her as she ran down the hall and then down the basement steps. Once at the bottom of the stairs, she turned left and threw open the door to her room.

Her mother lay sleeping on her side, her back to the doorway. Yet feeling desperate, Deseré ran to her and began shaking her shoulder.

"Mama, wake up!"

Patsy didn't stir.

"Mama, *please* wake up!"

With one last mighty shake, Deseré forced Patsy from her side to her back. Patsy's eyes were open, but only the whites visible. Horrified, Deseré backed away. She stood quickly and began screaming. In moments, Masta Anthony was in the room. So discombobulated, Deseré hadn't heard him come down the basement steps.

Anthony rushed to Patsy's side and sat on the edge of the bed next to her. "Patsy," he said, gently lifting her head onto his shoulder. He softly patted her cheek, again saying her name. Anthony lowered her head, then raised one of her eyelids. "Deseré, get me some smelling salts!"

Deseré rushed from the room to the medicine cabinet a few yards away. She returned to Masta Anthony a few seconds later, grasping a little green bottle. After she handed it to him, he removed the top, releasing the pungent smell of ammonia, and then held it under Patsy's nose. She didn't move. He closed the smelling salts, placing them on the bedside table, then felt the inside of Patsy's wrist, and then her temple.

By now Deseré saw Emmett appear in the doorway.

****

Anthony slowly stood up. He turned to Deseré, then held her gently by the shoulders. "I'm sorry, Deseré," he said softly, "but I think... she's no longer with us."

Deseré stood mutely, only shaking her head. Then a savage scream tore from her throat. "No!" She cried, ripping herself from her master's grasp. She knelt at her mother's bedside and once again began shaking her, "Mama! Mama! *Please* don't leave me!"

"Emmett," Anthony said over Deseré's cries, "send for the doctor. We must make sure she's..."

Emmett nodded silently and vanished.

Anthony gingerly pulled Deseré from her mother. "Deseré," he said quietly, lifting the girl to her feet. At first she struggled against him, but then collapsed against Anthony in tears. For a long time he held her, stroking her hair, and let her cry as long as she needed. Yet after several moments she pulled away.

Glaring at him, her face puffy and red, and eyes swollen, she accused, "You did this!"

Anthony felt his eyes widen in the shock that penetrated his body. Deseré's rose petal lips, so lovely when she smiled, were curled in angry grimace and a mixture of sadness and rage filled her voice. Trying to soothe her, Anthony asked calmly, "Deseré, what do you mean?"

"As if you didn't know!"

"Know what?" He began to put his hands on her shoulders, but she backed away.

"You conjured her!"

Gasping could be heard and Anthony turned to see two servants, Addie and Sophia, hovering in the doorway. "Back to your tasks!" Anthony ordered the women, embarrassed for them to witness Deseré speaking to him with such blatant disrespect. When the servants were gone,

Anthony turned back to Deseré. "Conjured?" he asked.

"You had someone cast a spell on her to *kill* her!"

Anthony took a deep breath. "Deseré, you're not being rational. You know — conjuring — isn't possible. Mr. Simmons told me you and your mother were too sophisticated to believe in all those superstitions, and besides, I'd never do anything to hurt your mother."

Deseré said nothing for several moments, then, "Maybe not, but you took William away from me!" She burst out crying again. "You can't deny that!" She wept loudly, nearly convulsing with sobs.

Anthony couldn't bear the sight of her crying and once more tried to comfort her. With caution he put his arms around her again, which she allowed. Still crying, she slumped against him. Anthony, consumed by guilt, was torn as to what to say or do. Deseré had lost the two most important people in her life, one being the man she loved. Now she was in the arms of the man who owned her. Poor consolation, Anthony thought, and he was sure she hated him. But he'd do whatever he could to change that.

Chapter 17

On Monday night, Patsy, with her hair fixed and dressed in her Sunday best, lay in the sick house. Her body had been cleaned and its cavities stuffed with myrrh. With coins on her eyelids, she was placed in a pine coffin constructed by Shamus. It was a rough looking affair, hastily made, and Deseré, sitting next to her mother in a simple pine chair, couldn't help but wish that William had crafted it instead; then it would've been fit for a fine white lady.

It was just before dark and all the slaves on the plantation had gathered at the sick house, meandering in and out for a last look at Patsy before her burial. Amidst the weeping, several chanted, "Praise the Lord." The May evening was cool, yet the sick house, filled with those who'd come to mourn, was warm, and filled with the heavy scent of sweat, the lighter fragrance of lilac, and the sweet nuttiness of myrrh.

A family member usually sat with the body from the time of death until the burial, watching for a sign of life. And that's what Deseré had done, swatting away the swarming flies, ever since Dr. Dawson, owner of a neighboring plantation, had tried to convince her that her mother was indeed dead. He'd placed a stethoscope on Patsy's chest, but heard no sign of a heartbeat. He'd held a mirror under her nose for several minutes, which never appeared to fog up, and then he'd pinched and pulled on Patsy to no avail.

When Deseré still wasn't convinced, the doctor had said the last thing he could do was pour scalding water on Patsy's arm. Deseré couldn't bear the thought of that, so she'd begged Masta Anthony not to bury her mother right away—just in case she really was still alive. Sunday passed, and a prayer service was held for her. Yet by the end of the day with no change in Patsy's condition, Deseré had sadly accepted the fact that her mother had died. She was no longer in bondage, Deseré thought mournfully. God had called her home. At least *she* could celebrate.

"Mama," Deseré said softly, looking into the face of her mother's corpse, "if only I could go with you..."

Deseré wiped her eyes with a cotton handkerchief. Now she had no one. Her face felt puffy from crying and she longed for William. Sundown had approached just as Eulee and Shamus walked into the sick house.

"It's time, Dezray," Eulee said sadly. He fit the lid onto the coffin. "We'd best get on to the graveyard."

With a hammer, Shamus drove in only a single nail, assuring Deseré, "Without it bein' sealed complete, her soul won't be trapped inside."

Deseré nodded. As she walked outside, she tried to appear grateful for that slight bit of comfort, though she knew it to be only mere superstition.

Moments later, Eulee appeared at the doorway of the sick house. "Come on," he motioned to some of the men. Four hurried inside and carried out the coffin to load it into the bed of a waiting wagon. George sat on the wagon seat, and once the coffin was procured, cracked the lash. While its reins jingled, the mule began to plod forward in heavy steps over the dusty dirt path.

With Addie's arm around her, Deseré wept and followed the wagon, along with the men, women and children who'd gathered at the sick house. Behind the grinding wagon wheels, they marched in a procession two deep that stretched nearly a quarter of a mile, and about each fifteenth person down the line carried an uplifted torch that burned bright orange in the darkness.

Addie squeezed Deseré's shaking shoulders. "It'll be alright, honey. Your mama's with the Lord now."

Jax walked behind them with April, and in his deep quavering voice led the procession in a mournful hymn:

When I can read my title clear
To mansions in the skies
I bid farewell to every fear
And wipe my weeping eyes

Should earth against my soul engage,
And hellish darts be hurled,
Then I can smile at Satan's rage,
And face a frowning world.

The procession slowly made its way down the long carriageway out toward the public road. They turned north, taking it all the way to the rut road that led them to the lonesome graveyard of the slaves. Once there, the corpse was lowered into the ground then, as a last act of kindness and farewell to the dead, each person threw a handful of dirt into the grave. While this was being done, Jax sang:

Hark! From the tombs a doleful sound
My ears, attend the cry;
Ye living men, come view the ground
Where you must shortly lie.

Princes, this clay must be your bed,
In spite of all your towers;

The tall, the wise, the reverend head
Must lie as low as ours!

A soft chorus of "amens" and "Yes, Lords" arose from the crowd, and afterwards, Eulee prayed:

The Lord is my shepherd; I shall not want.
He maketh me to lie down in green pastures: he leadeth me
beside the still waters.
 He restoreth my soul: he leadeth me in the paths of
righteousness for his name's sake.
 Yea, though I walk through the valley of the shadow of
death, I will fear no evil: for thou art with me; thy rod and
thy staff they comfort me.
 Thou preparest a table before me in the presence of mine
enemies: thou anointest my head with oil; my cup runneth
over.
 Surely goodness and mercy shall follow me all the days
of my life: and I will dwell in the house of the Lord for ever.

It's over, Deseré thought, as she listened to Eulee's recitation of the twenty-third Psalm. The life that she'd known was gone. As two hands commenced shoveling dirt into her mother's grave, Deseré gazed off into the distance away from the graveyard and the procession of negroes. Looking toward the road, she saw a lone figure cloaked in the darkness holding a torch. The flame reflected a white face. It belonged to Masta Anthony, and Deseré feared that he was determined to destroy her.

Chapter 18

As Anthony walked out the back door of the big house, he was just in time to see Lily coming down the outside steps from the second floor. Dressed in a blue home-spun dress and white turban, the girl, a little younger than Deseré, was as thin as a wheat stalk.

"Pardon, Masta Anthony," she said, as she passed by him carrying a pail containing the contents of his emptied chamber pot.

"Quite alright." He quickly moved out of her way, as she had spilled it once before.

Lily was the new house girl, a bit clumsy, but she was better suited to house chores than cooking. That was according to her mother, April, the Pleasant Wood cook herself, who requested that she be moved from the kitchen to the house after Patsy's death nearly a month ago. Despite her awkwardness, the girl had been quite helpful. So far she'd only broken two plates.

As she started down the steps from the back porch, with her clunky wooden shoes clanking, Anthony asked, "Where's Deseré?"

"At the soap house, Masta."

Anthony started down the steps behind her, but Lily turned back to him. "That's not right, sir. That was yesterday. Today she's in the sewing house. She's so many places I can't keep track of her."

"I suppose neither of us can," Anthony said, watching the girl precariously carry the bucket, and praying she wouldn't slip over her shoes. "Careful with that," he warned.

"Yes, sir," Lily said, as she reached the bottom step and then went on her way to empty the bucket into the creek.

Anthony headed toward the sewing house and on his way passed by the kitchen house and inhaled the soothing aroma of nutmeg and cloves. Jasper and Darcy, the two hounds, ran from around the front of the house, briefly nipped at Anthony's booted heels, then made way for the pasture.

Anthony gazed up into the live oaks spreading above him. Although the hot summer sun broke through in glistening shards, he was thankful for the shade. Anthony had given Deseré time to grieve, but since her mother's death, she'd made a point of avoiding him by leaving the majority of the household chores to Lily, claiming she, Deseré, needed to oversee various other duties in her mother's stead.

As Anthony walked, he stood taller and straightened his cravat. Then he patted his breast pocket, ensuring that he'd placed the important legal document, money and tickets there. This morning, he was a man intent on a mission, and he'd make sure Deseré was aware of it. Perhaps what he was choosing to do was a bit spiteful, but her avoidance of Anthony had wounded him.

By the time he reached the sewing house, he could hear Deseré's voice. The door was open in the heat, but upon hearing the word "Paris," he stopped to eavesdrop on the conversation inside.

"Anna at the Dawson place went to Paris?" Deseré asked.

"Uh huh," Addie, the seamstress replied. "Long time ago, near 'bout ten years. But, honey, when she came home, you shoulda seen the fabrics she had to work with. Silk, smooth as water, satin, soft as butter. Mistress Dawson even bought some for Anna to make a dress for herself."

"I'd do anything to go to Paris," Deseré sighed.

At this, Anthony smiled. Addie and Deseré chattered on, but he no longer listened. Instead, he began planning, and in moments felt himself beaming at his idea. Deseré would do anything to go to Paris; his uncle had wanted to take her there to buy fabric. Now she could possibly have her wish. Remembering the task at hand, Anthony replaced his smile with a look of stern business and made his presence known by walking through the open doorway. "Addie, Deseré," he said. The two women, along with the four younger girls assisting them, almost stood, but Anthony stopped them. They worked with jeans cloth sewing the new winter pants to be distributed for the men at Christmas. "Deseré, come here for a moment, please."

She frowned slightly but walked outside to meet him. "Yes, Masta?"

"I'm on my way to the Wesley place with some important news, but I wanted to tell you first. I received word of William's freedom from the legislature yesterday."

Deseré's brows rose and her eyes welled. The sure sign of a broken heart.

"I realize you've been avoiding me, but I felt this news important to share, so you wouldn't hear it from the grapevine. William will be leaving this state as a free man, and going to Ohio, Cincinnati to be exact, and he'll never set foot here again. Do you understand?"

Pursing her lips, Deseré did her best to hold back tears, yet one escaped in a sparkling trickle down her delicate cheek. She quickly wiped it away. "Yes, Masta." Now Anthony felt guilty about bearing the news he'd so looked forward to delivering. "Tell him...I'll always love him," she said forlornly.

Anthony's guilt evaporated. "As you wish," he said sternly, "but remember, he chose freedom over you."

****

Anthony followed Hamp, Norris Wesley's butler. The thin man raised a hand, the color of bronze, to gesture Anthony should enter Wesley's parlor.

"I'll tell Masta Norris you're here," Hamp said.

The room smelled of tobacco and furniture oil. Not long after Anthony began studying the seascape above the ornately carved mahogany mantel, he heard the patter of footsteps. He turned just in time to see Norris Wesley walk into the parlor.

"Anthony Sinclair," Norris smiled jovially. Norris was of a solid build, but short, probably not more than five foot two, with a balding pate and long side whiskers. His suit jacket strained slightly across the middle and he appeared to teeter over his fine leather shoes.

"Good morning, Norris," Anthony smiled.

After they exchanged pleasantries, Norris said, "I sent Hamp to fetch William. I tell you, Anthony, that buck has been as excited as a jaybird in June about his freedom, and when your boy arrived yesterday with your message that you'd be here today with his papers and travel arrangements, he was happy as a dead pig in the sunshine. I suppose any negro would be as happy, but William wasn't even half as excited about getting married to that pretty little wench of yours. But the thing is," Norris prattled on without taking a breath, "I think he's still hung up on a girl he escaped with years ago from Kentucky. Now, I didn't think negroes could form attachments like that, but I think William actually wants to look for her. Talk is, she was his wife, but you know how that goes with darkies, marry one here, marry one there."

Before Anthony could ask any questions regarding this stunning revelation, William appeared in the doorway.

Dressed as a free man, he wore a suit with the chain of his gold pocket watch visible. He also held a hat in his hand and set a carpet-bag down on the hardwood.

"William!" Norris said with a large smile. William wasn't invited in to join them. Instead, the two white men walked to the doorway. "I'm sure you know why Mr. Sinclair is here."

"Hello, William," Anthony said.

William tipped his head slightly. "Masta Sinclair."

Anthony pulled William's freedom papers from his breast pocket. "I have your papers." As he placed them firmly in William's hand, William smiled just as broadly as Norris. "Now, you're officially a free man."

"Thank you, sir," William beamed.

Norris said, "Look at that smile, I told you he was excited as could be!"

"Yes, indeed," Anthony agreed, looking at Norris. Then turning his attention back to William, he said, "Just make sure you guard those papers with your life. Cincinnati is a haven for runaways from Kentucky." He eyed William up and down, thankful the handsome threat to Deseré's affections would no longer be present. "I must say, though, you hardly look like a runaway. I see you're dressed to accommodate your new circumstances."

"Thanks to Masta Norris," William said.

"I gave that suit to him as a going away present," Norris said proudly.

"Well," Anthony reached into his breast pocket again and this time removed a thick envelope. "Another present." He handed it to William. "This holds your steamer tickets and enough money to get you started in your new life."

"Praise God!" William declared, his smile broadening even more.

"My friend, Mr. Braithwaite, is expecting you," Anthony continued, almost flummoxed by William's unabashed enthusiasm. "You'll be staying with him until other arrangements can be made. Mr. Braithwaite knows a negro carpenter who's interested in meeting you."

"I can't thank you enough, Masta Sinclair. You'll never know what all this here means to me."

"You're welcome, William. Now, if you'll come with me, George is waiting for us in the wagon. He'll be taking you to Beaufort for the first leg of your journey, and I'll accompany you there."

They said their goodbyes to Norris, then left through the back door.

As they walked toward the wagon William said, "What you're doin', sir, is surely an answer to my prayer. If I could say thank you a million times, it wouldn't be near enough."

"Living your life up North will be thanks enough for me," Anthony said. Then he slowed his pace and stopped walking. "Are there...any parting words you have for Deseré?"

William stopped as well. His beaming face fell in a mixture of awkwardness and guilt. Anthony wouldn't dare humiliate Deseré by giving him her message, *I'll always love him.* William lowered his head for a moment, then meeting Anthony's eyes he said, "Tell her...I regarded her highly."

As they resumed their walk toward the wagon, Anthony rationalized that he'd helped William, as well as Deseré. He'd given William his freedom, which would thus allow him to find the woman he'd loved. Therefore, Anthony had saved Deseré from the heartbreak and misery of marriage to a man whose heart she could never fully possess, no matter how hard she tried. Yet, would Deseré ever see it that way?

Chapter 19

A few weeks later, Anthony stood bent over in the potato field, planting slips alongside the field hands. He wore trousers and only a linen, with his shirt sleeves rolled to his elbows. With a straw hat perched atop his head, he stopped for a moment and wiped sweat from his brow with the back of his hand. It was the heat of the day, twelve noon, and Jesse Flanagan, the new overseer, could be heard ringing the bell announcing dinner for the hands.

Eulee's face shone with sweat. "I think you done good, Masta Anthony," he said. Several hands put down their tools and passed by on their way to the quarters for dinner. "You caught on right quick to plantin' those slips."

"Two feet apart, push them into the soil," Anthony said. "I'm sure I'll dream about it."

Eulee smiled, as he started off. "After the work you done today, you be sleepin' hard. You won't be rememberin' no dreams."

Eulee was the last of the hands to leave the field, and as the man walked away, Anthony set down the long two pronged tool he'd used to push the slips into the soil. Although he'd only worked for two hours with the hands, it was more manual labor than he was used to, and now in the burning heat, he felt as if he'd perspire to death. He walked a small distance from the fields to the shade where he tethered his uncle's horse, Boaz, earlier. After untethering him, Anthony mounted the animal's back, then turned him in the direction of the vineyard and took off at a good trot.

The summer months in St. Helena were extraordinarily hot, and because of the increased possibility of illness, several families chose to summer away in the nearby resort town of St. Helenaville or further away in Beaufort. That's where the wealthier families stayed, like the O'Malleys, who owned a very fine home there. Along with the plantation, Anthony had inherited a small house in St. Helenaville where his Uncle Jeremy had summered. But Anthony had chosen to stay in St. Helena to learn as much as he could about the crops, including learning how to work the fields.

What enthralled him most about the plantation was the vineyard, and after a good ten minute ride, he found himself among the well cared for wooden arbors. They were large and strong, covered with vines and spread over several acres. The grape harvest had been completed in April. Several varieties were grown here, including muscadine and scuppernong.

Anthony's fascination had started when he'd first learned about Pleasant Wood's vineyard. Then the allure had increased even more when he'd found a book on wine making on one of his Uncle Jeremy's bookshelves. Anthony played over in his mind some figures he remembered: one ton of grapes would yield over seven-hundred bottles. One acre on a low yielding vineyard could produce about two tons of grapes or fourteen-hundred bottles, while a high yielding vineyard could produce ten tons or seven thousand bottles.

Anthony harbored a crazy notion. Perhaps he should concentrate on growing more grapes instead of growing more cotton. Could he possibly become a winemaker? It could be lucrative, he mused. After all, alcohol was healthy; it wouldn't make a body sick like spoiled milk or foul water. He had the vineyard, but he lacked the knowledge of winemaking, and what better place to gain at least the rudiments of the craft than in France?

This harebrained scheme wasn't crazy enough to prevent him from writing to his mother and imploring her to request that his stepfather ask his acquaintance, the winemaker Nicholas Longworth of Cincinnati, to write Anthony a letter of introduction to a winemaker in Burgundy. Now he had to make a decision: would he travel to France or not? He'd always wanted to go back there. Out of all the places he'd been on his Grand Tour after graduating from college, Paris had been his favorite destination.

Anthony wondered if he would be biting off more than he could chew. He was still trying to master the art of cotton production, as well as a multitude of other crops. Yet a journey to France would be twofold: not only to learn about the winemaking process in Burgundy, but to woo Deseré in Paris, a place she'd always wanted to go. Thinking of Edith Emory's wedding and her planned tour of Europe with her new husband, Anthony mused that he could provide an even grander tour of the most splendid place in all of Europe, perhaps even the world, for Deseré. Besides, he wanted to make Deseré love him. Anthony believed he was losing his mind over that girl. He hadn't wanted to, but he'd fallen in love with her—a servant, a negro, a slave girl—and she despised him. Would she ever love him? Perhaps courting her in Paris would allow that to happen... Paris, the city of love...

Anthony inhaled deeply while taking one last look at the vineyard, then turned Boaz in the direction of big house so he could head back for dinner. Lost in thought, he gazed straight ahead as Boaz, whose red coat glistened gold in the sunlight, trotted over the dark gray soil. But in moments, Anthony heard another horseman approach from his left.

Anthony stopped, once he'd turned to see Flanagan approaching him on his large dappled gray gelding, Whiskey. The tall bulky man, dressed in a gray vest over a white shirt, almost matched his horse. Even the gelding's gray dapples were similar to Flanagan's black hair, now mostly streaked with silver.

Flanagan slowed Whiskey to a trot, then stopped near Anthony. With authority, he said, "Mr. Sinclair." Whiskey gave a firm snort, as if echoing his owner. Boaz snorted back, then looked away.

"Yes, Mr. Flanagan," Anthony replied. He peered into the overseer's face, shaded by a wide brimmed straw hat. The man's rough-hewn chin and cheeks were covered with a beard more gray than black, and his high forehead and glassy gray eyes were swathed in a series of tiny lines and wrinkles. His heavy dark brows were bushy, his nose long and slightly crooked, and his lips pale and thin. Flanagan wore a serious expression, but for an overseer seemed a good humored sort.

"I see you were workin' out in the fields today." Flanagan spoke with a slight Irish brogue.

"That's right."

"I wouldn't recommend that you become so familiar with your niggers by workin' alongside them like that." Whiskey nodded his head, as if in agreement. Boaz continued to look away but stomped one of his front feet.

"Would it pain you to call them negroes?"

Flanagan smiled, but the smile didn't reach his translucent eyes. "Leprechauns, fairies, pixies, I'll call your niggers whatever ya please, Mr. Sinclair. You're payin' me."

"Negroes will do. And as far as my working alongside them, I'm only trying to learn the land."

"That's what you have me for. And your nigger Eulee, I mean your *negro* Eulee, knows a thing or two."

Anthony was sure Eulee knew more about the plantation than Flanagan ever would, but he kept that thought to himself. "You're knowledgeable about crops, Mr. Flanagan, but do you know anything about wine or winemaking?"

Flanagan smiled, and this time his crinkly eyes sparkled. "Drinkin' it, yes. Makin' it, 'fraid not. But I could make you a fine Irish ale."

Anthony smiled. "I might be traveling for a while, Mr. Flanagan, to Europe." Six days to New York, he thought, and nearly twelve overseas, and at least a month's stay, perhaps two. "I'll probably be gone for two to three months."

"I'm worth my pay, Mr. Sinclair. The place will be in capable hands while you're away."

"I haven't made a decision as to whether or not I'll be going."

"Well, if you do go, sir, the place won't fall to pieces while you're gone."

"I'd appreciate that."

"But, you know, Mr. Sinclair, I could get a lot more out of your land if you'd allow me to use the lash, get the work day started earlier and extend the hours later into the evening."

Anthony frowned. "I don't approve of the lash," he said sharply. "We'll leave things as they are for now."

Flanagan sighed, exaggeratedly, not making an effort to hide his disapproval. "As ya wish, sir." Whiskey let out a loud whinny. Boaz looked back at Whiskey and sounded a low grunt before turning his head away once more. Flanagan tipped his hat, then turned his horse around. As Whiskey trotted off, manure plopped from his rear.

Anthony resumed his ride to the big house. By the time he neared the stable, he saw Deseré leaving the kitchen house. As she walked toward the other outbuildings, she looked in Anthony's direction, but upon seeing him, her gaze hit the ground.

That convinced Anthony then and there that he was taking Deseré to France, where she could no longer ignore him. He'd allowed her time to grieve over her mother's death and the loss of William, and he'd kept his distance. But it was going on two months and he could bear it no longer. A chance to travel overseas would surely please her, as well as ease her grief. But most importantly, it would put William's memory to death.

Chapter 20

At nine o'clock that evening, Deseré lay in fear, as she waited for sleep to come, as she had for the past two months. A night breeze swept through the open window offering a bit of relief from the humidity. What would she do if Masta Anthony came through her door? He'd made a show of compassion, being sweet as a brandied peach after her mama had died, but then he'd been slick as a weasel the very same day, enticing William with the gift of freedom.

Tears burned Deseré's eyes. Of course William would choose freedom over her, but couldn't he have at least fought for her freedom, too? Then Deseré's heart began to beat rapidly. She shuddered at the thought of Masta Anthony's words, *I care for you...* He cared for her, all right, cared to have his way with her! Deseré would rather die. At this point she had nothing to live for.

She'd kept from his clutches as best she could, but it was only a matter of time before—

There was a knock at her door. Deseré didn't move. If it was one of the negroes, they'd say something.

For several moments Deseré heard nothing. Then there was another knock, soft at first, then louder...then a voice.

"Deseré?"

Deseré's heart stopped. It was Masta Anthony.

"Deseré, may I speak with you?"

Did she have a choice? Even if the other servants down here heard him attack her, they couldn't do anything to stop him. He owned them, and besides, if a slave struck a white man, he or she could be severely punished or even killed. Addie would venture forth to help her, Deseré thought, but she wouldn't want the woman harmed on her account.

Deseré slowly sat up. She lit the candle on her nightstand, then stood from the bed and grabbed a patchwork shawl slung over a pine chair in the corner of the room. She quickly wrapped the shawl around her shoulders to cover the shapeless cotton nightgown that nearly reached the floor. Now feeling well covered, Deseré hesitantly approached the door. If she didn't open it, he'd surely barge in.

"Deseré?"

"Coming, Masta." Once at the door, she opened it just a crack.

Masta Anthony smiled, but it was a foolish smile, like a possum eating a sweet potato. He held a single candle. Its flame eerily illuminated the planes of his handsome face, and the candle fire reflected in his eyes as if he were the devil himself. "May I..." he paused for a moment, as if uncertain of how to proceed. "May I come in?"

Even though his tone was kindly, again she asked herself, did she have a choice? Deseré gulped, then haltingly opened the door, yet remained behind it.

"Deseré, you needn't hide," Masta Anthony said gently, as he walked into her room. He placed his candle on the dresser. "I'd prefer we speak behind closed doors." He pulled the door from her grasp, causing the shawl to slip from her shoulders, then closed it.

Deseré adjusted her shawl, backing away from him, then bumped into her bed, its edge pressed against her legs.

Feeling trapped, like a bat with a broken wing cornered by a tomcat, she felt herself begin to tremble.

"I won't bite," he teased.

"Why are you here?"

The smile left his face as if he'd been offended. Deseré didn't care. "Because," he said, "I'm going to France, and I'd like to take you with me." His smile returned and he spoke with heightened enthusiasm. "I—I'd like to see Paris through your eyes. I want to share all the amazing sights with you and hear your thoughts."

Feeling frightened, Deseré's eyes widened. "I—I won't be the only *slave* to accompany you—will I?"

A look of stunned disbelief crossed his face for a moment, as if he'd been slapped. "Of course not. I thought that Addie would go as well. As a fellow seamstress, I know she'd enjoy a trip there. You're close to her, and I assume you've grown closer in the absence of your mother."

Deseré nodded silently.

"So that pleases you?"

What did it matter if it pleased her or not? She had no choice, but she nodded again anyway.

"I believe traveling would help ease the pain you've been subjected to these past months."

Pain that was mostly his fault, Deseré thought. Holding back tears, she took a deep breath. "What will be expected of me?"

He appeared surprised. "Only that you enjoy yourself. You'll be my traveling companion."

Unsure of what to think, Deseré felt her eyes widen again.

"Take all your beautiful dresses, and once there, I'll buy you more. I'll also take you shopping for fabric so you can create all the beautiful dresses you please. If my uncle had lived, he would have taken you there. This is the trip he'd promised you."

Deseré couldn't concentrate on beautiful dresses or Parisian fabric. "Traveling companion? But I—I—couldn't—

I—what would people—"

"We'll be in Europe," Masta Anthony said. "No one will know either of us. And Addie will act as chaperone."

Deseré said nothing, but only wondered if he was sincere. As his *traveling companion*, could she really keep him away from her, even with Addie as a chaperone? Despite any pretenses, she was his slave. Paris? It might as well be hell!

****

Anthony had had a glass of wine—well, three glasses—before he'd descended the basement steps to Deseré's room. Now all he could think was that she was a vision from heaven to behold. Perhaps the wine enhanced her beauty, but surely not by much.

She smelled of lilac, and in the candlelight her skin glowed like the rays of the setting sun through breaking clouds. Her thick blond tresses shimmered in a sleep braid over her shoulder, creating a glistening halo around her face, a face he was certain more beautiful than any Renaissance Madonna's. But it wasn't just her beauty that entranced Anthony and caused him to love her more each day. It was everything; her strong spirit, her cleverness, her intelligence.

In her luminous blue eyes, he sensed the lingering grief over her mother's passing, and her unhappiness because of losing William. That boy wasn't worth her thoughts, and Anthony would make her forget him.

"Deseré," he said, "I realize you're still distraught over William." He took a deep breath, then continued, "And I hesitate to even mention this...but not only did he choose his freedom over you, according to Mr. Wesley...there was another woman."

Tears immediately sprang to Deseré's eyes and spilled down her cheeks. He was satisfied at the result of this revelation, yet his heart broke at the sight of her pain. Perhaps he shouldn't have been so blunt. He'd fix it.

"Deseré, I'm sorry," Anthony said, "but that only proves that William didn't appreciate you, your fire, your radiance, your passion, but I do... I care for you."

Deseré sniffed. "Me? A slave? Then you..." she looked down, mumbling the rest of her words so that he could barely hear her.

"You say I have no self-respect?" he asked, but Deseré remained silent. Her words stung, but he'd put all aside for her, including his self-respect. "Deseré, I — I —"

"You what?" She looked up at him, her face tear-stained.

"Deseré," Anthony moved closer to her, gently placing his hands on her shoulders. She stiffened, backing herself further into the edge of the bed. Then, with no where to go, she began creeping along the edge of the corn husk mattress. He crept with her, yet the wine caused him to take leave of his senses. She froze, as his hands, as if by their own accord, slid from her graceful shoulders to her swan-like neck, then cupped her fragile Madonna's face, lifting it to his. She squirmed uneasily, yet he ached to kiss her. Feeling his insides melt like ice cream in the hot summer sun, he said, "Deseré, could you...could you ever care for me?"

She pulled from his grasp, only managing to fall onto the bed in a sitting position.

Now Anthony towered over her. Deseré sat ramrod straight, clutching the shawl tightly around her. She looked up to him, then breathing hard, her voice broke as she said, "Get out.

"But, Deseré —"

"You're drunk. I can smell the wine on your breath."

Embarrassed, Anthony said, "I had a little, but I'm hardly inebriated."

"Don't hurt me."

Anthony's brows rose and he knelt before her. She gasped, as this seemed to startle her. Incredulous, he asked, "Hurt you?"

Deseré dropped her head and began to cry.

She looked like an injured sparrow. Bewildered, Anthony said, "Why are you be afraid of me? Why do you think I'd hurt you?"

Weeping harder, Deseré cried, "For two months, I've been terrified that you'd come down here—and—and violate me! Now here you are and there's nothing I can do about it."

Devastated, Anthony said, "Deseré, you actually think I'd—I'd hurt you that way?"

Wiping away her tears, she rapidly nodded.

Dumbfounded, Anthony finally managed, "I—I couldn't—I wouldn't!" Then he lowered his head.

****

Deseré looked down at Masta Anthony. Not only was he drunk, he was crazy. She sat still as he blubbered, "I'm sorry, Deseré, but you must believe me. Never would I ever do anything to hurt you! I only came down here to tell you about Paris. I thought it would please you—that's all I want—to please you."

He sniffed. This alarmed her. And when he raised his head to look at her, his eyes glistened with tears. As one began to roll down his cheek, Deseré stared in disbelief. Did he truly care for her? She lifted her fingers, as if to brush the tear away, then caught herself, quickly pulling back her hand. Drunkenness was a terrible thing. He had to leave. Deseré stood from the bed. Speaking slow and steady she said, "Masta Anthony, we can talk about Paris tomorrow, but now," she swallowed hard, "will you—will you please go?"

He gazed up to her from his knees. "I will," he said slowly. His eyes were red and his face flushed. Appearing chagrined, he quickly wiped the stray tear from his face. "I wouldn't want to...unnerve you any further. Forgive my heartfelt display of folly. And I'm sorry... I shouldn't have put my hands on you. I promise I won't do that again. And it wasn't my place to deny you William, despite the circumstances. So the only thing I ask from you...is your forgiveness. Do I have it?"

Once more, Deseré asked herself if she had a choice. She wasn't ready to forgive him where William was concerned, and didn't know if she ever would be. But if that's the only thing he wanted to take from her by force, she'd pretend to give it willingly. "Yes, Masta."

Chapter 21

Deseré's hands trembled. Looking in the mirror mounted on the wall, she studied her complexion. Fair, yet dusky. "Addie," she said, turning toward the woman, "what if somebody finds out I'm not white?"

Addie seemed not to hear Deseré's concern as she looked around the state room onboard the steamship. "It ain't big, but it's right nice," she said.

To Deseré, the confines were a bit too close for comfort. The chamber was narrow with a wash basin and a closet and drawers built into the wall. There was just enough room for a chair to stand between the edge of two berths, which were situated one above the other.

Deseré could hear water slosh against the outside of the ship, and though anchored, it felt unsteady, as if it weren't on solid ground. Then she reminded herself, it wasn't. Deseré felt more than just butterflies in her stomach. She was certain grasshoppers and cicadas were wreaking havoc inside her, as well.

She wore a bonnet made of leghorn straw with a large pink bow tied at her chin, and her dress was a red on white calico with fitted sleeves and a pleated bodice. Yet despite her clothing, light skin and blond hair, she worried that once among the passengers, her deception would be on full display.

Deseré asked, "Addie, did you hear what I said?"

They were in Charleston, waiting in the stateroom on board the steamship that would begin their journey up North to New York. And it was here that Masta Anthony had insisted the charade begin. Deseré would pass as white, and Addie would be her mammy and chaperone. "If anyone should ask our relationship," he'd said, "Deseré, you are my charge, an orphan traveling to meet your relatives in France." Masta Anthony had a state room for himself next door.

"Oh, chile," Addie said, "we ain't seen anybody we know from Saint Helena or Beaufort, so quit your frettin'. Besides, Masta Anthony ain't gonna let nothin' happen to you."

Deseré grimaced at the thought of how obvious it was that he *cared for her*. Yet she was afraid of his kind of caring, which only increased the cloud of insects plaguing her stomach.

Addie took a quick look in the mirror and adjusted her turban. She was a bit plump and in her forties, but despite her advanced years, Deseré thought her an attractive woman. Her skin was golden and her eyes light brown. With a heart-shaped face, pleasant smile, and soothing disposition, she was just the calming influence Deseré needed.

"Now we still got a lot of time 'fore we set off," Addie said, "and Masta Anthony said to meet him up on deck once we done got ourselves situated. So, let's go — *Miss Deseré, ma'am*."

"Oh, hush!" Deseré chided, as Addie handed her a shawl.

After Deseré draped the shawl around her shoulders, Addie said, "Come on." Then she grabbed Deseré's arm and led her from the stateroom. Deseré picked up her skirts, maneuvering her petticoats, as they left through a ventilated door that opened directly into the cabin, a common area for eating and socializing, lined with long tables and benches. "Pretend you an uppity southern belle, like Miss Careen," she murmured as they strolled past the other white passengers and negro stewards.

"But she's nice," Deseré whispered.

"Then act like her mama."

Deseré frowned, turned her nose up high, and threw back her shoulders, trying to appear as haughty as possible.

"That's it, girl," Addie said softly. "Now you look so high and mighty, you'll scare all the white folks."

Deseré almost giggled, but forced herself not to, as she and Addie walked upstairs to the upper deck in search of Masta Anthony. Several other passengers were still boarding the ship. The ocean waves crashed loudly, seagulls flew above cawing, and the sea air smelled of salt, fish and soot. Deseré saw black coal dust lingering around them, but slowed her pace when Addie squeezed her arm and whispered, "Look."

Deseré peered overboard where Addie indicated, toward a neighboring ship. Both looked on in horror as a drove of about forty slaves chained together were herded from the vessel like animals.

There were men and women anywhere from eighteen to forty years of age, filthy and bedraggled. Weary, with heads downcast and torn clothes, they appeared to have never known happiness, and that any semblance of hope had been drained from their beings. They wore no shoes. The thick metal chains around their ankles could be heard clanking in a slow mournful rhythm with every heavy step.

As they were taken from the ship, none of the passengers around Deseré and Addie, nor any people standing on the wharf appeared to notice them. Deseré reckoned that seeing a drove of slaves disembarking from a southern steamboat in the land of cotton and rice was apparently a common occurrence in these parts.

Deseré gripped the rail on deck tightly as she watched, her fair knuckles now white. "I didn't think I'd ever see that," she whispered to Addie. Feeling her chest tighten, she tried not to look at the sorrowful mass, but then realized she couldn't not look.

"They been sold down South," Addie said sadly. "I ain't never seen it either."

"I wish there was something we could do for them," Deseré said.

"Prayins 'bout the onliest thing we can do," Addie sighed.

Both women lowered their heads and sent up a silent prayer.

When Deseré opened her eyes, she found a bearded gentleman staring at her with down turned lips and a scowl in his eyes, as if insulted that such a horrific sight should unnerve her. Or perhaps he suspected something about *her*...

Deseré felt a surge in her stomach. "Addie," she said suddenly, "I feel sick. I need to go back to the room. When you find Masta Anthony, tell him—just tell him I'll be back up in a little while." She quickly turned from Addie, leaving her alone.

"Pardon me, Miss," a negro steward said, when Deseré nearly knocked him over as she fled down the stairs to her state room. Other passengers walked through the hall, but Deseré recognized one couple as she approached her room. She'd seen them when she'd first boarded the ship. The woman was beautiful. Her features were delicate, her hair was dark, and her eyes large, brown and long-lashed. She looked distressed, and the man leading her by the arm appeared angry. Deseré assumed they were husband and wife. They walked into a room a few doors from Deseré's and the man shut the door. That's when Deseré heard shouting and didn't have to venture at all from where she stood to overhear bits of their exchange.

Over a burst of steam the man yelled, "You listen to me!"

"No!" the woman cried.

A bell began to clang, but Deseré heard the man shout, "And you'd better do..." Then his voice dropped to a murmur. Deseré stood outside her room. Wanting to continue listening, she opened her reticule and began rummaging through it, pretending to look for something.

"No!" Deseré heard the woman clearly.

"I got you this fancy state room..." The man's voice rose again angrily, before he quieted himself.

"I don't care!" The woman sounded hysterical and her shrieking became incoherent. A couple being led by a steward turned their heads toward the room curiously as they passed by.

The man's voice rose above the woman's. "It isn't like you have a choice..." More bursts of steam blocked out what the he said, but then Deseré heard, "...be my housekeeper, or I'll sell you off..." A group of laughing passengers walked by drowning out the argument, but after they passed Deseré heard, "Then you'll be a field hand at the worst plantation I can find!"

The woman began to cry, and Deseré gasped as she heard bits and pieces of the man's lewd intentions toward her. Deseré now understood that the woman wasn't his wife, but his slave. And just like Deseré, she was light enough to pass.

Through weeping the woman cried, "No, no, no!"

Now the man was so irate that Deseré could hear him in between several bursts of steam and the bell. "Think about it, you black wench!" he said. "Your fate is in your own hands!"

A moment later the man left the room. As he slammed the door behind him, Deseré quickly opened her own door and ducked inside. She left the door open just an inch and watched the man trudge off. For a brief moment, Deseré, sympathizing with the woman, felt compelled to comfort her. Then, however, self-preservation wildly unleashed itself. That woman could give her away, Deseré thought, so it was best to leave worse enough alone.

Feeling sicker, Deseré's whole body began to tremble. She was nothing more than chattel and she could end up chained and sold to a slave trader just like the poor souls she'd seen earlier. Did the same fate lie in store for her as the poor woman who'd cried at the hands of that monster? Give in or be sold... Masta Anthony had asked could she care for him. But if she never did, would she be sold? Or would he become a beast and force himself upon her...then sell her just the same?

"Deseré?"

She jumped, backing away from the door, and her stomach twisted inside out at the sight of Masta Anthony's face.

"Are you alright?" he said through the crack in the door. His voice was filled with what sounded like kindly concern. "Addie told me you felt ill." Deseré saw Addie's face beyond Masta Anthony's shoulder.

Although he'd promised never to hurt Deseré or touch her as he had the night he'd informed her of the trip to France, she remembered William's words, "A white man's promise ain't worth piss."

"I'm fine, Masta," Deseré said.

He whispered, "Remember, call me Anthony."

Chapter 22
Over Three Weeks Later
Riviere de Vin
Burgundy, France

"You'd think with Masta Anthony bein' here a week he would've learned how to make every kind of wine there is," Deseré sighed.

With bonnets on their heads and shawls wrapped around their shoulders, she and Addie walked down the dirt road of a rolling hill in Riviere de Vin, a small vineyard of less than ten acres, situated in the middle of Cote de Nuits, in the Burgundy wine region.

Acres of grapevines stretched beyond them on either side with stems so large at the base they resembled narrow tree trunks. Their leaves were bright green. Succulent clusters of crimson grapes burst from the vines, filling the air with a fruity freshness.

"I don't think it's that easy," Addie said.

For the past week, Etienne Gautier, the winemaking contact provided by Nicholas Longworth of Cincinnati, had taken Masta Anthony through several vineyards in Burgundy and let him experience the wine making process first-hand. Masta Anthony had insisted Addie and Deseré accompany them. This vineyard was the last tour Gautier would provide. To escape from hearing another word about wine, Deseré had requested that she and Addie walk the grounds instead.

Now on level terrain, Deseré shaded her eyes from the gleaming sun and looked up into a pale blue sky dotted with puffy white clouds. "I don't care," she pouted. "I just wanna get back to Paris."

The steamer had arrived at Le Havre, the great port of Paris at the mouth of the Seine. They had traveled the one-hundred and ten mile journey southeast from Le Havre to Paris in a diligence, a cumbersome vehicle pulled by five horses that was equal to two and a half stage coaches in one.

The journey had taken about twenty-four hours. The level farm country along the valley of the Seine was a pleasant change of scenery from the ocean they'd sailed on for nearly two weeks. The river had been in view much of the time, broad and winding, dotted with islands. Every field appeared perfectly cultivated.

There had been a stop at Rouen halfway to Paris to see the great cathedral in the center of town. The structure stretched high into the sky. It was built of limestone and was centuries older and far more monumental than anything Deseré had ever seen in Chalreston, let alone Saint Helena. Thinking about it now, she could only remember it as breathtaking. The image of carved stonework, immense pillars and rainbow colored windows played through her mind.

The journey by diligence had continued for another eighty miles beyond Rouen, and after arriving in Paris, they'd spent the night at the Hotel Bedford. Leaving the majority of their luggage in storage there, they'd taken a week's worth with them the next morning when they'd left by stagecoach to ride to Burgundy.

"I wish we could've seen more of Paris that morning before we had to leave," Deseré said. "Looking at all those sights along the Boulevards was so exciting! I loved seein' all the cafés with the tables outside and the men sitting at them with those long mustaches and their ladies just a smilin' away, wearin' all those pretty clothes...and some didn't even wear bonnets! And you could hear that different sounding music from the gardens in the back! It was like bein' in another world."

"I know," Addie said. "I was there. But it looks like you forgot about what we saw when we first got there. All those filthy, smelly streets runnin' every which a way, those old dirty buildings black with soot, and folks so poor they didn't look no better off than the worse off slaves in Saint Helena."

"At least they ain't owned by anybody."

"True. But I sho' 'nuff saw more rats than I seen at home."

That part of Paris was far removed from the magical part where their hotel was located, and Deseré sighed again thinking about it. "I just want to go back... Now we're stuck out here in the country," she mumbled, looking down at the dirt. "I'm mighty glad this is our last vineyard stop, because if we had to see another one I just might scream."

"Oh, stop your complainin', Deseré!" Addie said. "We'll be goin' back to Paris tomorrow and we'll be there a long while." Then she smiled. "And I don't care what you say. I've enjoyed seein' the vineyards. They been fun, and they coulda been more fun for you if you'd tasted the wine."

Deseré lifted her chin. "The devil's poison."

"Now, Deseré, my mama used to say wine is from God, but the drunkard is from the devil. A little won't hurt."

"Masta Anthony always has more than just a little, then he looks at me—that way."

This time Addie sighed. "Wish I was you."

Deseré gasped.

"Masta Anthony's a decent man," Addie said, "even if he

is white. They all not the same — think of Masta Jeremy."

"Addie! Aside from Masta Jeremy, a white man's a white man! Besides, Masta Anthony drinks — and more than just wine!"

"I didn't say he was perfect...but I suspect, like his uncle, he has a heart of Jesus."

Deseré frowned. "You mean like Mr. O'Malley's evangelical nigguh huntin' hounds? As far as I'm concerned, Masta Anthony doesn't have a heart — not after what he did between me and William!"

"Hush, chile," Addie scolded. "You and William wasn't meant to be anyway. You told me Masta Anthony said he left you for another woman."

"I know, but — "

"The Lord says in His word, 'And we know that all things work together for good to them that love God, to them who are called accordin' to His purpose.'"

"Then why are we slaves?"

"I ain't got no answer for that, Deseré. But that's gonna change... One day we all gonna be free."

"How do you know?"

Addie hesitated. "I don't...but I feel it in my spirit." Addie grasped the crook of Deseré's arm. "Let's just enjoy our last day in Burgundy. The surroundings here ain't like the Paris Boulevards, but they're awfully nice, even if they are just quaint and simple."

"Humph," Deseré snorted, "those folks look mighty simple, and not any better off than the poor buckras on Saint Helena." She gazed at the white laborers harvesting grapes and placing them into large baskets. With wide brimmed hats on their heads, they wore their trousers baggy and their shirt sleeves rolled to the elbow. Many eyed Deseré as she and Addie walked by. They smiled and tipped their hats politely.

Both women smiled and nodded back. "Well they sure is nicer than all those poor crackers," Addie said. "And look at all of 'em. White, toilin' in the soil just like nigguhs. Ain't it been somethin' not bein' looked at like you ain't less than nobody? Ever since we rode over on the steamer 'cross the ocean, I done felt like I's as good as anybody else! 'Course *you* been feelin' that way since you started passin' for white in Charleston."

"Not really," Deseré said. "I was afraid, 'til we left New York, bein 'round all those other folks. I ain't never heard so many languages or seen so many different types of people. Masta Anthony said there were a hundred passengers on that ship, but most of 'em weren't even Americans."

Addie said, "Bein' on that ship was the first time I'd ever seen Africans that wasn't slaves."

"Um-hum," Deseré agreed.

The two women walked silently for a few moments, then Deseré said, "I never could figure out where that brown-skinned man with the long mustache came from." She playfully bumped into Addie's shoulder. "He took a likin' to you."

Addie rolled her eyes. "Don't remind me."

"Ya'll didn't speak the same language," Deseré laughed, "but you made him understand you weren't interested." Deseré blew out an exasperated breath. "Just like I'm not interested in Burgundy and all these blame vineyards!"

"Now I know you sick of hearin' everything there is to know 'bout wine, but Masta Anthony's tryin' to learn all he can, 'case he wants to make it and sell it."

"But do you really think he will?" Deseré asked.

"I ain't got no inklin' one way or the other."

"Well if he does, you think he's gonna have the field hands crush the grapes?"

"Maybe," Addie said. "Who else he gonna get to do it?"

"But they do the crushin' with their feet," Deseré said distastefully. "You think white folks would drink wine crushed by nigguhs' feet?"

Addie laughed. "Mr. Gautier *said* they do it with their

feet, but I wanna see that with my own eyes. Can you imagine what that feels like? I'd think..."

As Addie talked on, something caught Deseré's eye in the distance. "Lord have mercy," she said, grabbing Addie's arm with one hand and pointing with the other.

"Good, God Almighty!" Addie exclaimed.

"You done said you wanted to see it," Deseré said. "They're crushin' grapes with their feet alright, but they ain't got no clothes on."

At three different locations that they could see, vats had been brought into the vineyards and filled with whole clusters of grapes and naked men were stepping into them to begin the crushing process.

Addie gulped, as she clutched Deseré's arm. "And I think we both seen enough," she said, turning the younger woman away from the sight. "We'd best head back to the winery and stay inside 'til Masta Anthony's ready to leave."

Deseré swirled back for one last look, but Addie yanked her away from that direction. "Don't be gawkin' back there, chile. You keep your eyes innocent. Um, um, um. I ain't never seen a sight like that, and I hope I die never seein' one like it again."

"Well," Deseré said, "Masta Anthony won't *ever* get me to taste any wine now. And if he wants to crush any grapes," she shook her head rapidly, "it won't be like that!"

"Sho' 'nuff," Addie agreed. "It ain't Christian!"

****

"I have a feeling I've been mistaken about my capabilities regarding this venture," Anthony said to winemaker Etienne Gautier and Claude Boucher, the owner of Riviere de Vin.

They stood in the cellar of Boucher's winery, a large stone farmhouse. The cellar's walls were made of stone, its floor with slabs of gray slate, and sturdy dark wood beams crossed the ceiling. The air was moist and filled with a wet fruity aroma infused with yeast and alcohol. Over twenty wine casks lined the walls, stacked by twos.

"Not if you have ze time and ze determination," Boucher said with a thick French accent. He was stocky and solid, of medium height, and had bushy graying hair. He wore spectacles, yet despite a stern expression, his face easily gave way to a gregarious smile. "Wiz zat comes experience."

"Oui," Gautier agreed. Tall and lean with a thin mustache and jet black hair, Gautier was a graceful man who fluidly moved his hands through the air as he spoke. His accent was just as pronounced as Boucher's. "And wine making requires savoir-faire and experience. As a wine maker, you are an artiste, and a lot of zings will determine ze taste and ze quality of your art."

"Such as land, climate, and your choice of grape," Boucher said.

"Ze barrel or cask you use can make a difference," Gautier went on, "as well as how long you ferment ze wine. Zere is no unique method, which is why I say, winemaking is a most exquisite art!"

"I appreciate all you've taught me throughout this week," Anthony said, "but I'm beginning to realize my dream of making a profit from this venture may not come to fruition."

Although Nicholas Longworth had enjoyed great success in Cincinnati, Anthony believed financial success for him in this realm was unattainable. It would cost a great deal of time to become skilled at the art, as well as a large amount of money to invest in all the additional materials he'd need such as casks and the building of a winery.

Anthony would continue to only grow the grapes and ship them up North and to the local markets. Winemaking could be a gamble in which he'd make much, or nothing if the crop were to fail, and he'd already suffered enough failure in his life. Yet an area in which he was determined not to fail was in securing Deseré's love.

"But you already have your vineyard, your grapes, and your servants to harvest, de-stem and crush zem," Gautier encouraged.

"Yes," Anthony said, "so I believe as a hobby, I could perhaps very much enjoy wine- making."

"Tout ce qui sera sera," Boucher smiled broadly. "Whatever will be, will be. You never know what ze future holds."

Just then the men heard footsteps coming down the narrow stone stairwell.

"Ah, madame," Boucher said cheerfully, upon seeing Addie on the steep cellar steps. She walked sideways, coming down one step at a time. Anthony strode over and climbed the first two steps to offer his hand as she descended. Boucher asked, "Did you enjoy walking in my vineyard?"

"Why, yes, sir," Addie said. She thanked Anthony for his gentlemanly assistance, then added, "The grounds are just as pretty as can be."

****

Deseré saw Anthony near the bottom of the steps. Addie was way into her forties, practically an old woman. Deseré wasn't, and besides, she'd come down the steps like a white lady since that's what she was pretending to be. Rather than inch down sideways, one step at a time, she'd put on her finest airs. Using both hands, Deseré picked up her skirts and started her descent. She moved quickly, but by the time she was mid-way down, she lost her footing and started to fall.

"Deseré!" Anthony said. He rapidly moved up a few more steps to catch her and, in seconds, she fell into his arms.

Addie, Boucher and Gautier ran to the foot of the steps.

"Mademoiselle, are you alright?" Boucher asked. "I am so sorry. My cellar steps are steep."

Deseré found her head crushed into Masta Anthony's broad chest, while her arms held fast around his neck. Holding her tightly around the waist, he helped her to the bottom of the steps. Once her feet touched the floor,

Deseré's arms slid from around his neck, settling onto his arms. Then she gazed up to him and saw a look of worry in his eyes, as if he genuinely did care for her. Deseré's heart began to pound.

"I'm fine, Mr. Boucher," she said. Although Deseré addressed Boucher, her eyes were locked on Masta Anthony.

"Are you sure," Masta Anthony asked, the concern still evident on his face, a face that suddenly seemed more handsome to her.

She nodded, feeling herself begin to melt. "Thank you for catching me," she said softly. Then Deseré turned to Boucher. "I just wasn't paying attention like I should."

"I am so glad you are not hurt," Boucher said. "And I hope you enjoyed my vineyard as much as Madame Addie."

"Indeed, I did," Deseré said, realizing she still held onto Masta Anthony's arms, the strong arms that remained around her waist. She let go of him, then discreetly removed herself from his grasp. Anthony picked up her shawl from the floor. It had fallen from her shoulders when she'd stumbled. When he gently placed it around her shoulders, Deseré felt her face redden. "Thank you," she said quietly, letting her gaze linger on him. She'd lost her train of thought where Mr. Boucher was concerned, but then remembered and addressed him. "Your vineyard is quite beautiful, Mr. Boucher. As a matter of fact," she moved her eyes to Addie's, "we saw a *whole* lot more than we expected."

The two women chuckled.

Chapter 23
Paris

So many shops, Deseré thought, as she walked through the Passage des Panoramas with Masta Anthony on one side of her and Addie on the other. She'd never seen a market so big, nor one like this, which was a covered passageway filled with an assortment of stores.

"We'll visit the fabric shop and then the dressmaker the hotel recommended first," Anthony said. "Perhaps tomorrow the shoemaker and the milliner."

"But there's so much to see," Deseré said, as she strolled, slowly gazing in all the stores and inhaling a variety of aromas.

"That ain't a bad thing," Addie said, just as taken with the market as Deseré.

Anthony smiled. "We can come back as often as you like."

Several people walked about between the shops that lined each side of the gallery, their footsteps echoing continuously. Windows lined the ceiling, letting in bright light that vividly illuminated the pavement. Brightness glowed from white globes, red lanterns and lines of blue gas flames. And even more brilliance shone from giant plate-glass windows of stores displaying gold and glassware. A line of little round windows were above the shops. With their signs bright, the stores were arranged with no rhyme or reason, but to Deseré it all seemed a fascinating adventure. The rich scent of tanned leather wafted in the air, floral sweetness and savory musk floated from a perfumer's shop, and a candy-maker prepared confections fragrant with the scents of chocolate, vanilla and cinnamon. All the smells combined created an intoxicating thrill.

"Here we are," Anthony said, stopping in front of a shop called Tissu Premier. More dazzle emanated from its large plate-glass windows from a display of brightly colored silk and satin.

Upon entering the shop, Addie said, "Good, gracious day! Looks like we in high cotton now!"

Shelves lined the store from front to back, overflowing with bolts of fabric suitable for anything from clothing to furniture. Deseré stood in stunned disbelief, her mouth open in awe.

Anthony smiled. "I suggest both of you pick out enough fabric for the dresses I promised, plus some additional to take home."

As Addie quickly bustled off toward the fabric, Deseré walked as if in a trance toward the shelves. With arms outstretched she ran her hands over the plushest velvet she'd ever touched, appreciating its nap and feel. Deseré closed her eyes for a moment imagining it as a cape fit for royalty. Her fingers moved along the shelves feeling the silkiest of satin and the sleekest of silk, and she envisioned them as the grandest of party dresses. The shelves seemed never-ending, filled with more fabrics from vividly printed cotton and sheer muslin to ornate brocades and artistic tapestries. Deseré sighed contentedly, feeling as if she were in paradise.

****

Over two weeks had passed since their return to Paris, and now Deseré gazed at the splendor of the magnificent masterpieces that covered the twenty-foot walls from top to bottom beneath arched panes of glass that allowed a view of the sparkling blue sky above. "Your Uncle Jeremy told me about this museum," she said to Masta Anthony as they strolled through the Louvre. Addie walked alongside them on tessellated wood floors waxed to a gleaming shine. "I just never imagined it to be so big."

"Well," Masta Anthony smiled, "it was a palace."

"Humph," Addie said. "They must have at least five-hundred folks to clean it."

"And this is known as the Long Gallery, or Grande Galerie," Masta Anthony continued.

"That's the God's honest truth," Addie quipped. "This gallery must be near a quarter mile long."

Deseré didn't care how long the gallery was. She was enjoying the art, she was enjoying Paris, and to her astonishment, she was enjoying Masta Anthony more than anything.

When they'd returned to Paris from Burgundy, Masta Anthony had taken Deseré and Addie shopping for dress fabric, Parisian dress patterns and bonnets. In addition, he'd commissioned new dresses and shoes for them.

Today, Deseré wore a lace edged shawl draped over a lavender cotton dress that had tiny mother of pearl buttons down the front; its bodice fit smoothly against her body. The sleeves were three-quarter length, trimmed by one lace tier that matched the lace tier at the hem of her skirt. Like some of the fashionable Parisian women, Deseré, after much thought, decided not to wear a bonnet, at least for one day. Addie's dress was a simpler cotton creation with vertical stripes of pale pink, green and gold with full length sleeves. Her shawl was a matching shade of green, and a bonnet covered her head.

During their time abroad, Masta Anthony had been

nothing but a gentleman, and Deseré was beginning to think that Addie was right. Perhaps Masta Anthony *was* a decent white man. Deseré felt that her heart had actually softened toward him because he'd treated her, as well as Addie, as he would any white lady while they'd traveled. He'd shown kindness to each of them, and he'd curtailed his drinking to no more than two glasses of wine per day.

Now Deseré didn't even mind the way he looked at her anymore. Her body had begun to tingle at the sight of him, as it once only had for William.

Perhaps the uncontrollable feelings for Masta Anthony flourished within her because in France, she hadn't felt in the least like a slave. Yet once back in South Carolina, she knew things could never remain as they were here. Deseré had to keep reminding herself that she was his property to do with as he pleased. Selling her was always a possibility, and if he married a white woman of his own station, Deseré would never be anything more than his concubine. Her heart beat rapidly at the thought of her fate, yet the only thing she could do now was make the best of things.

"The Long Gallery," Anthony said, disrupting Deseré's thoughts, "contains some of the finest paintings in the world."

Gazing at the numerous paintings, Addie asked, "So did they take all the best art and leave nothing behind?"

"I assure you, Addie," Anthony said, "there's more than enough artwork in the world to go around."

As Deseré strolled by the paintings with her white gloved hand in the crook of Anthony's arm, she noticed several artists, men and women, sitting at easels copying the masterpieces. Some were completing their work and leaving, some were in progress, and others just beginning. As Anthony walked on, she let go of his arm to watch a young man as he worked on a reproduction of Raphael's *Saint Catherine of Alexandria*. Masta Anthony had explained that she was a martyred saint.

Deseré was impressed by how the artist's work so closely resembled the original. The girl on his canvas appeared life-like as she gazed upward to a cloud-filled sky, radiant with beams of sunlight. The colorful folds of her garments looked so real, that if touched on canvas they could be felt.

The man turned from his work to look at Deseré. His eyes widened slightly, as if in surprise. He smiled. For a brief moment, Deseré was taken aback by how handsome he was. He was probably twenty-one, with wavy dark hair falling beneath his ears.

"Beautiful," Deseré said, indicating his work with a nod of her head.

"Bien moins que vous," he replied.

"Deseré." Masta Anthony approached her. Then guiding her away by the arm, he said, "I'm sure the artist would prefer not to be disturbed."

"If you say so — Anthony." She had to keep reminding herself to call him that. "But he didn't seem to mind my compliment."

A while later, Addie took a particular liking to Carravagio's painting, *The Fortune Teller.*

"What do you think of this one, Deseré?" she asked quietly, while Masta Anthony stood a few feet away from them in front of another painting. "That man's *supposed* to be gettin' his fortune read," she chuckled.

Deseré studied the canvas for a moment. "I like it," she whispered. "Looks like that girl's stroking his hand, but he doesn't have sense enough to know she's stealing his ring."

"Seems he's too taken with her to realize she's takin' advantage of him."

"Guess she's doing what she has to do to survive," Deseré said.

"Like any woman," Addie sighed.

When they passed da Vinci's *Mona Lisa*, Addie said, "With that smile, what you think she's got up her sleeve?"

"No telling," Deseré said, "but it must've paid off, if that's all her property in the background."

After the three of them had walked down both sides of the hall, Addie said, "So what sight will we take in next?"

"We've only just begun, Addie," Anthony said. "There are six more rooms to explore right here in the Louvre."

****

Several hours later, they approached the long flight of marble stairs that led to the first floor to leave the museum. "I still can't believe we didn't see everything," Deseré said. Wearing a new pair of beige flat-soled leather half-boots that Masta Anthony had had made for her, Deseré's feet hurt from all the walking. But she was getting used to aching feet and legs since they'd walked innumerable miles to do sightseeing since arriving in Paris.

"We'll come back to finish touring before—" Anthony started, but was interrupted when a man called to them.

"Monsieur, madame, et mademoiselle!" The voice echoed, as did running footsteps over the marble floor of the enormous hall.

When they turned, Deseré recognized the man as the artist whose work she'd admired earlier in the Long Gallery. He was tall, and although French, his looks were similar to the swarthy men she'd learned were Italian. His skin was what they called olive, his large eyes were a deep brown, his nose sharp and his lips full. He carried one of his paintings.

The artist began speaking in French, but Anthony stopped him. "Je ne parle pas Francais," he said.

"Non?" the artist asked.

"Un petit peu," Anthony replied. "Je parle Anglais."

The man smiled and began slowly in English, "Ze young lady, I see her when you...come in...long ago. Je pense qu'elle est tres belle," he said quickly, then stopped and continued in halted English trying to think of the correct words. "Very beautiful. Une ange. Avec pastel...I paint her." He held up the canvas, revealing a portrait of Deseré. "A gift," he said to her. "When you see, zink of Paris."

Dumbfounded, Deseré's eyes grew large as she beheld the image created by the artist on a canvas that was about a foot-and-half wide and two-feet long. He moved it closer for her to take.

"Is it wet?" she asked.

"No," Anthony said, "it's done with pastels. They're like chalk. Just be careful not to smudge it. Perhaps you'd better remove your gloves."

Deseré quickly slipped off her gloves and handed them to Addie. Then she held the portrait by the edges, thinking it a fine likeness. It was lovely, serene, almost angelic. In her mind she could hear her mother scolding her for the sin of vanity. Yet she wasn't admiring herself, but the image that stared back at her.

Deseré wore her hair in ringlets on each side of her head. However, the artist had painted her golden tresses in loose tumbling waves about her shoulders. The portrait's radiant blue eyes were the exact shade of hers, and the lips he'd painted appeared lush and pink. The face she gazed upon was beautiful, more beautiful, Deseré believed, than she actually was. She wondered if Masta Anthony saw her this way.

Deseré smiled at the artist, then finally said, "Thank you, I mean, merci," she corrected herself, as Masta Anthony had taught her the few French words and phrases he knew.

"Oui," Anthony said abruptly, then possessively put an arm around her. "Merci beaucoup." The grasp of his hand was firm on her shoulder. Deseré's heart beat rapidly at his touch, and she felt a rush of blood through her body.

"You come again here?" the artist asked, dreamily gazing into Deseré's eyes. "Ze portrait, I paint from memoire," he pointed to his head, "after I see," he ran his fingers over his face, "your visage. It is not perfect, not complete. If you sit for me, I finish and —"

"We won't be coming back," Anthony blurted. Then he reached into his pocket and removed his leather wallet.

"Non—a gift!" the artist protested, upon seeing that Anthony wanted to pay him.

"I insist," Anthony said, passing the young man a handful of francs. The artist refused again until Anthony took one of the artist's hands and forced the money into it. "Buy some more paints—pastels—or something. Now, au revoir." He clutched Deseré by the elbow and hurried her out of the museum with Addie quickly following behind them.

"I'll carry your...gift," Anthony said sourly.

"No, sir," Addie said. "I'll carry it. I gotta look like a good mammy to her."

Deseré chuckled. "Thank you, both, but I'll carry it myself. I wanna look at it some more." She gazed at the painting. "I never thought I'd have my own portrait." Then Deseré glanced over her shoulder. She smiled at the artist who still stood where they'd left him, mesmerized. "And my, my, my, to have it painted by such a handsome man."

"You mean a penniless swine," Anthony grumbled under his breath. "We won't bother coming back here again," he said shortly. "There are too many other sights to see."

Upon stirring Anthony's jealousy, Deseré felt a slight sense of power. Though not far-reaching by any means, she realized it could be a usable asset.

Chapter 24

The next morning as they strolled the boulevards under noble chestnut trees, Anthony saw a sign that read *Bijoux*. Although his French was limited, he knew that meant jewelry. "If you ladies will pardon me for a moment," he said to Addie and Deseré, "I'm going to stop in here." He motioned toward the tall glass door of the store. "I'd like to purchase a little something for my mother. Keep strolling and I'll catch up with you shortly."

It wasn't until later in the afternoon while in the Garden of Tuileries among many other promenading Parisians and tourists, that he revealed the true intention of his visit to the jeweler's shop. As the three of them walked around a large circular pond with a spewing fountain in the center, Anthony excused himself from Addie, this time taking Deseré with him. "I'd like to speak with her privately," he said, over the chatter of children, who ran about playing happily, their immaculate Swiss maids not far away, keeping careful watch over them.

"Stay in plain sight," Addie said. "I gotta do my job as chaperone and keep an eye on her." Just then, a ball landed at her feet. She tossed it back to a child of about five, wearing a flat cap along with his blue and white sailor suit, who had come running to fetch it.

"Merci beaucoup, madame! Maintenant, je peux continuer a jouer!" the child shouted, then scurried off.

Addie shook her head in wonder. "Amazin' how these little whippersnappers can speak French."

Anthony laughed. "We'll be only mere yards away," he said, walking Deseré to a shaded bench nearby under a towering tree. Deseré closed her parasol. After they sat down, Anthony pulled a small white box from his pocket. "This is for you."

****

With hands clasped in her lap, Deseré looked down at the box. A mixture of excitement and fear caused her heart to race. Lifting her eyes to Masta Anthony's she asked, "What is it?"

"Take it," he smiled.

Deseré's shoulders stiffened. Although she'd warmed to him, and even now felt goosebumps in his presence, this box surely implied the door to something more, a door she wasn't yet willing to open. An elderly couple walked by. They nodded towards them, smiling. Thankful for the distraction, Deseré smiled back, then reluctantly returned her attention to Masta Anthony and the box. "But what is it?"

He smiled again. "You'll have to open it and see."

Deseré hesitantly took the box, then slowly lifted the lid. She gasped upon seeing a cameo pendant. The shell background was blue and the woman, carved in profile was white. Her face was pretty and her hair up-swept in curls. Pearls were around her neck and a teardrop dangled from her ear. A rose blossomed near the bottom right edge. Deseré wasn't sure what the frame was, but she guessed it to be white gold. It was accented with tiny blue crystals which sparkled in the rays of sunlight streaming through the overhanging branches above them.

"I tried to find something blue to match your eyes," Masta Anthony said.

Deseré smiled at him, feeling her heart swell, yet she was silent for several moments. "It's beautiful," she finally said, "but...but I can't take it." Now feeling her stomach churn, her mother's words reverberated through her mind about trinkets from a white man to a slave woman: *If they don't take by force, they'll give to get, but either way, they'll put a yellow baby in the nest.*

"But I insist," Masta Anthony said, interrupting Deseré's thoughts. "Besides, it's not only a pendant, but a watch, as well."

"A watch?" Deseré leaned forward to examine the pendant more closely.

Anthony removed it from the box to show her. The attached chain, made of tiny links of white gold, glistened. Then he opened the cameo to reveal the small clock inside. "It will help you keep track of the time."

"Why, fancy that," she said, amazed at the small abalone timepiece. But then Deseré gently pushed his hands away, letting her fingers linger on his a moment longer than necessary. Looking into Masta Anthony's deep brown eyes, she said, "No, I can't take it. It's — it's much too nice."

He closed the cameo, then held her gaze. "You'll cut me to the heart by not taking it. It's just a small token I purchased."

Deseré smiled. "But Anthony, you didn't have to buy me anything. That artist from yesterday, he meant nothing to me. Just because he painted my portrait didn't mean you had to buy me this."

"Regardless," he said, standing up, "I wanted to. Now, turn around. Let me try it on you."

"Oh..." Feeling her face flush, Deseré shook her head. "No."

"What harm can it do just to try it on?"

She gazed up at him, feeling her breathing deepen, then

said quietly, "I suppose none." Deseré turned away from Masta Anthony, allowing him to lean down and place the pendant around her neck and fasten it. The touch of his fingers sliding against her skin caused more goosebumps to flare. When she eased around to face him, his eyes dropped to her chest. The pendant lay nestled between her breasts, which were covered by the turquoise colored muslin of her dress.

"It's beautiful on you," he said, letting his eyes linger on the cameo.

"Thank you," Deseré said, as he sat down next to her. This time, he was so close, she could feel his steely thigh through her petticoats. Her heartbeat increased. Then Deseré lifted her wrists to unfasten the cameo. Anthony gently grasped her hands, causing her heart to flutter even more wildly.

"You have an objection to wearing a watch?" He softly caressed her hands.

"No, but—but it wouldn't be appropriate for me to take such a fine piece of jewelry from you."

Still holding her hands, he said, "I expect nothing in return, only your appreciation."

After several seconds, Deseré looked in Addie's direction. The woman certainly took her role as chaperone quite seriously. While vehemently shaking her head, she stood with hands on hips wearing a stern expression aimed at Deseré. Seeing this, Deseré quickly slipped her hands from Masta Anthony's and slightly inched away from him. He had noble intentions, she rationalized. He expected nothing in return, so she'd just have to explain that to Addie. "Well...I—I suppose I can wear it—but only to keep track of the time."

Chapter 25

"What do you think?" Anthony asked as he walked arm and arm with Deseré while touring the grounds of the Palace of Versailles.

They'd taken the train twelve miles southwest to the small village earlier that morning. In one hand, Anthony carried a copy of *Galignani's New Paris Guide.* He continued to make the most of his time in France with Deseré and never tired of showing her the sights. She'd become more at ease and relaxed around him, and he actually believed she was beginning to fall in love with him. He wasn't positive regarding this, however, and hoped he wasn't merely fantasizing.

Before Deseré could answer what she thought of Versailles, Addie said, "A thousand folks must clean that place!"

The sprawling palace, with its many wings, seven-hundred rooms and more than two-thousand windows was opulent, and the exquisite gardens designed in alleys, leading to innumerable groves, never-ending.

"I think it's splendid," Deseré said. Fresh flowers of

several varieties and colors burst around them as they casually strolled among the numerous fountains and countless lifelike statues of gods and goddesses.

Anthony thought Deseré appeared no less a goddess herself, in a pink pin-stripe dress with long bell-shaped sleeves. She also wore a bonnet he'd purchased for her, adorned with pink silk roses and pink satin ribbons trimmed in lace. The blue stones of the cameo around her neck glistened to match the sparkle in her eyes.

The scent of fresh flowers swirled around them, as well as the metallic smell of water from the fountains that gushed, spewed, streamed, and cascaded in fizzing jets. Now as they walked west of the Water Parterre they saw two fountains of fighting animals. To the north was the Evening Fountain, which depicted two massive lions, one bringing down a wolf and the other attacking a wild boar. To the south was the Daybreak Fountain, which showed a tiger assailing a bear and a bloodhound besieging a stag.

Many other tourists walked the grounds, including a matronly British woman, who said as she passed by, "One can easily get lost here, so it's best not to separate. I haven't seen my husband for over an hour."

Anthony smiled, as the woman trudged on in search of her spouse, then perused his *Galignani's Guide*. "It says here that Versailles was the seat of power for France's kingdom starting in 1682 when Louis XIV moved the royal court from Paris." He read further. "It also says that the palace is now unoccupied, and that no ruler has taken residence here since Louis XVI and Marie Antoinette were driven from it by the mob from Paris on the eighth of October, 1789." Word for word, he read, "'Time had produced its revolution in opinion and Versailles could not again exist under the conditions of the monarchy of Louis XVI.'"

"Musta been like what happened with Nat Turner, leadin' that rebellion against the white folks in Virginia," Addie said, as they stopped at the Daybreak Fountain to admire the realistic animals.

Addie's remark unsettled Anthony, but he tried not to show it. The Nat Turner rebellion had occurred a mere fourteen years earlier. He'd been fifteen at the time and living with his mother in Ohio. She'd been relieved to read of Turner's capture and execution after he'd killed over fifty whites. She'd said that Turner wanting to spread terror and alarm among whites could have negatively influenced even the most docile of negroes, turning the nation on its head.

Anthony feigned a study of the stag carved into the fountain. With antlers high, it was low to the ground, hooves curled beneath it. Water spewed from its agonized mouth into the fountain's lower basin. Although large and powerful, the stag had been conquered by a bloodhound less than half its size. The fearsome hound with a thick, decorative collar, was mounted above the stag with its sharp claws embedded into the flesh of its prey. It appeared to bark in triumph, gushing water from its mouth into the fountain's upper basin.

Deseré followed his gaze. She pointed to the hound and said, "Back home, that dog would've been bringin' down a negro."

"Sho' 'nuff," Addie agreed.

Deseré's comment, along with Addie's earlier remark, had reminded Anthony for the first time since he'd been overseas that he was a slave owner. It wasn't exactly that he'd forgotten, he just hadn't felt like he was an actual owner of people and now a willing participant of something so evil, bloodhounds tracked human beings, and so oppressive as to lead to revolt. Anthony's feelings overwhelmed him at times. So as not to stir discontent among his people, he'd do his best to remain a benevolent slaveholder, but how could he not, since he'd fallen in love with a slave?

He'd given up on the prospect of winemaking. Perhaps he should abandon the idea of owning a plantation with slave-labor, as well. He could sell the land and free the people. Yet everything led him back to Deseré. As long as he owned her, she was his.

Another couple approached the fountain, but immersed in his thoughts, Anthony paid them no mind. Deseré mentioned to Addie that she wished she had something Anthony had left at the Bedford, but not listening to the women chatter, his mind continued to wander. Then above the fountain's spewing water, he heard his name.

"Anthony?" a woman said. "Anthony Sinclair? Is that really you?"

Anthony met the eyes of the tourist addressing him, and was struck dumb.

"It *is* you!" the woman exclaimed, smiling broadly.

"Why yes...yes indeed it is...Edith."

Anthony felt the blood drain from his face. Edith Emory, the woman he'd once intended to marry, stood before him on the arm of a thick behemoth of a man, whom Anthony assumed to be her new husband. Edith was as beautiful as ever, in a pale blue dress, although not quite as beautiful as Deseré. A bonnet covered her chestnut hair and her brown eyes twinkled gaily. Edith's upturned nose was small, and her pale pink lips bow-shaped.

"Imagine running into you here! Why the world is such a small place. Allow me to introduce my husband. Abraham Weld, this is Anthony Sinclair."

Freeing him for a handshake, Deseré discreetly took Anthony's guide book and passed it to Addie.

"Pleased to make your acquaintance," Anthony said stiffly, to the man whose head seemed welded to his shoulders in the absence of a neck.

The man grunted a reply as Anthony extended his hand, only to receive a most crushing handshake in return. Abraham Weld had been described in their wedding announcement as an industrious architect. Yet with his bald pate covered by a top hat, hard black eyes resembling well-beaten nail heads, and the down-turned lips of a scowling ape, to Anthony, this son of a beer brewer looked more like a criminal.

Pushing his distraction aside, Anthony said quickly, "And allow me to introduce Miss Deseré ..." he scrambled to think of a French surname, and that of the hotel's Suisse came to mind "...Crete, and her mammy, Addie. Mr. and Mrs. Abraham Weld."

After an exchange of pleasantries, Anthony noticed Edith studying Deseré, as if noticing her beauty for the first time. The smile left her round face. Anthony felt Deseré's grasp on his arm grow tighter.

"Ya'll must be Yankees by the way you speak," Deseré said brightly, sounding like a most pampered southern belle. Now both of her hands grasped Anthony's arm. He glanced down at her, and for a brief moment Deseré looked up to him. She appeared to beam.

"Why, yes," Edith said, her voice lacking the luster it once held. "And you..."

"Deseré's family owns a neighboring plantation in South Carolina," Anthony lied. "They're here visiting relatives and invited me to join them." Upon meeting someone he actually knew, he'd had to change his fabrication regarding Deseré. Claiming she was an orphan in his charge wouldn't seem quite that credible to Edith.

"Oh?" Edith looked skeptical.

"Yes," Deseré said, "since Anthony and I are..." she paused, gazing up at him for several seconds this time, her wide blue eyes brimming with adoration, or at least a believable impression of it.

"Are planning to marry?" Edith said, incredulously.

"Uh—that's right," Anthony blurted. What else could he have said? He noticed Addie turning her head away to cough, but another look revealed that she was trying to disguise a laughing fit.

"Oh..." Edith said, unsmiling. "Oh, my... Well, congratulations." She nudged the block of granite next to her. "Congratulate them, Abe."

"Congratulations," Abraham said, sounding like he'd swallowed a tablespoon of gravel.

After Anthony and Deseré thanked the Welds for their good wishes, Edith said, "I'm surprised I've heard no mention of your impending nuptials in Cincinnati." He noticed a slight suspicion in her tone.

"It's a...very recent engagement," Anthony said, feeling the last of the blood drain from his face, probably leaving him paler than the underbelly of an albino cat. "Aside from Deseré's family, you're the first to know, I asked her only yesterday. So please keep the news to yourself. I'd like my family to hear it from me first."

Edith smirked. "Of course."

"So your family and Anthony's family are friends?" Deseré asked. "I don't recall him ever mentioning your name at all."

Edith flinched ever so slightly, as though she'd been pricked by a pin. "That's because I'm Edith Weld now. Anthony knew me as Edith Emory. Perhaps *that* rings a bell."

"No," Deseré said, pressing her body firmly into Anthony's, "it doesn't."

Anthony could have dropped to the ground and kissed Deseré's feet.

"Oh." Appearing almost disheartened, Edith's lips drooped slightly. She seemed to catch herself, then flashed a loquacious smile. "So, Deseré, what does your family's plantation produce?"

"Cotton," Deseré said, then frivolously waved a hand through the air. "Acres and acres of cotton."

"Well then, you must own several slaves," Edith said condescendingly, "including that one," she pointed to Addie as she would a pet.

"Why, yes'm," Deseré said, "but we're good to our people. Isn't that right, Mammy Addie?"

"Oh, yes, ma'am, Miss Deseré, ma'am," Addie said in exaggerated good humor.

"See?" Deseré said, sounding like the epitome of oblivious southern womanhood.

Anthony didn't know if he should be insulted, appalled or amused as he watched the charade being played before him, because he actually felt as if a joke were being played on him. Deseré so skillfully portrayed a southern belle, and Addie, complicit in her role of mammy, performed deftly as well. He felt as if he were seeing them for the first time, as human beings, mocking the life he'd known as a boy and now wished to rekindle. He had to ask himself, were slaves not actually happy in the role that life had assigned them, even under the care of a kindly slaveholder?

"Well," Edith raised a brow, "if you'll pardon my saying, as a northerner, I don't approve of the institution, and I'm still rather surprised that Anthony has become a slaveholder himself." Her brown eyes held his.

"I have." Anthony said awkwardly, trying not to sound ashamed.

"Well, your mother told me you'd gone to live on a plantation you'd inherited," Edith said. "Now I can tell her I've seen the proof with my very own eyes."

"You're...in touch with my mother?" Anthony asked, feeling even more unsettled.

"We still see each other on occasion, socially. Speaking of which, perhaps you and Deseré and her family can join my husband and I for dinner this evening."

"Well..." Anthony said, feeling trapped, and wondering how he could extricate himself from this situation.

"It's just so nice to see a familiar face while traveling abroad," Edith went on. "Won't you say yes? I promise to keep my anti-slavery opinions to myself."

"I'd have to, of course...check with Deseré's family, and see—"

"Darling," Deseré said, tugging on Anthony's arm, "we

can't."

"No?" His eyes widened, looking at her.

"We have plans," Deseré said. "Remember? The opera."

"Oh, yes, the opera," Anthony nodded.

"The opera?" Edith said. "Which one?"

"Uh—" Anthony began.

"*La vestale*," Deseré said, "at the Salle Le Peletier." They'd seen it two nights before.

"Oh. We haven't seen that one yet, "Edith said. "We saw *I puritani* at the Theatre Italian. Well, perhaps you can join us tomorrow for dinner."

"Tomorrow?" Anthony felt a trickle of sweat stream from his hairline. Edith wouldn't give up.

"You're staying at the Hotel Bedford?" Edith asked.

Anthony froze for a moment. "How—how did you know?" he stammered.

Edith grinned like a pixie. "I believe I heard Deseré mention the Bedford just before I recognized you. So perhaps we can make arrangements to meet you there. Wouldn't that be—"

"Edith," Abraham said in his gravelly voice, "Not possible, we leave for Germany early tomorrow."

Edith clucked her tongue. "Oh, yes. That completely slipped my mind. Seeing Anthony here at Versailles of all places has utterly befuddled me. It's a shame we can't spend more time with you later. I'd just love to visit with you and meet Deseré's family. Will you be going to Germany? We'll be staying there until—"

"It's been nice meeting you folks," Abraham interrupted bluntly, "but I think we'd best move on, let you get back to your sightseeing. Busy day ahead of us, Edith."

"Abe," Edith snapped, "I wasn't finished talking to Anthony."

Keeping his voice low, he mumbled something to Edith that sounded like, "But he's *been* finished talking to you for quite a while."

Turning pink, she frowned, then forced a tight smile. "I suppose we should let you get back to enjoying the sights. Perhaps we'll see you sometime in Cincinnati."

"Perhaps," Anthony said. "Goodbye, Edith." He tried not to sound too relieved at her departure. "It was nice meeting you, Mr. Weld."

After all the goodbyes were said, Weld led Edith away, yet she looked over her shoulder one last time to wave a final farewell.

Anthony patted the sweat from his brow with a handkerchief. To Deseré he said, "I certainly appreciate your assistance from a trying situation."

She smiled. "It seems Miss Edith is sorry she let you go."

For a moment Anthony said nothing, then, "How do you know anything about her?"

Deseré hesitated. "Just a guess."

Addie said, "A blind man could see that if she wasn't on the arm of that big slab of cement, she woulda been on you like white on rice, Masta Anthony."

A slight smile curled his lips. "I suppose Mr. Weld is a rather...critical looking man."

"By critical," Deseré said, "do you mean he got hit with the ugly stick?"

"No," Addie said, "it means he got whooped with the whole forest."

Anthony laughed, but then said seriously, "Deseré, back to your knowledge of Miss Emory, or rather, Mrs. Weld..." He felt her stiffen against him. "Can you...read?"

Deseré pulled from Anthony's arm. "Read?" she asked, stepping away from him.

"Read?" Addie repeated.

"It's — it's against the law for a slave to know how to read, sir," Deseré said.

"So we don't know nothin' 'bout no readin'," Addie shook her head adamantly, then opening the guide book, she turned it upside down. She and Deseré looked at the words wide-eyed, as if clueless. "See, we ain't got no idea what all this here means."

When Addie closed the book, Anthony looked at Deseré. "I was aware that your mother could read. She claimed not to know much beyond the basics, but I believe she was lying... I'd prefer you *not* read my letters. "

Deseré bit her lower lip. "Yes — Anthony."

"And Addie," Anthony said, "I assume you can read, as well."

"No, si—" Addie began.

But Deseré interrupted, "She can indeed."

Addie looked sharply at Deseré and muttered, "You done it now, girl."

"That's alright, Addie," Masta Anthony said. "Reading will...certainly make for easier communication between us." After a moment of silence he looked back at Deseré. "Despite your prying eyes, thank you for collaborating with me in taking satisfaction during a most unpleasant encounter."

Deseré smiled, the mist from the fountain creating a rainbow around her. "My pleasure."

Chapter 26

"Deseré, if I could stay here in Paris, I would," Addie said, over the rattle of cabs and the rumbling of omnibuses, the giant horse drawn public conveyances that clattered over the cobblestone street in front of them. "It's so beautiful! There ain't no drunks reelin' around all afflicted and nobody spittin' tobacco."

The two women sat at a sidewalk cafe across the street from their hotel having breakfast. Several other tables surrounded them filled with fashionably dressed Parisians conversing in French, or enjoying the solitary company of a newspaper or book. Some titles, such as *Les Trois Mousquetaires* and *Les Frères Corses,* she'd learned were written by a man named Alexandre Dumas, and his grandfather was a negro. The white folks certainly wouldn't believe that back home.

Addie, wearing a pale pink turban and matching shawl, felt just as fashionable as the Parisians. She wore a cotton dress patterned with a floral design of pale pink, lavender and turquoise blue. The bodice was high at the neck and the sleeves long. She even felt pretty because a very handsome older gentleman sitting at the table next to theirs had smiled at her when they'd first arrived. He stood out because he was dark, with coppery brown skin. Here in Paris, there were people of every kind, from every place.

Addie inhaled, taking in the heavenly scent of Parisian coffee and fresh baked bread which momentarily overpowered the smell of urine and horse manure that abounded in the streets, although the piles were fastidiously cleared by garçons paid to clean them. Addie poured hot milk into her coffee, then took a bite of her petit pan. The slender biscuit was crisp and warm, tasting like bread and cake combined. "But mostly," she said, "everyone's so polite, so civil-like. We've been waited on hand and foot in our hotel, in restaurants, treated like queens. We can go anywhere, any time, without a pass... I wanna keep livin' like a free person, bein' respected. Shoot, I almost forgot I was a slave 'til last week when that heifer, Edith, pointed to me like I was a dog."

Batons de marche, cannes... A street vendor called politely as he walked by their table, pushing a cart filled with a variety of walking sticks and canes.

"It is different here," Deseré sighed wistfully.

"At least you have a future when you go back to South Carolina."

"What do you mean?"

"As if you didn't know," Addie said. "Masta Anthony loves you." Deseré stared at her, wide-eyed. "Now don't be gawkin' at me like that. Even though you're his slave, I can tell he loves you by the way he looks at you. And I seen the way you been lookin' at him. It's 'cause you love him, too."

Deseré blushed. "No I don't... Well...maybe I do...I don't know. But sometimes...I still think about William and what could've been."

"Shucks," Addie said, "William's gone and you ain't never gonna see him again!"

Deseré nodded sadly. "But I still think that if he'd stayed in South Carolina, maybe he would've forgotten that other woman, and sooner or later...he would've fallen in love with me."

"Chile, that's a dream."

Deseré stayed silent a moment. "I suppose it is. I'm being foolish to think he could've grown to love me, when his heart belonged to someone else. I should be thankful that Masta Anthony saved me from sorrow and despair."

"Sho 'nuff." Addie took a sip of her cafe au lait.

"And I do find myself thinking about Masta Anthony...and wanting to be with him...more and more, but—"

"Now, if you had a choice," Addie leaned close to her, "would you stay here or go back to South Carolina with Masta Anthony and take your chances as his high yalla slave mistress?"

Torn, Deseré looked into Addie's kind face. Before she could answer, the brown-skinned man who'd been seated next to them approached their table. Addie saw that in addition to being handsome, he was quite tall. He appeared to be in his sixties, and was a bit heavy-set.

The man addressed Addie, "Pardon me, ladies." His deep baritone sounded American.

Puzzled, Addie and Deseré looked at each other for a moment, stunned by the realization that he'd probably understood every word they'd said.

The man removed his top hat and bowed slightly. His long mustache and slick black hair were liberally threaded with gray. "My name is Dr. Vincent Chenault. I hail from Louisiana. I...couldn't help but overhear your conversation. I want you to know that under the French anti-slavery law, we negroes are all free here."

Addie's eyes widened. "Really?" Then she thinned her lips at the smooth talking negro, who most likely thought them nothing more than ignorant American slaves. Dismissing him, she lifted her chin. "You're just playin' with us, so go on 'bout your business."

"Oh, no, madame." Chenault looked at her intensely, his dark eyes boring into hers with purpose. "I wouldn't dare tease you about so serious a matter. What I'm telling you is the absolute truth."

Addie hesitated, then glanced at Deseré, her large blue eyes filled with apprehension. After studying the man for a moment, Addie patted the chair next to hers. He seemed genuine, and talk of freedom from a fine looking negro gentleman sounded good to her. "Why don't you set a spell and tell us more," she said.

Chenault thanked her and sat down.

"Addie," Deseré cautioned, "Masta Anthony will be joining us soon."

"Never mind that, chile." Addie brushed away the girl's concern with a wave of her hand. "Pardon my manners, sir, but I'm Addie, Addie Albright, and this here's Deseré."

"It's a pleasure to meet you both." Chenault smiled at Addie.

Fleurs... Another merchant passed by them, pushing a cart of brightly colored flowers. Chenault stopped him and bought two pink roses, giving one to Addie and the other to Deseré.

The ladies gasped in appreciation and thanked him, then Addie said, "We are a little pressed for time..." she smelled the rose, its fragrance sweet and delicate, "...so maybe you could quickly explain our, um, bein' free."

"Well, under French law," Chenault began, "you can petition for your freedom. That's the way of the French. You see, our revolutionary constitution abolished slavery. 'Liberte, Eglite, Fraternite.'"

"What's that mean?" Addie asked

"'Liberty, Equality, Brotherhood.' The slogan of the French Revolution," Chenault explained. "So, in other words, you have the legal right to remain here in France as a free person. Of course if you go back to America with your—*masta*—it will be as a slave. You have a choice."

"Deseré, you hear that?"

"Yes, but," Deseré moved her eyes from Addie to Chenault, "...but Dr. Chenault, how did you come to live here?" she asked.

"I was born a free man in New Orleans, and I came here to study medicine at the Faculty of Medicine of the University of Paris in the Latin Quarter. As a Creole, I spoke enough French to quickly learn how to speak properly. Studying here with no restrictions upon my person seemed the most logical choice. I finished my studies years ago, and decided to stay. Although a free man of color in Louisiana, I was looked upon as no better than a slave."

Deseré nodded, listening, then said, "Dr. Chenault, I'm sure your family possessed means, but for us, just deciding to live here won't be that easy."

"Do you have a skill?" Chenault asked.

"We both sew!" Addie said.

"Can you read?"

"Both of us can," Addie said.

"Well," Chenault leaned toward Addie, "there are several dress shops in which you could find employment, and you can learn French. Being around it constantly will see to that. In addition, you could hire a tutor, or... I'd be happy to teach you, free of charge."

Addie looked at Deseré, feeling hope well within her chest. "Deseré, we could be free."

"You *are* free," Chenault corrected. "As long as you're on French soil."

A man playing a hand organ sauntered by, playing what was true music to Addie's ears, the sound of freedom. "Deseré, I don't want to give this up! Masta Anthony's a lawyer. He'll understand that he *can't* make us go back, because we're free!"

"But we don't know anybody here," Deseré whined.

"Both of you know me now." Chenault lightly touched Addie's hand for a moment.

"That's right," Addie said, sitting tall. "We know Dr. Chenault."

"I'd be happy to help you both," he said.

"But we don't speak French," Deseré said. "We don't have any money."

"Deseré, this is an opportunity at having our freedom and livin' good as the white folks!"

"Young lady," Chenault said, "you should listen to Miss Addie. Wouldn't you rather live here than go back to living in bondage? In New Orleans, I knew of plenty of young girls, just as pretty and fair as you, sold to the fancy trade by their masters looking to make a tidy profit. And love between a master and a slave girl? Doomed when he marries and the new wife insists he sell off his..." he trailed off, embarrassed. "I'm sure you understand what I'm implying. Nevertheless, I know lots of people, and I'd be happy to help both of you in your new life as free women every step of the way.

"As I mentioned, there are several dress shops in need of seamstresses. Also, there's an order of nuns, known as the Daughters of Charity, that provides a temporary home to women. You could stay there until you earn enough from working to afford your own lodging. Just think, Miss Deseré, you work, *you* get paid." He turned his attention back to Addie, "I understand that you don't have much time to talk right now, so is there a time that you could meet me later?"

"We'll be with our masta all day, but 'round six-thirty he likes to go to that English bookstore," Addie said.

"Galignani's," Deseré added. "He likes to read the papers there before we dine in the evening at nine. While he's there, Addie and I usually go to the Passage des Panoramas to browse in the shops."

"Alright, then," Chenault said, " will you be able to meet with me at seven?"

"We can do that," Addie said.

"Where are you staying?" Chenault asked.

"Right across the street," Addie motioned with her head toward the Hotel Bedford.

"Here's what we'll do," Chenault looked serious and spoke with urgency. "I'll pick you up. Pack a trunk. Bring whatever belongings you can."

"You mean we can start bein' free now?" Deseré asked, uncertain.

"As I told you moments ago, Miss Deseré, you are free here already. I'm only expediting the getaway from the clutches of your master."

"Oh," Deseré said softly.

"I have a good friend who's a lawyer," Chenault said. "He'll be with me when I pick you up. He can better explain the process of petitioning for your freedom. I tend to the medical needs of the ladies at the Sisters' Home, and I know for a fact that a room is available that could accommodate the two of you. I'll alert Sister Marie Catherine of your arrival and I'm sure, after hearing of your circumstances, she'll approve you to stay for as long as you need. Meanwhile, I'll have my sister-in-law make inquiries at some of the dress shops in the area."

"So you're married, Dr. Chenault?" Addie asked, feeling a bit crestfallen. She'd been flattered by his attention.

Chenault sighed, "My wife died a year ago."

Addie, feeling relieved and none too guilty about it, offered her condolences, as did Deseré.

"I appreciate that, and I also appreciate the opportunity to help my sisters in need. As a person of color, I feel it is my mission. I attended the Peace Conference in London a couple of years ago, and that opportunity heightened my motivation to promote peace and freedom wherever possible. So consider me at your service." Chenault reached into his breast pocket, then placed a calling card in front of each of them. "Contact me at any time, and I'll see you this evening to start you on your journey to freedom." He stood and replaced his hat. "Good day, ladies." And with that, Chenault took his leave.

"I'm already giddy 'bout bein' free!" Addie said, "And what a nice man that Dr Chenault is. Handsome," she sniffed the rose again, "and charming too. I didn't even know there was such a thing as a negro doctor. What would the white folks in St. Helena think about that?"

"Addie," Deseré's brow furrowed with worry, "I—I don't know about this. I mean... Masta Anthony brought us here; he's been so kind, all the money he's spent... I just can't see us—"

"All the money he's spent?" Addie snapped. "What about all the years I been a slave and ain't seen a cent? Deseré, I'm taking *my* chances here! I ain't got nothin' except the same if I go back. And bein' that you told Masta Anthony I could read is just one more strike against me."

"What?" Deseré blinked.

"Don't tell me you don't know what the white folks'll do if they find out a slave can read! The lash ain't touched your skin and may it never, but I could be whooped, maybe even to death, and the crackers would say I done *died* under a moderate correction! Or else I could be sold, ending up just like those chained up nigguhs we saw gettin' off that ship!"

"Masta Anthony wouldn't allow that, besides, he doesn't mind that we can read."

"That man'll protect you, but I'm fair game if he tells anybody."

"But he won't tell a soul."

"Maybe not while he's sober, but he *does* like to crook his elbow."

"*You're* the one that said he only likes to drink a little."

"Wasn't no harm in that when he didn't know I could read," Addie said. "You bein' hesitant 'bout your freedom shows you're sidin' with the enemy now."

"He's the enemy? But you like Masta Anthony—you said he had a heart of Jesus."

"Well, the white folks is the enemy, and you look just like 'em."

"But I'm not—"

"Just hear me out, Deseré. If Masta Anthony says somethin' to somebody while he's drunk as David's sow, like the new overseer Flanagan or that Mr. O'Malley, no tellin' what they'll tell Masta Anthony to do—or they could even convince Masta Anthony to let them handle things, bein' that Masta Anthony's a green horn at runnin' a plantation."

"No, Addie," Deseré shook her head. "It—it can't be that bad."

"Not for you," Addie said. "Masta Anthony loves you. And the only reason you ain't jumpin' at the chance to be free is 'cause you love him back."

Looking down, Deseré sighed. She lifted the cameo pendant she wore around her neck, then opened its face to reveal the watch inside. Clearly uncomfortable with the topic of conversation, she said, "It's just past nine. Masta Anthony should be here any second, then we can catch the omnibus to Notre Dame."

"Just what did you have to do for that cameo?" Addie asked snidely.

Appalled, Deseré exclaimed, "Nothing!" She closed the pendant. "And you know that! You saw him give it to me, and I told you the whole story! I told him I didn't want it. But he insisted I take it to keep track of the time."

"Or is he tryin' to keep track of you?" Addie mumbled.

"What?"

"Nothin'," Addie frowned. "But he loves you, alright," she insisted. "Didn't force himself on you; just gave you that cameo. No chance of him sellin' you off as a fancy. He wants you for himself. I could tell the first day he arrived at Pleasant Wood, the way he started slobberin' like a hound once he set eyes on you."

"Addie!"

"And maybe ninety-nine out of one-hundred white men

wouldn't have the nerve to love a negro woman as a wife, but I think he's the one that would."

Deseré's eyes watered. "What if he can't love me like that?" she almost whispered.

"I think he's willing, and I think he brought you here to make you fall in love with him."

"Oh, Addie—I'm—I'm so confused."

"Well, missy, it's time for you to grow up. You love him now. Admit it."

"Maybe I do, but I still don't know."

"Then give him an ultimatum. Tell him the only way you'll go back is if he gives you your freedom."

"What if he doesn't agree to that?"

"You stay here."

"But—but I don't know if I really want to..."

Addie smirked. "Well I know what I want! You been pampered all your life; doted on by Masta Jeremy, loved by Masta Anthony. I ain't had none of that! So I'm tellin' you right now, girl, I'm stayin' here. I'm done bein' a slave and I'm done bein' your mammy!"

"Addie, why are you being so mean to me? It wasn't my idea for you to play my mammy."

"Oh, hush up!" Addie glanced across the street toward the large plate glass windows and balconied rooms of their hotel that overlooked the boulevard. She'd seen Masta Anthony leave through the hotel's tall glass doors. As he navigated his way through horse drawn vehicles across the stone-paved street, she said, "Now Masta Anthony's comin', and I don't wanna hear you mention one word 'bout Dr. Chenault."

Chapter 27

Deseré climbed, maneuvering her petticoats with every step. She felt as if she were running away from something, but she didn't know what. Addie was behind her, and Masta Anthony in front, as they wound their way up the spiral stairwell to the top of the bell tower at Notre Dame Cathedral.

Deseré wasn't sure what unnerved her most: the prospect of staying in Paris, returning to Saint Helena, Addie's attitude, or Masta Anthony's intentions. She had to make a choice, but was remaining in Paris the right one?

The narrow stairwell they climbed was stone and the slender steps fan-shaped. It seemed an endless spiral, winding round and round. The three had begun their ascent at a doorway in the north tower, around the corner from the main entrance where a dead rat lay sprawled, a common sight every now and then that they'd grown accustomed to.

"It's nearly four-hundred steps." Masta Anthony looked back at them as they climbed. "Are you ladies sure you wish to continue?"

"Masta Anthony," Addie said, "we done walked all over

Paris, so we can certainly do this. Isn't that right, Miss Deseré, ma'am?"

Deseré didn't miss the sarcasm in Addie's tone.

"Yes," Deseré replied stiffly. She didn't like the new Addie, fortified by the prospect of her freedom. Not that Deseré didn't want that for her; she did. But now Addie had seemed to have turned on her. Deseré wanted her own freedom, too, but not necessarily in France, where she'd never see Masta Anthony again. Did that mean she really *did* love him?

Deseré didn't want to be Masta Anthony's slave, or his slave mistress, but in a way, she did want to belong to him, if that made any sense. She wasn't sure it made any to her, because the only way a woman *wanted* to belong to a man was as his wife, which would mean she loved the man in question. Regardless, the marriage of a master to a slave woman was impossible. However, becoming a master's mistress would be a high level of achievement in what existed of the slave hierarchy. Deseré sighed at that prospect, realizing that a master's marriage to a white woman would topple that achievement.

As Masta Anthony moved on, Addie seemed to move slower. Deseré stayed with her, her skirts preventing her from moving that much faster. By the time they were half-way up the tower, Masta Anthony was out of sight. When the women came to a high-ceilinged stone chamber, they paused to glance briefly at their surroundings, then walked on toward another door that opened to an upper staircase in which they continued their climb to the open gallery of the north tower.

Addie said, "We're on a new path, Deseré. Paris is my path, but you gotta decide for yourself what you gonna do." Her words reverberated against the circular stone walls as they climbed.

"Addie," Deseré turned to face her for a moment, putting a finger to her lips, "shush. We can't let Masta Anthony overhear us," she whispered. "I don't know what I'm going to do yet. But if you stay, won't you miss everybody back home?"

"Well...maybe some more than others." Addie started quietly, then her voice rose in volume. "But Dr. Chenault will introduce me to a bunch of new folks over here."

"Quiet," Deseré cautioned, keeping her voice low. "We only talked to that man for ten minutes."

"It doesn't matter. My mind's made up."

They trudged upward in silence for several minutes, then Deseré said, "Paris is exciting, but it's not home." As her pace slowed, she said, "You'd really give up everything...just like that?"

Addie clucked her tongue. "Chile, you mean give up bein' a slave for bein' free?"

"No—I mean—I mean—give up...home."

"What's there to give up besides hoedowns, log rollings and corn shucking parties? I want freedom and respect. Now's my chance to have it."

Deseré sighed. She wanted freedom and respect too, and the drudgery of slave life in St. Helena paled in comparison to the excitement of a free life in Paris. However, that free life included the fear of the unknown, living in a strange place, not understanding the language. They had no money and Dr. Chenault was their only connection to Paris. Although Dr. Chenault had assured them that they could enjoy their freedom through gainful employment, what was the allure for Deseré to return home, if that was indeed what she wanted? Distracted from her thoughts, Deseré heard an awkward footfall behind her.

"Dang blasted!" Addie exclaimed.

Deseré turned to look at her. "What is it?"

"I done stumbled and hurt my ankle."

"Oh, no! Can you walk?"

Addie leaned against the wrought iron railing, then lifted her skirt just slightly above her ankle. She moved her injured foot, covered by a light brown half-boot, up and down, then took a step up with it. "Ouch," she said. "It hurts a little, but I can walk on it, just not very fast."

"Maybe we should turn around and go back down," Deseré said.

"No! Since we're here and we've come this far, come hell or high water, I wanna keep on goin' so I can see the top of this place."

"Then let me help you."

"You just a bit of a thing," Addie scoffed. "Go get Masta Anthony. I can lean on him without knocking him down. And hurry. That keeper of the keys said he only let's three folks up there at a time, so I don't want us holdin' up the show for the next group of folks."

"Right!" Feeling a slight surge of energy, Deseré turned and moved up the steps as quickly as she could, just as the bells in the north tower began ringing, sending vibrations throughout her entire body.

Not long after, she came to a narrow walkway that led to the south tower. She skittered across it, glimpsing down at the hideous looking drain spouts, or gargoyles, that protruded from the building. She thought the winged creatures resembled scary looking critters, loosed from hell. Once at the south tower, Deseré gazed toward the Emmanuel Bell up high in the belfry. It appeared big as a barn to her, but hurrying by, she didn't stop to climb the steps of the belfry to touch it.

Although slightly off key, the north tower bells continued tolling, adding urgency to Deseré's mission to find Masta Anthony. She squeezed her way up a corkscrew staircase to the viewing platform atop the south tower. Yet by the time she reached it, her pace had slackened considerably, her legs ached, and her breathing had become labored.

Feeling a strong gust of wind, Deseré almost doubled over, out of breath. Then she called to Anthony, but couldn't hear herself above the discordant ringing of the bells. She took a deep breath, then for a brief moment gazed beyond the edge of the platform. The spectacular view of the city dazzled her. The Seine River and all of Paris, gigantic as it was, seemed beneath her feet.

Deseré had read about this very sight in Victor Hugo's *The Hunchback of Notre Dame*. Though she hadn't appreciated the novel as a small child, when she'd read it again last year, the chapter devoted to the view from the towers had fascinated her. And now here she was, thanks to Anthony! Remembering the task at hand, Deseré again picked up her pace. She raised her skirts a bit higher, careful to avoid the numerous bird droppings, and once more began searching for him.

Finally, she saw Anthony emerge from the opposite side of the viewing platform. He wore a black suit that enhanced his broad shoulders, and somehow, he seemed taller, and his dark good looks even more dashing than before. His black hair blew in the wind, swept away from his chiseled face, and his brown eyes met hers with a look of concern—for her.

Breathless, feeling flushed, and covered by beads of sweat, Deseré pushed herself to move rapidly toward him. He walked quickly to meet her, then shocked her by holding her face in his hands. As he gazed into her eyes, the smell of him, sandalwood and cloves, infused Deseré's senses. Then Masta Anthony further surprised her by kissing her full on the mouth.

Forgetting about Addie, Deseré didn't resist him. Apparently, she hadn't known that much about kissing either. William's kisses had been chaste and short, only longer when she'd held onto him, and he'd always kept his mouth closed. But Masta Anthony's kiss was long and sensual, and he'd opened his mouth and probed inside hers with his tongue. Being caught too off guard by Masta Anthony's ardor, she didn't embrace him, but instead stood with her arms slightly outstretched at her sides, as though trying to maintain her balance. Deseré enjoyed the sensation, but just as suddenly as Masta Anthony began, he stopped. She felt dizzy as he stepped away from her, his face bright red. With his lips slightly parted and brows raised, he appeared apologetic, as if he wanted to beg her forgiveness.

Yet Deseré grabbed his broad shoulders and pulled him to her lips, kissing him back, surprising herself by her unbridled boldness. This time, she held him close, embracing him around the neck. The ringing bells caused their bodies to pulsate in unison. Anthony wrapped his arms around Deseré's tiny waist, kissing her longer, with even more intensity, forcing the floodgates of passion to burst through her from the brim of her bonnet to the soles of her shoes. When she released him, even more breathless than when she'd reached the top of the tower, Anthony looked deeply into her eyes, so deeply her soul ached for him.

The bells finally stopped.

Masta Anthony said, "Deseré...I...I..."

****

I love you, is what he wanted to say, but Anthony couldn't bring himself to do so.

"You what?" Deseré asked, as a flock of pigeons cawed, flying above them.

Lightly, he stroked her cheek. A breeze swept over her, swirling the golden curls that sparkled beneath her bonnet. She was so beautiful...so innocent... "I..." Anthony became lost in the depths of her clear blue eyes. His heart pounded rapidly. He'd give his life to make love to her at this very moment. Anthony did love her, and she'd kissed him, more than willingly, in fact. Had he succeeded in his quest for her to love him? If he had...what now?

Did he have to remain a slaveholder? Since being in Paris, he wasn't sure. But if Anthony did sell his land and free his people, Deseré included, would she love him enough to stay with him, or would she seize her freedom and run off? Owning her guaranteed his possession of her. It wasn't right for him to think this way. It was selfish, as had been freeing the man she loved while keeping her in bondage. He wondered if, deep down, she hated him for that.

"Anthony?" Deseré prodded.

Lured from his reflections, Anthony could only say, "I...wanted to...let you know how much I'm enjoying being with you here...in this beautiful place."

"Oh," Deseré said, her eyes downcast.

Chapter 28

Deseré heard the bell tower of a nearby church chime seven times as she and Addie stood outside the Hotel Bedford waiting for Dr. Chenault. He was supposed to arrive for them at seven this evening. Deseré felt the empty hollow of her neck. She'd left the cameo pendant behind because it wouldn't have been right to take it. Other tourists, dressed in evening clothes and wearing expensive jewels, jostled by, or waited nearby for private cabs to take them to the theater, opera or ballet.

In moments, a four-wheeled enclosed carriage arrived. It was black, driven by a blond coachman in his twenties, and pulled by two large bay horses, reddish brown in color with shiny black manes. The coachman pulled to a stop, and seconds later Dr. Chenault quickly alighted along with another man who was white and about fifty years of age.

"Ladies," Chenault greeted them quietly. "Is everything alright?" he asked Addie. "And since you're here, I assume your master is nowhere near this place?" Addie assured him all was well and that Masta Anthony was at the bookstore. "Good," Chenault replied. "French soil means your freedom, so consider your chains of bondage now broken."

As Chenault said this, Deseré noticed one of the American tourists. He'd only been at the hotel a couple of days, but he'd seen Addie and Deseré more than once with Masta Anthony. She believed his name was Mr. Youngblood. Dressed in day clothes, the tourist appeared to be returning to the hotel from an outing. An older curmudgeonly sort, with a tall thin frame and a slight hunch, he walked toward the hotel entrance but moved more slowly than usual, as though eavesdropping. Only a few yards away now, he stopped by the entrance and stared at them suspiciously.

"Your belongings?" Chenault asked, looking at the small carpetbag at each woman's feet.

"We have more," Addie told him. "There's a large black trunk in the lobby with the name tag Albright."

Dr. Chenault said something to his white companion in French. The man nodded, then walked rapidly toward the lobby.

Chenault extended his hand to Addie to help her ascend the carriage step. She smiled at his chivalry. "We must make haste," he said, as Addie sat down. Then he extended his hand to Deseré. Once she was seated next to Addie on shiny black leather covering a firm cushion, he placed the carpetbags beneath their seat. "If you see your master before we load on your trunk," he whispered only loudly enough for them to hear, "just knock on the glass and shout 'Go.' The driver will understand."

Afterwards, Chenault shut the carriage door and disappeared into the lobby. Yet when the doctor was out of sight, Mr. Youngblood approached the carriage. Now he walked faster, as though twenty years had been miraculously slashed from his age.

Hook-nosed and mustached with silvery gray hair peeking from beneath his top hat, he put a scowling, mottled face to Deseré's open window. "Ya'll takin' an excursion some-whe-uh?"

Deseré tensed. His voice creaked like a hinge in need of oil, and she could now tell by his accent that he was a southerner. Panicked, she blurted, "To Burgundy."

The man's eyes narrowed. The feeling of living as a slave in the American South, which she hadn't felt in weeks, suddenly returned.

"Without you-uh *mas-tuh?*" he hissed.

Deseré put a knuckle to her lips, wondering if the duskiness in her skin had given her away, and this man had realized she wasn't white.

Addie leaned across Deseré to face the American. "What's it to you?" she asked rudely. "You ain't got no business with us, so just be on 'bout your way!"

Deseré's eyes widened, for freedom had gone too quickly to Addie's head and it could get them in trouble.

Youngblood's blotched face reddened. "How day-ah you —"

Chenault called something to Youngblood in French, as he and the Frenchman approached the carriage carrying the trunk.

Youngblood looked at Chenault, obviously surprised that a black man could speak French. "You wanna say that in English?"

Chenault feigned ignorance and spoke more French to Youngblood.

"I just heard you speakin' English a minute ago," the American said, "sayin' somethin' 'bout freedom, chains and bondage."

Chenault laughed, as he and the Frenchman loaded the trunk into the boot of the carriage.

Youngblood smirked. "Somethin' ain't right 'bout a nigra speakin' French and English, then pretendin' he can't speak English."

"Then wonders will never cease," Chenault said, as he

and the Frenchman stepped into the carriage. "Good evening." Chenault closed his door and the carriage speedily rolled away from the hotel, leaving Youngblood dumbfounded.

As the carriage jostled and trounced over the cobblestone street, Addie laughed. "That stupid old coot," she said, bouncing in her seat. "He ain't never gonna be the same havin' nigguhs talk back to him like that. *Free* nigguhs," she added with emphasis.

Slamming into Addie as the carriage took a sharp turn, Deseré pursed her lips, not thinking the situation funny at all.

"Ladies," Chenault said, his expression serious, "allow me to introduce Monsieur Maurice Jordan," he motioned to the man seated next to him.

Jordan nodded to them and smiled. He was a slim, sharp-featured man with kind blue eyes and thinning brown hair.

"He's the lawyer friend I mentioned to you earlier. I'll leave it to him to explain the legalities of your freedom. But first, I did talk to my sister-in-law. She has a wealthy friend in need of a seamstress. Miss Addie, I recommended you for that position, but you'll need to meet with her before a final decision is made. And Miss Deseré, my sister-in-law's favorite dress shop just lost a seamstress who married and moved from Paris. So that could be a possible position for you."

As Chenault asked Jordan to explain their legal situation, Addie smiled broadly upon hearing the news of her prospective seamstress position. Deseré, on the other hand, strained to smile in attempt to look pleased. If Addie worked in the home of a wealthy woman, most likely she'd be provided a room. Besides, she could tell that Dr. Chenault had designs on Addie and the feeling was mutual. Before long, Addie would be *his* wife, living under *his* roof.

Yet if Deseré worked in a shop, she'd eventually be

responsible for her own lodging. She couldn't live in a charity home forever. How long would it take for her to earn enough money to live on? And how long would it take for her to learn French?

While Jordan spoke in heavily accented English, Deseré's mind wondered further to Masta Anthony. What would he think when he couldn't find them later this evening? Would he be worried? Did he know that on French soil, she and Addie were actually free?

Deseré remained unfocused, only gleaning that there were legal documents Jordan could assist them with in order to petition the court for affirmation of their free status. Whatever else she'd missed, Addie could explain to her later. Glancing at Addie, Deseré noticed that the woman eagerly drank in all the information Jordan explained.

Deseré could think only of Anthony. She sighed with sorrow at the thought of not seeing him again. Would she *ever* see him again? Then from deep inside, she felt a longing for him. She missed him...dreadfully. Deseré couldn't deny it any longer—she *had* fallen in love with Anthony. Now was a fine time to realize it, running away from him like a fool! And that note she'd written... Addie didn't know about it, and now Deseré regretted leaving it for him. If only the letter had been a little kinder. Who was she fooling? It wasn't kind at all.

Deseré wasn't sure how Anthony felt. Addie had said he loved her. But if he did, why hadn't he told her? Deseré burned thinking of the reason, then held back the sting of tears. She was his slave, less than nothing. It was a good thing she *was* running away, and that she *had* left that note, because she'd only be used and tossed aside. Emboldened by the power of freedom, Deseré decided that she was doing the right thing. Why shouldn't she run away? If she did return to America, she'd be sold away as soon as Anthony married a white woman of his own status.

By staying in France, she'd have the power to decide her

own fate. And that's exactly what Deseré would tell Masta Anthony... *If* she had the opportunity to see him again... She felt her heart pound. Would that even be possible now?

Chapter 29

When they arrived at the Sisters' Home, Deseré peered from the carriage window. The building they stopped in front of resembled just another Paris dwelling probably built about a hundred years ago. Sandwiched between other buildings of a similar structure, it was five stories tall, made of white stone and had a tall wooden door inlaid with two glass panels. As Chenault helped Addie and Deseré from the carriage, he said, "This building was donated to the order by a wealthy widow. The sisters are quite fortunate to have it."

After Chenault removed the carpetbags, Jordan said in English that he and the coachman would bring in the trunk. Chenault thanked him, but then hesitated briefly before approaching the door of the Sisters' Home. "I must warn you," he said to Addie and Deseré, "some of the ladies that reside here have...shall we say...fallen on hard times. But they've been blessed to find their way here."

"Just how hard a time you talkin' 'bout?" Addie asked.

"Some of the residents," Chenault began, "are young girls, orphans of sixteen or seventeen. Others are...ex-convicts, some ex-prostitutes." Chenault must have noticed Deseré's eyes widen, because he hastily added, "However, keep in mind, this is only temporary lodging for you, just a place to start."

As he carried their carpetbags, Deseré glanced at Addie. The woman merely shrugged her shoulders, then followed Dr. Chenault to the door. Deseré slowly walked behind her, feeling her skin prickle at the thought of being surrounded by women of ill repute. Then she gasped as a rat as large as a cat scampered by her feet. Addie turned upon hearing her, then seeing the varmint said, "Ain't like you never seen a rat in Paris, or St. Helena either."

Dr. Chenault rang the doorbell and moments later, the door was opened by a young woman with large brown eyes set in a pleasant face. She wore the strangest bonnet Deseré had ever set eyes on. Deseré had seen nuns before, but not one dressed like this. This nun wore a long black dress with a big white collar, high at the neck that looked like overlapping rectangles, almost resembling a bib. She wore a white bonnet, low at the forehead, which covered everything but her face, and it had what could best be described as large wings sprouting out from each side. Looked like she could fly away at any moment!

After a warm greeting, Chenault said, "Sister Marie Catherine, allow me introduce my friends Madame Addie Albright and Mademoiselle Deseré Albright."

"How do you do?" Deseré said.

"Come on tally voo?" Addie said, practicing her French, although she butchered the pronunciation.

"Tres bien!" Sister Marie Catherine smiled at Addie's effort. "Bonsoir, mes amis. Entrez, entrez." She invited them in. "It is wiz much pleasure to meet you. Of your circumstance, Docteur Chenault has informed me, and at zis time we do have a room for you. Allow me to show you. Come."

Over the scent of body odor, Deseré smelled bread baking

and a stew of carrots, potatoes and onions simmering. She heard the clatter of pots and pans from what must have been the kitchen. Looking to the left, she saw a dining room with a very long table and several mismatched chairs, and on the right, a furnished parlor with a piano and threadbare pieces of furniture.

Two thin women, probably in their early twenties, peeked from the parlor doorway. Both wore faded gingham dresses that hung loosely on their gaunt frames. They smiled crookedly, their expressions generating more coolness than warmth.

Sister Marie Catherine introduced them. Yvette's gray eyes were sunken in a sallow face. "Bonsoir," she said, her voice low and husky. She was missing a front tooth, and her blond hair was shorn close to her head.

The other girl, Claudette, was hollow cheeked with a scar along the side of her face that looked like a knife wound. A thin braid of dull brown hair fell over one shoulder, almost resembling a rat's tail. She coughed while nodding in greeting toward the newcomers. She grumbled to her companion, "Une négresse."

"Negress," Addie whispered to Deseré. "Is that a fancy way to say nigguh?"

Yvette then covered her mouth with a bony hand and mumbled, "La blonde apporte l'argent sale de ses passes."

Sister Marie Catherine frowned. "Yvette, Claudette, taisez-vous!" she admonished for whatever they'd said. Then the nun led her new guests and their benefactor through a dimly lit entrance foyer with peeling paint to a narrow, musty smelling spiral staircase that was even darker.

"I am sorry," the sister said, "but it is," she raised her hand high, "at ze top."

As the ascended the stairs, Deseré's legs wobbled a little from the bell tower climb. She noticed Addie was limping.

"Sister Marie Catherine mentioned that one of the rooms

in the attic is available," Chenault said.

"Oui," Sister Marie Catherine agreed, "ze attic."

"Least we won't be in the basement like at Pleasant Wood," Addie said.

By the time they'd climbed the five stories, Deseré's legs throbbed with fresh pain. The smell of food had completely vanished now, but the pungent smell of human filth was ever present. Sister Marie Catherine opened a door with a skeleton key. She lit an oil lamp revealing a room with dreary gray walls. As Chenault set down their carpetbags, Deseré observed that the ceiling was low, and at a slight incline on one side to accommodate the roof. Windows slanted on the incline were hinged open to relieve the stuffiness in the room. The space accommodated one thin cot that could fit two small people. Deseré grimaced. Addie wasn't huge, but she certainly no longer possessed the slimness of youth.

The gaslight was very old and sat next to the bed on a small unvarnished table. Against the wall was a five drawer dresser, probably made around the turn of the century, and in the corner stood a wash stand with a cracked white basin on top. There was also a little fireplace and one small closet. No splendor here, Deseré thought to herself as she noticed a large brown cockroach crawling up the wall, not fancy by any means. She'd ascended from the basement of the Pleasant Wood big house to the attic of a maison in Paris. Yet the more she looked at the cramped quarters in front of her and recalled the questionable women she'd met earlier, the less she wanted to be here.

"I know these surroundings hardly compare with your hotel," Chenault said, "but I'll do my best to make your lives in Paris worthwhile."

Sister Marie Catherine handed each of them a set of keys for the front door and the room, then she and Chenault conversed in French for a few moments. Afterwards, Chenault explained that all the residents helped with cooking and cleaning and the general upkeep of the place.

"That ain't no different from what we're used to," Addie said, "but at least we won't be owned by anybody—aside from ourselves."

When Monsieur Jordan and the coachman entered the room with the trunk, Sister Marie Catherine told Addie and Deseré that dinner would be served at ten. "So," she smiled, "I will see you zen and introduce you to ze ozer girls." Then she excused herself and left the room. Jordan politely excused himself and the coachman, telling Chenault they'd be waiting outside.

"Dr. Chenault," Deseré said, "just what did that girl say? The one that was missing a front tooth."

Chenault straightened. "I'd rather not tell you. It might offend you."

Addie laughed. "We're slaves, or we were. We've been offended more than once."

"Addie's right," Deseré said, "and we should be privy to what these women think."

Chenault hesitated, then said, "Alright, but forgive me. These are her words not mine. She said something to the effect of 'the blonde would bring high dollar as a prostitute.'"

As Deseré's face reddened, Addie said, "Good, gracious day! Well, they look like they been rode hard and put away wet to me." Then she squeezed Deseré's shoulder. "They don't know you, or me for that matter, and we won't be here that long, so don't you give those buzzards a second thought."

"I won't," Deseré said tightly. Then pursing her lips, wishing to change the subject, she looked at the trunk. "We'll have to get that back to Masta Anthony." Now more than ever, especially after being compared to a prostitute, Deseré *was* having second thoughts about living here.

Addie put her hands on her hips. "What did you say?"

"Oh, Addie, you heard me," Deseré said. "We can't keep

that trunk. It would be stealing."

"Stealing? Are you out your mind, Deseré? How many years of my life have been stolen from me by bein' a slave?" Addie exclaimed. "Us keepin' one trunk ain't gonna make no difference to Masta Anthony! Besides, we ain't got nothin'. We can at least claim that as a possession now. Shoot, you takin' it back to him would be like stealin' it from me!"

"Well..." Deseré hesitated, "perhaps *I* should go back and explain what we've done." The note she'd left didn't go into detail. It was more like a slap in the face, and she was feeling guilty about it now. Anthony did deserve more of an explanation.

"Absolutely not!" Chenault declared.

"You must be outta yo' mind!" Addie exclaimed.

Just then, a woman of about thirty with reddish-orange hair popped her head into the room. Unkempt curls were piled high on her head like rusty springs, and her pudgy pink cheeks were flushed. Frowning she said, "Que se passe-t- il? Pourquoi tout ce bruit?" Then she smiled, reaching a veloptuous arm around the doorway that clutched a bottle of wine. "Prendriez-vous du vin?"

"Everything's fine," Dr. Chenault said quickly, walking to the door. "I'm sorry about the noise and we don't want any wine, but thank you. Now, if you'll excuse us."

The woman looked at him, not understanding. Chenault then repeated everything in French before shutting the door completely.

"We can't just disappear!" Deseré insisted, picking up where she'd left off, now determined not to stay here! Not after yet another encounter with a fallen woman, who from the looks of things, resided next door. "Masta Anthony will be sick with worry wondering where we are."

"There ain't no need to see him again!" Addie said.

"But we know we're free here," Deseré went on, "so he can't make us stay with him. You said so yourself. He's a lawyer; he'll understand."

"Miss Deseré," Chenault said, "Miss Addie is absolutely right."

"But, Dr. Chenault," Deseré said, "I'd — I'd like to see him — just one last time. I believe that would only be right."

Chenault said, "He'll say anything to lure you into going back with him. Remember, you're an investment to him. He'd rather sell you and have money in his pocket than let you remain here."

"I know why she's so eager to see him," Addie said, "and no matter what you say, Dr. Chenault, you won't change her mind. Ain't that right, Deseré?"

With tears in her eyes, Deseré nodded. "I — I think I love him — I *do* love him!"

"Umph," Addie snorted. "'Bout time you admitted that."

Dr. Chenault crossed his arms. With brows creased, he said, "He'll take advantage of that. He'll make lavish promises he can't keep. He'll entice you with ludicrous notions. He'll tempt you as the serpent tempted Eve and nothing good will come of it."

Addie looked down for a moment. "He ain't a bad man," she said.

"Is he white?" Chenault smirked.

"As far as white men go," Addie said, "he ain't bad. And I think he loves her too."

"A white man's love for a slave girl doesn't reach far," Chenault said. Then he looked at Deseré. "What would he be willing to give up for you? A respectable name? His social status and position? A pedigree for his future children?"

"I don't know," Deseré said through tears. "Maybe nothing."

Chenault shook his head, then clasped his hands behind his back. "Just what do you expect by seeing him one last time?"

At a loss, Deseré shook her head. "I couldn't say."

Chenault was silent for several moments. "If your freedom is what you truly desire, you will not see him again," he said firmly. "So it's best you forget he ever existed."

"But I can't," Deseré cried.

"Think about your life, Miss Deseré. Back in America it won't belong to you," Chenault said.

Deseré looked down, saying nothing.

"When I was younger," Chenault went on, "I had a dream of going back to America to help my enslaved brothers and sisters by working as an abolitionist. But I became too involved with my own life, living as a man judged on my merits, not my color. So going back to America as an abolitionist never happened. I regret that. Meeting the two of you has given me a chance to procure your freedom and give you a new lease on life. So why would you ever want to go back to your master and bondage in America?"

"Perhaps...he'll free me," Deseré said, "if he loves me."

Dr. Chenault sighed. "But you'll have no guarantee that he will—even if he *does* love you." Silence hung in the room for several moments until Chenault said, "God brings good things out of bad situations... The only possible good I could see coming from you going back to your master would be that you could somehow convince him that slavery is wrong and to free his people. If you could then convince him to become an abolitionist, *that* would be a miracle."

"She could be one too," Addie said. "White as she is, she can read. They could work together."

"That would be a true miracle indeed," Chenault agreed.

Deseré felt as if her eyes had grown as large as saucers. "Maybe I can convince Masta Anthony to free just me, but everybody? And talk him into bein' an abolitionist? I don't know if I could... And *me* bein' one too? I couldn't! I'm not brave enough...I'm not brave at all."

"We don't know what we're capable of," Chenault said,

"until faced with adversity. But I must say," he smiled, "it certainly takes bravery to start a new life in a strange place. Perhaps you should just concentrate on being a free woman here in Paris."

Chapter 30

As Anthony entered the hotel a little after nine that evening, he was greeted by Mr. Youngblood, a planter from North Carolina. "Mr. Sinclay-uh, Ah must have a wurd with you." Reeking of tobacco, the old man walked Anthony to the corner of the lobby. "It's a good thing Ah caught you. You-uh," he cleared his throat, "*lady* friend and her survant ah no longuh residin' in this particular establishment."

Anthony frowned. "What are you talking about?"

"Well, Ah'll tell ya," he drawled. "They left with a French-speakin' colored fella who said somethin' 'bout them bein' free in France. Drove off with 'em of their own will and they looked happy to go. Two healthy pieces of property flown the coop! It ain't none of my business, but seems you were paradin' around a yalla gal as a white woman. Now that behav-yuh is bettuh left behind closed do-uhs. Ah s'pose in France —"

"What do you mean they drove off with some French-speaking colored fellow?" Anthony interrupted.

"Why, suh, just what Ah say-ed! There was the colored fella and a white man too, and those gals took a trunk filled with they-uh things."

"How long ago did this happen," Anthony asked, "and what was that fellow driving? Which way did they go?"

"It was 'round seven, two hou-ahs ago. The fella had a black carriage." Then looking toward the hotel entrance, Youngblood pointed. "They went south. But no tellin' whe-ah they were headed. Befo-ah they left, how-evah, Ah confronted the young one. She said they were goin' to Burgundy, but Ah'm shu-a that was a lie. And that old wench, why *she* had the nurve to *back-talk* me!"

Anthony hastily excused himself from Youngblood's presence. The man was old, perhaps senile, yet Anthony had to know if the he was telling the truth. Anthony ran up the four flights of stairs to the second floor, which was illuminated by wall sconces and crystal chandeliers. He rushed down the hallway over a thick Oriental runner that lined the hardwood floor. Once he reached the room next to his where Deseré and Addie stayed, he began knocking frantically and calling their names. After several moments, he used his key to enter the room. Anthony looked in the closet and dresser drawers, seeing that the majority of their clothes were gone. Then he spotted a note on the desk next to the cameo pendant he'd given Deseré. Written in a flowing script, it read:

Anthony,
  I have chosen to embark on my life as a free woman in Paris, over bondage as your slave in America.
Deseré

Crushed, Anthony stared at the note. He re-read it once, then twice. It was true... Deseré was gone. Anger, sadness and despair stabbed through him, slashing his rapidly beating heart to shreds. She couldn't leave him. How could he have driven her away when he'd brought her here to fall in love with him? Anthony stuffed the note in his pocket, then fled the room in search of her.

****

That night at dinner, Sister Marie Catherine sat Deseré and Addie next to Marianne, a French girl fluent in English. An old brass chandelier burned above them while they ate dry crusty bread and a thin vegetable broth that, though flavorful, lacked body. Sitting in a hard, high-backed wooden chair in the dining room, Deseré studied Marianne. With thick brown hair piled in a bun on top of her head, she appeared to be in her early twenties. Dressed decently in a brown frock, she didn't resemble the sickly thin girls, nor those who had indulged in less than acceptable lifestyles. The girl explained that she'd lost her factory job, and then her husband had died after being trampled by a horse. She hoped to be in the charity home for only a short while.

"My sister works for a rich family," Marianne said. "She zinks zey will hire me as a servant. Do you have skills?" she asked Deseré and Addie.

"We sew," Deseré said. "We're seamstresses."

"Cootooreeays," Addie added, when Marianne appeared not to understand.

"Oh, couturieres" Marianne smiled, making a sewing motion with a pretend needle and thread. Addie and Deseré nodded. "Good skill to have. You see Simone," she pointed to a quiet girl across the table and a few seats down. She was thin and pale with light hair almost the same pallor as her complexion. She kept her head down, eating silently while holding a spoon with crooked fingers. "Simone is a— *seamstress*," she said the word slowly, "or she was. She worked in a shop, but she needed more money. Ze pay was not good—not enough. So she took a, how do you say? A lover. A very rich man who could *give* her money. But he was bad. He ruined her, beat her. Broke her fingers. Zen she could not work. He was ze cause of her losing her job, and zen he left her." Marianne shook her head. "C'est la vie."

Deseré had never worked for money, but as a seamstress in a shop, she now doubted that she could make ends meet. If a native girl couldn't, what were her chances?

****

The hotel put Anthony in touch with La Surete Nationale, the criminal investigative bureau of the Paris Police, but when it was determined that Deseré and Addie weren't taken by force, they could do nothing to help. The hotel, however, did allow Anthony to place Deseré's portrait in the lobby with a brief note posted below it written in French and English:

Deseré. Missing. Last seen with her servant and two unknown male individuals driving away in a black carriage. Please contact hotel management if you see this young lady.

Paris, well lit by gas lights in the evenings, allowed Anthony to wander through the streets for hours in search of them. However, after a fruitless expedition, he gave up, deciding to resume his search the next day.

Now after midnight, he sat in a café not far from his hotel. Too distraught to eat, he sat at the bar drinking his fourth glass of wine, while inhaling the rich scent of coffee intertwined with the sweet aroma of chocolate. There were many mirrors around him, behind the bar and on the walls, remarkable in their size and height. Their reflection of the tall glass doors, gilded furniture and chandeliers combined to make quite a dazzling effect. The tables in the room were covered with snow-white tablecloths and filled with men and women engaged in lively conversation sipping liqueurs from small crystal glasses, or demitasse served in small china cups, or chocolate from slender ceramic mugs.

Anthony had postcards he'd purchased earlier in the day in his pocket. After pulling one out, he asked the barkeep if he could borrow the pencil stuck behind the man's ear. As Anthony drank, he wrote. He was no poet, but tonight felt compelled to write Deseré something. He knew he'd find her, and when he did, he wanted to have something to convince her of his love. Something to convince her to come back to him. If only he'd said he loved her at the bell tower.

After the fourth glass of chardonnay, he wasn't thinking with his head, only his heart, and that was all that mattered. He loved Deseré and couldn't live without her. What was she worth to him? Everything. Anthony began to write...

Where choosing to run, but in what realm,
And of my heart so true, I am not at the helm.
Where logic found but lost in love,
Yet wins the fight and flies above.
I match the dream but with a day,
To climb and climb and create a way,
To Deseré ...
Surely will I falter; surely will I fall,
Lead my hand to your heart, of this I call.
My dream I see, my mind derives,
A path we take, diverts our lives.
Perplexed is my life and I ponder it still,
Understand it no more, yet follow through, I will.

"What's that you're writing, ol' boy?" an Englishman said, looking over Anthony's shoulder.

"Poetry," Anthony said. "Of some form or fashion."

The man read it and smiled. "Speaks of love, I see." He patted Anthony on the shoulder. "Whoever she is, she'll fancy it."

****

By the time dinner was finished at the Sisters' Home and cleanup completed, it was nearly midnight. After retiring for the evening, Addie slept soundly, snoring softly, yet Deseré couldn't rest. Not only did Addie take up most of the bed, the room was steamy and Deseré heard scratching in the walls, most likely emanating from a family of varmints living inside them.

Deseré was determined to get out of here...or was she?

She wanted to go back to Masta Anthony — Anthony... But why? To be his slave? She didn't want to be his slave, but she did want to be with him...because she loved him. But did she love him enough to take her chances and go back where her freedom wasn't guaranteed, or should she stay in Paris where it was. She'd be a fool to go back to him. She didn't deserve to be a slave! Not after tasting real freedom, so she'd stay here. But was she really too afraid to stay here? She could learn to speak French. It just might take a while. But working in a shop as a seamstress wouldn't pay well. How long could she stand living in this hell-hole? How long would she even be allowed to stay here? She'd be nothing but a whore if she took a lover to help pay her way. She'd never do that. But she was young and pretty. She could find a husband, but she wanted Masta Anthony as she'd once only wanted William. Anthony cared for her...Addie said he loved her...and he'd free her if he loved her, wouldn't he?

Deseré sighed, then looked over at Addie, sleeping peacefully. Despite the woman's uppity attitude toward her lately, Deseré loved her. She said a silent prayer over Addie, asking God to bless her new life in Paris with Dr. Chenault. Then she whispered, "May that, Lord Jesus, lead to marriage." After several moments, she added, "And Lord, please make it possible for me to be with Anthony...in some way."

Sleep never came to Deseré that night. By two a.m., she was up. Using the light of a single candle, she put on a pale green dress, wrapped a shawl around her shoulders, and placed the bonnet on her head that Anthony had purchased for her with the large pink roses. Then she re-packed what belongings she could in her carpetbag, and quickly scribbled a note using a pencil gnawed with teeth marks she'd found on the dresser. On the back of Dr. Chenault's business card she wrote:

Addie,

The uncertainty of my life here in Paris is too great. Therefore, I have decided to take my chances and return to America with Master Anthony.
Deseré

After leaving the note on the dresser, Deseré gazed sadly at Addie, knowing she'd never see her again, then quietly slipped from the room.

****

Anthony awoke to a knocking at his door. He hardly remembered stumbling to his room last night after leaving the café. Now his mouth was dry. His eyes felt as if glued shut. He struggled to open them. When he did, he reached for his pocket watch on the bedside table. It was after eight a.m. He heard the knocking again.

Last night he'd removed his shoes, vest, jacket and cravat, but hadn't gotten much further than that. He appeared to have slept on top of the covers in his shirt and trousers with his suspenders lowered. His head felt like a hammer was on the inside trying to pound its way out. He'd finished an entire bottle of wine and was now suffering the consequences. More knocking.

Why had he done something like that? For Deseré he'd curtailed his drinking. What had made him start again...? Then he remembered. Deseré. She was missing. He scrambled to his feet. She'd come back! He fell to the floor, but grabbed onto the bedpost, pulling himself up. Once standing, dizziness overtook him, but he struggled to steady himself and moved as quickly as he could from the bedroom to the small sitting room, feeling as if he were walking on shifting sand. Upon reaching the door he flung it open, prepared to embrace Deseré at once and vow his undying love to her.

"Good morning, Anthony."

Anthony stood, nonplussed. Then when he tried to

speak, he couldn't. Finally, after several seconds he said, "Good morning...Edith."

Chapter 31

Anthony felt as if he were dreaming. Edith couldn't actually be standing at his door, could she? Her familiar scent of jasmine, sharp and sweet, told him she was.

"I'd rather not stand out here in the hallway," Edith said. She wore a pale yellow dress with a pattern of large pink roses. A row of abalone buttons ran from the lacy neckline to the band of fabric encircling her tiny waist. "Do you mind if I come in?" Edith didn't wait for an answer, as she brazenly walked into Anthony's hotel room and shut the door. The sunlight streaming through the windows hurt his eyes a little, yet it glistened on the golden highlights of Edith's chestnut hair. She wore it pulled from her pretty round face in a large bun at the nape of her neck.

"Where's your husband?" Anthony said, backing away from her.

"Abe?" she smirked with a sigh. "He's still in Germany. I told him I wanted to come back to Paris and do some more shopping. He said fine, so I left him behind with his block-headed lager-drinking relatives."

"You're traveling alone?"

"No. I hired a French speaking servant to accompany

me."

"Edith, I doubt your husband would appreciate you standing here in my hotel room, and I do have a pressing matter I must attend to this morning, so if you'll excuse me."

"I'm aware of your...*pressing matter*," she said. "It's Deseré. I arrived earlier this morning and saw the portrait and the note in the lobby. I'm sure you're worried. By the looks of things, you didn't sleep well."

Anthony noticed her eyes wander over him, taking in his disheveled hair, the stubble on his face, his wrinkled clothes. Feeling self-conscious, he raised his suspenders, then as discreetly as he could, tucked his shirt into his trousers.

"Did you...sleep in your clothes?" Edith asked. Before he could respond, she said, "Never mind that. Anthony, people run away because they want to." She took two steps toward him, he took two steps back. "Besides, this is fate." Edith smiled, hope twinkling in her brown eyes. "We traveled to Paris at the same time! What's the likelihood of that happening if it wasn't meant to be? I encountered you at Versailles, yet right before I recognized you, I overheard Deseré mention your hotel. Then I took my chances coming back to Paris and booking a room here, and now Deseré is gone. What does that tell you?"

Anthony took a deep breath. "That you're married," he said flatly.

Unfazed, Edith's bow-shaped lips curled in a half-smile. "That's only a minor infraction, but a positive one nonetheless, since I *am* married and now know what's expected of a wife."

"Edith," Anthony said sharply, "it's hardly appropriate for you to be here, and say such things, so I must ask you to leave!" Not only was this woman impulsive, Anthony thought, but now he was seeing that she had nerve and no scruples. He recalled thinking of Edith as a she-devil, but only after she'd rejected him. Thank God, she had! Had he really loved her as much as he'd remembered?

"Anthony," Edith said firmly, raising her upturned nose, "I'm not going anywhere until I tell you why I'm here. It was a mistake for me to leave you. It was a mistake for me to marry Abe. I was a fool, because I still loved you—I still *love* you. Whenever I'm with Abe—in that way—I envision him as you. Do you understand what I'm saying? I'm here, because I want *you* that way."

Flabbergasted, Anthony felt his face flush. "Edith, stop embarrassing yourself."

"Anthony, I'm twenty-one, but Deseré's young, she's just a girl, she doesn't know what she wants, her running away should prove that. She has French relatives, perhaps she's just gone off with them for a while because she couldn't tell you she no longer wanted to marry you. Her American family most likely knows where she is. Perhaps they're not telling you because she asked them not to."

At first Anthony couldn't fathom what Edith was talking about, then he remembered the lie he'd told, that Deseré was from a neighboring plantation and he was here with her family visiting French relatives.

Yet just as Anthony began connecting the dots, Edith began unbuttoning her dress.

****

When Deseré awoke, she couldn't recall anything, and she didn't know where she was. Her vision was blurred. The ground was cool and hard beneath her. All she could see was the flame of an oil lamp. It burned brightly near her feet. She inhaled, smelling moldy air. Her head throbbed at the crown. She reached to touch it, feeling a lump underneath her matted tresses. Blinking her eyes, her vision cleared. Sitting up, she gazed at her fingertips. There was blood on them. She saw her shawl balled up a few feet away, along with her bonnet, but her carpetbag was gone. That missing item was the least of her worries. Then looking around, Deseré screamed a blood chilling cry upon seeing a multitude of bones scattered about her. Human thigh bones, arm bones, skulls...

Perplexed, she couldn't breathe as she gazed at the skeletal remains surrounding her. Gulping, Deseré thought she'd been killed and gone to hell. But who'd wanted to kill her, and why had she been condemned to hell? She hadn't been bad, aside from having some mean thoughts about Masta Anthony, but that was before she'd fallen in love with him.

Coming to her senses, Deseré realized she wasn't dead, nor was she in hell. It was too cool. She *was* underground, though. But how had she gotten there?

****

In astonished disbelief, Anthony watched Edith pull the top of her dress from smooth shoulders, revealing a camisole with pink ribbons. It covered a corset that she wore over a lace trimmed chemise, and from it welled creamy breasts, smooth and round, like orbs of white marble.

"Anthony," she said, releasing her arms from the sleeves of her clothing, "things can resume between us." Then she pulled pins from her chestnut hair, letting it tumble in heavy waves beneath her shoulders. "I'll divorce Abe," she said simply.

"Divorce him?" Anthony said, astonished, not only at her words, but her state of undress.

"Yes," Edith said, as if that were nothing out of the ordinary. "Then we can be together as we should have been from the start."

Anthony quickly dropped his eyes to the floor, averting them from her near nakedness. "Edith, cover yourself. I don't want you here. What was between us is over. That's what you wanted and now you're another man's wife."

"I told you, I'm willing to divorce Abe. I'm willing to *scandalize* myself for you."

And she was off to a grand start, Anthony thought. Still looking down, he said, "Edith, I no longer love you."

"Anthony—you—you can't mean that!" Disbelief curdled

her voice.

"But I do."

"Why?" she asked angrily. "Because you're captivated by Deseré? Are you captivated by her family, her land, her slaves! Is that the life you want with her, being an owner of human souls?"

Her words cut him. Did he really want to be an owner of human souls?

"You should leave that despicable existence behind you and be done with it," Edith ranted on. "And be done with her! You *don't* love her!"

"I *do* love her," Anthony said, sorrowful that Deseré *was* one of the human souls he owned in that despicable life he led.

"Well, she doesn't love you!" Edith shouted, her voice rigid with wrath. "She ran away from you! And besides, she's a child. She couldn't love you, not like a real woman. But I can." Her tone softened. "And I can show you how much."

Anthony wouldn't dare raise his eyes. He didn't want to humiliate Edith anymore than she'd already humiliated herself. With eyes remaining downward, he said, "Edith, your husband loves you, and you must love him. You married him. You made a vow. I've continued on with my life. I am not interested in what you have to offer."

"What I have to offer!" she shrieked. "How dare you insult me! You make me sound like a prostitute! Anthony I *love* you and you love me!" she yelled, as if stating it vehemently would make it true. "You told me countless times! You said you'd die for me, you said no woman could ever compare to me, you told me I was everything—that I was the world to you!"

"Edith, I no longer feel that way. I'm sorry."

"You're sorry?" she asked. Anthony could hear the hurt and near desperation in her voice. "Then if you're sorry," she went on, "make love to me as a parting gift."

Anthony's eyes, still gazing downward, widened upon hearing this. Trying to remain calm, he said, "No, Edith."

However, in seconds, the woman hurled herself at Anthony, embracing him tightly around the neck, pressing her lips firmly into his. Taken by surprise, Anthony was so stunned by her wanton determination, he couldn't move for a moment. Edith felt soft against him, yet her kiss was hard, and her jasmine fragrance wild. Taking hold of himself, Anthony forcefully pulled her strong and unyielding arms from around his neck.

"Edith!" he pushed her away. "I won't give you anything! The least you can do is leave now with your dignity intact!"

Standing half-clothed before him, Edith gazed at Anthony with tears in her eyes. Then, as if hearing him for the first time, she said, "You really want me to leave?"

Anthony inhaled deeply. "Yes," he said.

Tears rolled down her cheeks. "You really...*don't* love me anymore, do you?"

In spite of himself, Anthony felt almost sorry for her. "No," he said, "but I did at one time, very much." He could at least give her that. "Now your husband loves you and you're his."

Edith hastily pulled up her dress top and buttoned it. Then she left Anthony's room without another word.

Chapter 32

Deseré brought her knees to her chest, holding onto them with one arm, while cradling her head with the other. She'd been struck there and the searing pain was sharp. Had she been mistaken for dead and dumped here? That couldn't have happened. Someone's body wouldn't just be unceremoniously thrown underground and left to decay.

Looking at the bones, Deseré shivered and panic began to set in. She had to get out of here, but how? Standing, she picked up the oil lamp. Gazing down, she saw cobwebs and dirt adhered to her dress. Deseré surmised that she was in a cavern. But when she turned, she gasped, feeling the hair on her arms and neck prickle in a cold jolt of fear.

Surrounded by empty wine bottles, a massive giant of a man rose slowly from the ground. Bald, and leering viciously, he unfolded to a towering height well above six feet. His head was large, his face unshaven, his jaw hard-edged and square. The slash of his mouth revealed widely-spaced teeth, no more than blackened stumps.

"Mademoiselle," his voice was deep and guttural, as if he'd risen from a swamp, "votre cri m'a réveillé." With feet the size of shovels, he took one lumbering yet unsteady step toward her, knocking over one of the empty bottles. It clanked against the ground. Then extending hands as large as spades, he grunted, "Je te veux!"

Deseré's heart raced. The man was drunk, but hardly incapacitated, and though she didn't understand what he'd said, she instinctively knew his intentions were salacious, rather than benevolent. Holding fast to the lamp with one hand, she picked up her skirt with the other and ran from the cavern. Seeing three different passageways ahead, all resembling a dark abyss, Deseré kept straight, taking the one in the center. Not long afterward, she heard the thundering footsteps of the behemoth echoing in the tunnel after her. "Tu es à moi!"

Deseré ran faster and faster, inhaling decay and mustiness. Her aching head pounded with every footfall, feeling as if it would split open from the pain. With only the light of the lamp swaying to and fro, she felt as if the dark, narrow passageway with its low ceiling and stone walls was closing in on her. Yet despite this she kept running, feeling as if she were going nowhere. The passageway split in two.

Deseré veered left, scrambling through what appeared a smaller tunnel. It thinned around her even more than the first, yet she could still move quickly, though her skirts brushed roughly against the constricting walls. Now the ceiling was only inches above her head. She hoped the tightness and lack of height here would prevent the colossus from pursuing her. After several minutes that moved like hours, she no longer heard the massive man's footsteps. However, this passageway soon merged with a larger tunnel, and seconds later, a decorative archway bloomed as if welcoming her to a church. Then the walls transformed from stone to bone.

For a moment, Deseré stopped to catch her ragged breath. The bones, a ghastly sight, were arranged as if pieces of art. Deseré began to run again, seeing that the skulls, wearing the grisly grin of death, were horizontally aligned, then placed in circular patterns, or arranged in crosses against a backdrop of arm bones and thigh bones and bones stacked upon bones and more bones. The macabre display stretched endlessly.

Moments later Deseré saw large shovels leaning against huge carts heaped with additional skeletal remains. It then occurred to her that men worked down here arranging these horrifying works of art. Feeling a glimmer of hope she thought, *They can save me!* Relieved, she stopped running, placing a hand on her throbbing head. But where were the workmen? Just as quickly as the glimmer sparked, it diminished. It was Sunday, she remembered, the day of rest. No one would be working today. She was alone. Trapped.

"Tu ne peux pas te cacher, mon amour."

Deseré heard the man's rasping voice a good distance away. Arming herself with a shovel, she hid behind a column of about four feet in width, yet she stifled a scream once she felt the stickiness of cobwebs adhere to her face and hair. She hastily wiped them away, then extinguished the lamp, shrouding herself in darkness.

****

Anthony's mind still reeled from his encounter with Edith, as he descended the stairs to the lobby in search of Mr. Youngblood, the gentleman who'd informed him of Deseré and Addie's departure last night. Anthony needed a description of the men who'd taken them away. One was white and the other colored, but what had they looked like?

The old man was nowhere in sight, so Anthony approached the front desk.

"I'm trying to determine who the young lady left with," he said, speaking to the clerk at the desk. "The lady in the portrait, Miss Deseré." He pointed to Deseré's picture, on display not far from where they stood. "One of the men was colored, negro. Did you happen see a negro with her at any time before she disappeared?"

"Non," the clerk, a young man of about twenty replied.

He wore a black suite with gold buttons down the front. "I know only one Africain. He is from Marrakesh. But I have not seen him here, nor any ozer Africains."

Anthony pursed his lips nodding, then said, "I believe she was with a Frenchman, as well. Tall, perhaps dark-haired; Italian looking." He described the only white Frenchman Deseré could possibly know, the artist at the Louvre who'd painted her portrait.

The clerk shook his head sadly. "Non, monsieur. I only see her wiz you."

Anthony left the hotel, then walked to the Garden of Tuileries toward the Louvre, convinced that the colored man he was looking for had to be an American familiar with slavery. Anthony wondered if at some point, Deseré and Addie had gone to Louvre to speak to the artist and made him understand that they were slaves in America who wanted their freedom. Had the artist then put them in touch with an American negro familiar with their situation? Unthinkable, but Anthony had to start somewhere. That's why he'd decided to make the Louvre his first stop.

The morning sun sparkled through chestnut, elm and lime trees that yielded a deep shade, while dappled rays of light peeked through the foliage speckling the pavement. Leaves wrestled like tiny whispers as squirrels scampered across hanging branches, and birds perched high softly chirped, whistled and cooed.

There were other Parisians and tourists out for a Sunday stroll in the garden, numbering in the thousands. Sundays seemed to bring out the largest crowds, with no one appearing to acknowledge the Sabbath. For Parisians, Sunday was a day of enjoyment. Anthony reflected that he was probably the only one *not* enjoying himself, especially when seeing numerous couples walking arm in arm. He had to find Deseré. Distracted by thoughts of her, Anthony walked quickly by large circular basins surrounded by white marble statues of gods and goddesses that glistened brightly in the sun. Quacking ducks swam peacefully in the basins, and water in the center of the fountains sprayed upward, catching rainbows.

Anthony paid little attention to the scenery or the others around him, until he saw two colored people, a man and the woman who gazed adoringly at each other. They too walked arm in arm, entranced in conversation. As they strolled in his direction, the woman from a distance resembled Addie. And why wouldn't she? There weren't an abundance of colored women her age or any age in Paris. Anthony broke into a run. Where Addie was, Deseré had to be, as well.

"Addie!" he called, while peering beyond them, hoping to see Deseré.

The woman froze, as did the man with her. Looking toward Anthony, her eyes widened. It was indeed Addie. She clutched the arm of the man she walked with more tightly, appearing afraid as her master beckoned. Addie looked toward her companion and said something. He was large, older — and colored. The culprit!

The colored man stood straight and defiant like a fortified stone wall.

When Anthony caught up with them, he grabbed the man by his massive shoulders. "Where's Des—" he began.

But the colored man interrupted, "Unhand me, sir!" He brusquely knocked Anthony's hands away with both of his arms. Then, stepping in front of Addie, as though to protect her, he said, "Mr. Sinclair, I am Dr. Vincent Chenault. Your slaves are free on French soil. In other words, they are no longer your property!"

Two young, well-dressed couples stopped to stare at the scene created by Anthony and Chenault. They loudly whispered to each other in French, not understanding what had just occurred.

For a moment Anthony felt too flustered to respond. Trying to defend himself he finally said, "How dare you abscond with my...my..." My what? Anthony thought. My people, my property, my slaves? Abandoning that train of thought, he blurted, "Why, you're nothing but a scheming charlatan—out to—to..." to what? Edith's use of a word popped into his head. "...to *prostitute* these women!"

Beyond Chenault's shoulder, Anthony saw Addie's jaw drop. The colored man stiffened even more. His light-brown face reddened. "How dare you insult my *honorable* intentions!" Chenault said. "*I'm* concerned for Miss Addie's humanity, as well as Miss Deseré's!"

Anthony gazed in all directions around the garden expecting to see Deseré at any moment. "And just where is De—" he started, but Chenault cut him off.

"I'm concerned for their rights as human beings," Chenault insisted, "not as *slave* chattel to be auctioned off or used as a means of agricultural production or *breeding*."

A foursome of two middle-aged couples approached. A rather rotund man, shaped like a barrel, with an equally round lady, and a thin man resembling a scarecrow escorted by a lady just as skinny. "That's what slaves are made for," the large man said. His beard covered only one of his three chins. By their less stylish clothes, Anthony could tell they were Americans, and hearing the accent and sentiment just spoken, he surmised they were southern. He tried to ignore the southern man's remark, still focusing on what Chenault had said. Auctioned off, agricultural production, breeding...that was slavery. Yet put that way, it sounded so inhuman.

Again at a loss for words Anthony said to Chenault, "I beg your pardon?" He certainly didn't look at his people—or rather his fellow human beings—that way. "You have no right to—"

Before Anthony could finish, the large southern lady whose jowls jiggled as she spoke, said, "It's a disgrace to see those colored people walking about in this beautiful place where they shouldn't even be allowed."

"I agree," the skinny woman said, her thin skin stretched

tightly over sharp cheekbones. "But here they walk around like they're just as good as anybody else."

"You," Chenault said to Anthony, "have no right to them as your possessions. Miss Addie will not be returning to America with you!"

Anthony was breathing hard now, his frustration mounting. "But what about De—" he said, yet Chenault kept talking.

"Miss Addie," Chenault went on, "has chosen to remain here and work as a seamstress, and I've procured respectable lodging. Though you're a white slaveholder, Miss Addie says you're a good man, which I take to mean a kindly master. And a kindly master's true intent is to keep his slaves oppressed and ignorant since he views them as docile creatures dependent on his guidance and care."

"Any darkie's main use is as a slave," the thin man said. Spectacles balanced on his beak-like nose. "They need to have a master, but I wouldn't recommend a kindly one."

Anthony felt his cheeks burn and balled his fists. "I—I— I've heard enough of this nonsense!" However, he felt as if he were addressing Chenault, as well as the southerners. "Tell me where De—"

"I'll tell you what you've heard," Chenault said sharply, "you've heard enough of the truth!"

"You're gonna let that darkie talk to you like that?" the large man said. By now more French couples had gathered around to look upon the American spectacle.

"And why can't he," Addie snapped at the large man. "He's just as good as you!"

The southerners gasped, then the large man said, "Why, I never!"

"And you never will!" Addie quipped. The large man stood nonplussed with his companions as Addie stepped to Chenault's side, placing her attention on Anthony. "Masta Anthony," she said, ignoring the southerners, who now loudly spoke among themselves about uppity negroes, "I don't want you to take no offense at what I'm doin', it's just that it's a once in a lifetime opportunity. I ain't got nothin' against you. You're a fine man, just like your Uncle Jeremy. And I ain't got no dissatisfaction with you as a person. But I do have dissatisfaction 'bout bein' owned as a slave. Now I can do somethin' about it, thanks to you."

"That wench is your property," the thin man thundered, "and you should whip the daylights out of her for her show of blatant disrespect!"

"Watch your tongue!" Chenault said back to the thin man.

"Are you addressing me, boy?" the thin man asked Chenault.

"I most certainly am! To who else would I be speaking?"

"The nerve!"

The heated exchange continued between Chenault and the thin southern man as Anthony spoke to Addie, ending with Chenault speaking angrily in French. The Parisians in the crowd gasped and giggled as the thin man turned red, unsure of what was said.

"Thanks to me?" Anthony said to Addie, dumbfounded, now finding it hard to ignore the gathering crowd.

"I thank you for bringing me here," Addie said, "where there ain't no slavery and negroes are free."

"Free?" the southern women said in unison.

"Not if they're American negroes!" the large southern man said.

Anthony looked at Addie for a long moment. "With so little thought—you plan to stay here? Based on what this—*stranger* — has told you?"

"Masta Anthony," Addie said, "I know this is most likely a shock—but I've made my choice to stay in Paris, bein' as I'm free."

Anthony's jaw stiffened. "So *you've* made a choice," he said, now at his wit's end since Deseré had failed to appear, "but what about De—"

"She wasn't born free," the thin woman pointed to Addie.

"And she never will be," the large woman addressed Anthony, "unless you free her! Does she even realize that you won't be able to come back and get her at the drop of a hat?"

"You, sir," the large man said to Anthony, "have surely lost your mind! Why are you trying to reason with that wench when you could just whip her into submission?"

"If I were a believer in violence," Chenault said to the large man, "I would challenge you to a duel! Yet despite my views on violence, I've reconsidered! I *do* challenge—"

"Dr. Chenault," Addie lightly touched his arm. Then she looked at the large man, keenly holding his eye. "Don't dignify anything else that bloviating blowhard and his companions have to say."

The large man flushed, then said to Anthony, "Why—did you hear what she said?"

"As a matter of fact I did," Anthony said angrily, turning to look the large man squarely in the face. "I've heard everything she's said, and I find no fault with any of it!"

"He's *insane!*" the large man yelled, looking at his companions for confirmation. They nodded adamantly.

Addie smiled. "I knew you were a good man, Masta Anthony. Bein' here's like I seen the light of freedom. It's for me too, not just the white folks. I can learn the language and everything else I need to. I'd say that's a small price to pay for freedom."

Addie's words sliced from Anthony's mind to his heart, as had all of Chenault's, although he'd tried to deny their truth. Everything he'd heard had caused him to question his ownership of people. Now seeing Addie on the arm of a distinguished gentleman, looking like a woman in love, he sighed.

"If that's your wish..." then he realized that here in France, he no longer had control over her life—or Deseré's! He had to make her his! Although he'd been anxious about finding Deseré, now panic set in. "But what about Deseré?" he asked quickly, feeling his heart race. "Where is she?"

Addie and Chenault looked at each other, then at Anthony. "I thought she was with you," Addie said.

"What?" Anthony asked, feeling his chest tighten.

"Last night while I was sleeping," Addie said, "she left. I found a note she wrote this morning, and her carpetbag was gone. Deseré was headed back to the Bedford, because in her note she said she wanted to go back to America."

"But—but I haven't seen her!" Anthony stammered, confounded. "She's gone—something's happened!"

By now, over twenty onlookers had gathered, including Parisians, English and Americans. Several spoke all at once in French and English trying to assess the situation as two police officers approached wearing dark blue uniforms and matching caps. "Quel est le probleme maintenant?" one asked.

Dr. Chenault explained what had transpired in French to the officers. The formal investigation into Deseré's disappearance began.

Chapter 33

THUD...THUD...THUD...

In the darkness, Deseré listened. The man no longer ran. Winded, and coughing like a rusty rattling cage, he walked slowly, his large feet plodding his way through the bone-lined passageway. Deseré trembled. Her heart thumped wildly. Her palms, slippery with sweat and the sticky remains of cobwebs, gripped the shovel. Peeking from behind the column, she could see a dim light approaching.

Lord Jesus, Deseré prayed silently, *please help me.*

The light appeared to become brighter.

The man coughed, then grunted and spat. "Mademoiselle," he said in an angry voice.

In seconds, Deseré could see his enormous silhouette. He carried a brightly burning torch above his massive head that now glowed like a ghoulish jack-o-lantern. He rasped out more words in French as he looked around the skeletal passageway, its protruding skulls now eerily illuminated by the torchlight.

Deseré held tight to the shovel, peering around the edge of the column. The man's back faced her as she watched him place his torch in a wrought iron sconce mounted against the wall. It reflected a shadow nearly double his size, flickering in an evil dance. "Où es-tu?" he growled.

Deseré held her breath.

There was another column across from hers several yards away. The man slowly approached it, then lumbered around the whole thing. He said something else in French, sounding like a child disappointed at not finding a playmate during a game of hide and seek.

CLICK—CLACK—CLACK!

Bones fell from a cart near Deseré's column. She stiffened. Feeling like a lame fox chased by a thundering pack of hounds, her heart raced.

"Ah," the man said, slowly turning toward her hiding place. Deseré concealed herself. Looking down for a moment, she saw the hem of her skirt peeking beyond the border of the column. Gripping the shovel tighter, she hoped he didn't notice. Deseré couldn't see the man now, but only hear his approach. He edged closer and closer, his stench of grime, urine and alcohol overwhelming her. Then he put his big hands on either side of the column. Deseré saw dirty fingers the size of sausages.

She gulped, raising the shovel high.

He breathed deeply, wheezing, then laughed in a low rumble. "VOILÀ!" His ugly face, with eyes bulging and an evil lopsided smile, popped from around the column in a fetid haze of stale wine and rotting teeth.

Deseré screamed, her shriek reverberating through the passageway bouncing from the walls piercing enough to wake the dead. She bashed the shovel down hard on the man's head. He yelled so loudly his voice echoed like the cry of a thousand beasts. Bending over, he clutched his skull. Deseré whacked him again on the back, and once more on the head. The man fell to his knees, but as she tried to strike him again, he yanked the shovel away from her hands and tossed it across the passageway.

It clanked against floor as Deseré began to run, but in

seconds the man was behind her. He grabbed her by the hair, pulling so hard she felt as if he were ripping it from her scalp. Then, he roughly pulled on her shoulders, turning her toward him. He pushed her into the wall of bone so forcefully the breath was knocked out of her. The repulsive crush of skeletal remains pressed into her back and shoulders. The smell of mold became stronger as skull fragments broke loose, rattling loudly at her feet. Then the man's thick fingers encircled her throat in a hot, vice-like grip. His eyes blazed as he cursed her in French and began to choke her.

With heavy hands, the man shook Deseré's delicate neck, slamming her head into the wall over and over. The wall gave in more with each painful slam, releasing a shower of dust and tiny bone fragments that hit the ground like pebbles. Her airway blocked, Deseré struggled to breathe. Fighting for her life, she managed to scrape her nails into his oily face and claw her fingers into his blood-shot eyes. Angered by this, his grip loosened.

He smiled widely, revealing the black stumps of his teeth, then squeezed her neck again, this time raising her from the ground. Deseré felt as if her head would snap from her body. Then, as if she were nothing more than a rag doll, he flung her away. Deseré crashed hard into a cart before hitting the cold ground. Bones spilled around her. She tried to escape, but the man threw himself on top of her, suffocating her with his odor of filth. He kissed her savagely, covering her with dog-like drool, his rough face burning hers, while large calloused fingers tore madly at her clothes, scratching her skin like razors.

Striving to survive, Deseré desperately felt around the rough ground for something to defend herself with, hoping to find a bone, a jagged skull, anything to fight off the monster. Her hand finally managed to locate something, a tool, two-pronged and sharp like a claw. She clutched it by a wooden handle, then with all the force she could muster, brought it down onto the beast, landing its claw-like base somewhere beneath his back. She pulled the tool, scraping it through the man's clothes and skin.

The man yelled, recoiling off of her in pain. Deseré, still on her back, was able to scoot away a short distance using her heels and elbows while gripping the tool with one hand. Enraged, the man stood, arms raised, ready to pounce on her. Blood seeped from his clothing near the side of his upper thigh.

Deseré sat up, then using both hands, swung the tool, with its six inch metal prongs, at the roaring man. He grabbed it. In a loosing battle of tug of war, she pulled as hard as she could. As he wrestled the tool from her, Deseré quickly raised her leg, kicking him in his manhood. Clutching the tool, the man lost his balance. He fell forward, landing in a solid smelly heap beside her.

Deseré scrambled to her feet, ready to run, but the man didn't move. Then he slowly raised himself to his knees. Deseré froze, almost vomiting, upon seeing the sharp prongs of the tool buried in his stomach, while a patch of red bloomed beneath his shirt. Breathing hard, the man gasped, "Merde..." as blood dripped from his lips. Then he pulled the prongs from his flesh and collapsed to his side, blood pooling around him.

Regaining her senses, Deseré retrieved the torch the man had placed on the wall, then moved as quickly as she could away from him. She fled the bone-lined cavern the same way she'd entered in search of a way out. A smaller tunnel had led her here, by connecting to a larger one. Perhaps if she remained in the larger tunnel, and not split off into the smaller one, it would lead to a way out. Then again, maybe it wouldn't.

"Help!" she began calling frantically, while maneuvering herself through the large tunnel. "Help!"

One thing was certain, Deseré realized, she couldn't get out of here on her own. "Dear Lord," she prayed while slowly running, "please help me to find a way out, and please help someone to find me... Lord, please help someone to find me..."

Piecing together the events from last night, Deseré remembered that she'd left the Sisters' Home to return to the Hotel Bedford, but she could recall nothing further. That beast must have knocked her out from behind, then brought her down here to... Her stomach twisted in knots. She felt no pain in her nether regions and her undergarments were intact, so she hadn't been violated...at least not yet. Deseré had left the man in the dark, wounded and incapacitated, so there was no way he could possibly come after her now...or could he...?

"Help!" she cried. "Please, someone, help me!"

Chapter 34

It was Sunday and the police were short-staffed. So as they conducted their short-handed investigation into Deseré's vanishing, Anthony coordinated his own, with the help of Addie and Dr. Chenault.

"The best thing to do," he'd suggested to Chenault and Addie while still in the Garden of Tuileries, "is re-trace her steps."

Once they'd taken a short cab ride to the Sisters' Home, Chenault explained that this location was only about three miles from the Bedford Hotel.

"I suggest we walk to the Bedford from here," Anthony said.

"I agree," Chenault said, as they began walking. Then he asked Addie, "What time do you suppose she left?"

"We didn't turn in 'til well past midnight," Addie said. "I woke up around six. That's when I found the note."

"So she must've left sometime in the early morning hours," Anthony said. Looking at his pocket watch, he saw that it was now close to eleven. "But what could have happened?"

"Let's just keep walking," Chenault said.

They passed a bakery with a display of tarts and pastries in the window, and momentarily the smell of fresh bread overpowered the smell of urine in the streets. They continued heading down the boulevard, through the leisurely strolling Sunday crowds, passing by more large glass windows of shops and apartment buildings.

When they were a little over two and half miles from the hotel, Addie stopped. From the sidewalk, she pointed into the street. Look!" A pink silk flower was crushed into the cobblestone. "That looks like one of the roses on Deseré's bonnet."

After waiting for a swiftly moving carriage to pass, Anthony rushed into the street to retrieve it. Walking back to the sidewalk, he studied the flower, trampled and soiled, then felt his heart sink. Deseré did indeed have a bonnet with pink silk roses that he'd purchased for her in Paris. His breath caught as he remembered her wearing it, her lovely face framed by the large beautiful flowers. Anthony didn't want to admit that this mangled blossom, so broken and dirty, could be Deseré's, so he held it out for Addie to examine more closely. "You're sure this is from her bonnet?"

Addie carefully scrutinized the crinkled silk. "'Bout as sure as I can be," she said.

A feeling of dread overwhelmed Anthony, as he placed the flower in his pocket.

A moment later, Chenault gazed across the street. "I hesitate to mention this," he said, "but there's the Barrière d'Enfer."

"Which is?" Anthony asked, looking toward the two large buildings opposite them. Three stories tall and made of white stone, they resembled miniature palaces.

"The Gate of Hell. Those buildings were toll houses used to collect taxes, but because of the crime in the area, The Gate of Hell became an appropriate name. And," he added ominously, "the entrance to the catacombs is there as well."

"The catacombs?" Anthony asked.

"You see that small black structure attached to the building on the west side?" Chenault asked. Anthony and Addie nodded. "That will take you to the burial place of the Paris dead. The underground ossuaries—"

"But how easy is it to get into them?" Anthony interrupted.

"Not easy at all," Chenault said. "Men work down in them, but tours were discontinued a while ago."

"The silk flower from Deseré's bonnet was in the street." Anthony said. "It could have fallen off while she was headed in that direction." Or dragged, he thought. "We need to explore that vicinity." After the three of them crossed the street, a gnawing feeling began to overtake Anthony's insides. He headed straight for the entrance to the catacombs. It resembled a black shack decorated with Doric columns and was sealed tight by a locked black gate over a heavy looking black door.

"It would be impossible for her to get in here," Chenault said, "and why would she even want to?"

"But what if someone forced her down there," Anthony asked. "You said men work there."

"They're hardly savages," Chenault said, "just men doing honest work."

"Are there other ways to get in?" Addie asked.

Chenault hesitated. "Rumor has it that there are illegal entry points, but I wouldn't know how to begin to find them."

"Deseré was only three miles from the Bedford, but she never made it back there!" Anthony said. "And Addie, you said her intention was to return there."

Addie nodded, about to say something, then she gasped, covering her mouth.

Chenault placed a calming hand on her shoulder, as Anthony asked, "What is it?"

Addie dropped her hand to her heart, then pointed to the

bushes lining the side of the entrance. Hardly noticeable beneath the shrubbery was the green and beige fabric of a carpetbag. "That's hers," Addie said softly.

Anthony started quickly toward the bag, but then became distracted by something he saw beneath the gated doorway to the catacombs. Sunlight glistened from the barely noticeable object—the end of a pink satin ribbon, possibly another remnant of Deseré's bonnet. Anthony squatted down to pull out a half foot of lace trimmed ribbon for Addie to see. The saucer-eyed expression of shock and horror on Addie's face confirmed to Anthony all he needed to know. He shoved the ribbon into his pocket. "We have to get inside!" he said, immediately trying to break open the gate by ramming it with his shoulder. It wouldn't give.

"Stop that, Mr. Sinclair!" Chenault reprimanded. "We can't get in, so I suggest we alert the police."

"There's no time for that," Anthony said, removing a small pocketknife from his pocket. After opening the blade, he shoved it into the round lock. "I doubt this lock will be that difficult to pick."

"Mr. Sinclair," Chenault said appalled, "you can't defile a historic landmark such as this. I'm sure we can—"

"Now Dr. Chenault, I think we'd best let Masta Anthony break open that door. What if Deseré *is* down there in trouble?"

Chenault sighed. "I'm not saying we shouldn't explore the catacombs as a possibility, I'd just prefer we do it legally."

"Addie," Anthony said, continuing to work his knife in the lock, rattling the black gate, "fend off any onlookers." Anthony looked over his shoulder just in time to see an old man leaning on a cane slowly trudging by, gazing toward him wearing a quizzical expression.

"She is no longer your slave!" Chenault objected.

"Then *you* fend off any onlookers or flag down the police," Anthony snapped back.

"We will leave you to your criminal devices," Chenault said, "and seek the police so you can enter the catacombs legally."

"I'll stay here," Addie said. "I gotta bad feelin' about this, and Deseré might—"

"Miss Addie," Chenault said, "I insist you come with me. I'll keep you safe. No need for you *and* Mr. Sinclair to get in trouble."

Addie pursed her lips, then departed with Chenault.

Ten minutes later, Anthony managed to break open the lock. Feeling panicked, as if Deseré's life depended on him, he flung open the black gate, then turned the knob of the black door behind it. Locked.

Anthony cursed under his breath. Taking a deep breath, he kicked the door. It didn't budge. After a second powerful kick, wood splintered and the lock gave way. Frantic, Anthony pushed open the door to find a steep stairway, appearing to never end, leading to darkness. Unlit torches were placed in sconces by the entrance along with several oil lamps that hung from the wall. Before grabbing something to light his way, he yelled, "Deseré! Deseré! Are you down there?"

****

Deseré stopped. Was she imagining things or had she actually heard someone call her name? The voice was barely audible. It was Anthony—it had to be! Praise God, he'd found her! She began running weakly in the direction she believed she'd heard him. "I'm here..." she called with a voice cracked and parched from calling for help for what seemed like an eternity. "I'm here..."

****

"Qu'est-ce que vous fais ici?"

If Deseré had responded, Anthony hadn't heard over the loud voice yelling behind him. He turned to see a tall police officer, probably one alerted by the old man who'd passed by earlier. Yet before Anthony could explain anything, the lanky officer pulled him several feet away from the entrance. Then the man slapped Anthony on the chest with the back of his hand exclaiming, "Seuls les fonctionnaires sont autorisés dans les catacombes!"

"Je ne parle Francaise!" Anthony said, straightening his clothes. "Je parle Anglais."

"What are you doing here?" The policeman switched to English, his angular features hard beneath his blue cap. "Only government officials are allowed in ze catacombs! And you have broken ze lock and ze door! Off to ze jailhouse for zat!" The officer grabbed Anthony's wrists, preparing to place them in handcuffs. Passersby slowed their pace to look.

Determined to find Deseré, Anthony resisted, pulling his hands away. The blow seemed to come from nowhere, as the officer struck him swiftly on the side of the head with a baton. While Anthony was momentarily stunned by the cutting pain, the officer handcuffed him.

"Dastardly Englishman," the policeman muttered under his breath.

"I'm an American!"

"Zat's worse."

"You don't understand!" Anthony exclaimed.

"I see all I need to understand!" the officer said. "You broke your way into ze catacombs and were trying to enter."

"Yes!" Anthony exclaimed, the strike to his head easing somewhat, yet still painful. "But only because there's a young lady trapped down there! I have to find her!"

"How do you know a young lady is down zere?" A heavy mustache covered the policeman's down-turned lips and moved like a caterpillar as he spoke. "She could not get in."

"Masta Anthony!" Addie called, from a short distance away. "Here's one of the investigating police officers!" This officer was clean-shaven and powerfully built like a bull. He quickly moved toward Anthony, along with Chenault and

Addie, who'd lifted her skirts, revealing the white lace of her petticoats as she ran. Upon moving closer, Addie noticed Anthony's predicament of cuffed hands and most likely a lump on the side of his head. "Good, God Almighty!" she said. "What did he do to you?"

Once the threesome had reached Anthony and the other officer, the two policeman and Chenault spoke rapidly in French, Chenault pointing to Deseré's carpetbag peeking from the shrubbery. The investigating officer pulled the bag from the bushes, then opened it to examine the contents. Addie identified the items of clothing and folded fabric as Deseré's. The investigator said something in French to the other officer who then took the cuffs from Anthony's wrists.

Now with free hands, Anthony removed the flower and ribbon from his pocket, explaining where he'd found them and that the items had most likely fallen from Deseré's bonnet.

The two policeman conversed quietly among themselves. After several moments, the investigator said to Anthony, "Only ze Prefect of Police will allow you to enter ze catacombs. Ze roof and quarries are in a dangerous state and it is practically impossible for anyone to receive admission."

"Admission?" Anthony exclaimed. "I'm not interested in seeing this place as a tourist! A young lady could be down there! She could be hurt—God forbid, she might be dead! I have to find her!"

"Her bag could have been discarded zere by chance," the investigator said. "Ze ribbon blown under ze door by ze wind, perhaps. "Paris is a very large city. Zere is a very small possibility zat she could actually be five stories beneas ze ground in ze catacombs. So I am sorry, monsieur, but we must follow protocol."

"Protocol?" Anthony asked astonished.

"Oui. Zere are papers to sign," the mustached policeman said, "many signatures needed."

"The Prefect does not live far from here," the investigator said, "but it is Sunday, so he is in church."

"N'oublie pas la maîtresse," the mustached policeman smiled slyly, "avec qui il ne manquera pas de passer du bon temps."

Anthony only caught the mention of a mistress in that sentence, most likely belonging to the Prefect. Perhaps he spends time with her after church, the fine man of God. Anthony had to stop himself from rolling his eyes.

"I am sure zat after mass has ended," the investigator continued, "and he's taken care of his ozer...obligations, he will be happy to assist you."

The mustached policeman said something in French, calling the investigating officer's attention to the broken lock and door.

"He says you did zis," the investigator said, "so we must charge you for the repair of ze lock and ze door, or ozerwise arrest you on charges of vandalism."

"I'll pay for the lock! I'll pay for the door!" Anthony said angrily. "But I refuse to wait for anyone's permission to descend into the catacombs."

"But, monsieur, we could lose our jobs!" the mustached policeman declared.

"However," the investigator offered, "zere are certain ways to get access wizout following protocol." Both officers eyed each other, then jangled their pockets, awaiting a bribe.

Chapter 35

Deseré had begun to lose hope. She'd come to the conclusion that she had indeed imagined someone calling her name, because a good bit of time had passed and she'd heard nothing more.

Deseré sighed. She wanted her mother. Right now she'd give anything just to be held in her mother's arms. Tears began rolling down her cheeks at the thought. Mama always had the right words, always knew what to do. There was a verse she used to quote, Philippians chapter four, verse thirteen. Deseré remembered it, and though her voice was weak, she said it out loud. "'I can do all things through Christ which strengtheneth me.'" Then she repeated the verse and prayed.

"Please, Lord, give me strength. In Jesus's name, show me a way out. Let someone know I'm here..."

Exhausted, Deseré continued to pray and call for help, dragging her feet along the pitted earth floor of the tunnel. The torch she carried burned brightly above her head, illuminating the never-ending darkness that stretched before her like a starless night sky. When her right arm tired, she shifted the torch to her left, yet her whole body, especially her head, ached from the abuse she'd suffered at the hands of that deranged lunatic.

How badly was he injured?" she wondered. Would he regain his strength and come looking for her? Would she ever get out of here? Would she have to wait until tomorrow when the men resumed working? But what if they didn't resume work for several days? She placed a hand over her growling stomach and longed for a drink of water. How much longer would she be trapped here?

****

After paying off the two policemen who'd given him an hour to search for Deseré, Anthony descended into the catacombs. Ninety steps down, they'd warned him, so he'd best be careful. He held an oil lamp in one hand, while grasping tightly to a wrought iron railing in the other. The narrow, slippery stairway wound down to damp, pitch black vaults housing the disassembled dead. Anthony felt as if he were slowly sliding into the depths of hell.

"Deseré!" he called. "Deseré! Are you here? Are you alright?"

****

Deseré stopped walking and listened.

"Deseré!" a voice echoed through the tunnel.

Feeling her heart leap, Deseré now realized that someone *had* called her name, and it *was* Anthony! Thank you God, she said silently, then she called, "Anthony," straining for him to hear her.

"Deseré, are you hurt?"

"I'm alive."

****

Anthony began to run through the dark passageway as he could clearly hear Deseré's straining voice.

"I can hear your footsteps," she called.

In moments he saw torchlight several yards ahead, and in seconds, Deseré appeared like an injured angel in the light, her face smudged with dirt and bruises, the skirt and sleeves of her pale green dress torn, and her golden tresses a bedraggled mess. Upon seeing him, she stopped moving for a moment, as if to confirm that he was real and not an apparition. As Anthony continued to run, Deseré weakly picked up her pace, then upon reaching him, collapsed in tears against him, dropping the torch.

Anthony, teary-eyed and overwhelmed with relief, let the lantern clatter to the ground so he could pull her into him as closely as possible. Thankful to hold her again, he never wanted to let her go. Yet while Anthony embraced her tightly, relishing the feel of her body against his, he began to smell smoke.

"I'm on fire!" Deseré's scratchy voice strained loudly, upon realizing that the torch had begun to burn her dress.

Anthony immediately flung her to the ground, then threw himself on top of her to smother the burgeoning yellow flames of her skirt. He rolled with her on the damp earth to extinguish the fire. Then when it was out, Anthony, still on the ground with Deseré beneath him, kissed her, deeply and passionately, and she kissed him back, pulling him closely with desperate need.

Anthony only tore himself from Deseré when he heard the torch crackle a few feet away. He looked toward it and saw its fading brightness, then stood and stomped out what was left of its dying fire.

"Anthony," Deseré said, breathless, raising herself to her hands and knees. He rushed over to help her stand. "We have to get out of here." Her tone was urgent. "There's a crazy man—"

"Where is he?" Anthony asked, ready to kill him.

"Just get me out of here!"

Anthony clutched her arm, then grabbed the oil lamp from the ground. "This way." He held the lantern out in front of them, lighting the way. He moved swiftly, but slowed his pace so Deseré could keep up. "That man—"

"He's crazy, Anthony. He knocked me out and brought

me down here. Let the police handle him. I fought him; he's hurt, but I don't know how badly."

****

When Anthony emerged from the catacombs, the policemen were shocked to see Deseré, wounded and in tatters, clinging to his arm. As Anthony led Deseré to a nearby bench and sat down with her, the officers asked a series of questions in stunned disbelief as they gawked at Deseré, who shielded her eyes from the sunlight.

"How did she get down zere?"

"Where did she come from?"

"How were you certain she was zere?"

Addie ran to Deseré and gave her a gentle hug, careful not to hurt her.

"I'll get her some water." Chenault rushed off to a nearby café.

"You!" the inspector said. He addressed Anthony and walked toward him with mustached officer by his side. "Tell us how you found her!"

"And how you knew where to look!" the mustached officer added adamantly.

Anthony began telling them how they had retraced her steps from the Sisters' Home to the Bedford and found clues, but in the midst of his explanation, Dr. Chenault returned with a large glass of water and a piece of bread. Then, as Deseré greedily gulped down the water and ravenously devoured the bread, Chenault began assessing her injuries.

"In addition to being dehydrated," the doctor said, "the bruising on her neck indicates that someone tried to strangle her." Chenault then walked around her, taking note of the blood matted in her hair. He felt her head. She winced. "There's a good sized lump there from a blow to the back of her head," the doctor said. "A cold pack applied will relieve the pain and swelling. Bed rest, a bowl of soup and a dose of laudanum would be what I'd prescribe, but I suggest, Mr. Sinclair, that you have the hotel physician perform a thorough examination."

"I appreciate your advice, Dr. Chenault," Anthony said. "I'll see that she's given proper medical care."

"Alright," the inspector said impatiently, "now we need to know what is it zat happened!" he demanded of Anthony and Deseré.

Anthony told the investigator and the mustached officer everything Deseré had said, then Deseré filled in all the missing information. When she finished, the officers looked at each other gravely.

"Donc c'était vrai," the mustached policeman said to the investigator, "la rumeur du fou qui vit quelque part dans les tunnels."

The inspector shook his head, then said quietly, "Donc c'était ça."

"What are they saying?" Anthony asked Chenault.

"Something about a rumor regarding a crazy man that supposedly lives in the tunnels," Chenault said.

"Ils disent qu'il aurait travaillé dans les catacombes il y a bien longtemps, et perdu l'esprit par la suite," the inspector said to Chenault.

"He worked in the catacombs but lost his mind, according to speculation," Chenault translated.

The inspector continued, "Il a disparu, mais certains ont cru qu'il vivait dans la clandestinité, loin dans les tunnels."

"He disappeared," Chenault said, "but some believed he lived in hiding, far underground in the tunnels."

"Je descends le chercher. Vous, vous continuez à interroger l'homme et la femme," the inspector said to the mustached officer, who responded back affirmatively.

Chenault explained to Anthony that the inspector was going into the catacombs while the other officer would ask further questions. Then Chenault called something to the inspector in French.

"Non Monsieur, c'est trop dangereux. Préparez une ambulance," the inspector yelled back before lighting an oil lamp and beginning his descent into the catacombs.

"That man down there," Chenault said, "despite his criminal intent, needs medical attention. The officer won't allow me into the catacombs, but I will procure an ambulance, so if you'll pardon me."

Chenault rushed off, leaving Deseré, Anthony and Addie with the mustached police officer who said, "Some claim to have seen zat crazy man lurking ze streets late at night, but none of ze police ever have."

"He's down there," Deseré said.

"Oui, mademoiselle," the policeman said. "I believe you. Did he," the officer looked down for a moment, as if embarrassed. "Did he—how do you say—ruin you?"

Addie gasped at the question, and Anthony, shocked, put a consoling arm around Deseré.

"No," Deseré said. "He tried, but I managed to— incapacitate him."

"Een-co-pa-see-tate?" the officer asked.

"I hurt him," Deseré clarified. "Like I told you, he fell on some sort of tool I tried to fight him off with."

"You say you hurt him," the policeman frowned. "I know you said zat before, but you are small and weak, a woman." The officer looked at Anthony, "You went down zere. I would suspect it was *you* who hurt him, tried to kill him, perhaps."

Anthony gritted his teeth. "I'm ashamed to say it wasn't."

****

By the time Deseré saw Chenault return, the mustached policeman, who remained nearby, had finished asking questions. Deseré leaned heavily against Anthony, whose arm was still protectively around her shoulder.

"An ambulance is on the way," Chenault said, clasping Addie's hand in his. "Depending on the injury, the man could still be alive."

"I don't want to live with his death on my hands," Deseré

said, as tears rolled down her cheeks.

"It was an accident," Anthony said soothingly. "And besides, you were protecting yourself."

"Because of what that man did," Addie said smugly, "he don't sound like he's worth savin'."

"Mama would've said he's a child of God," Deseré sniffed.

Addie clucked her tongue. "That don't excuse what he did!"

Just as the inspector appeared from the depths of the catacombs, a horse drawn ambulance arrived, carrying two white-clad attendants, its wagon covered by a white canopy with a red cross on each side. The inspector called to the attendants, "Il est vivant," and in moments, they removed a stretcher from the back of the wagon and rushed toward the entrance of the catacombs to follow the inspector back down.

"He's alive," Chenault said.

"Somebody bad as that don't deserve to live!" Addie said in disgust. "I know that ain't right, and it ain't my place to say it, 'cause God is the final judge, but that's just my opinion."

"I'm relieved he's alive," Deseré murmured to Addie, "but he needs to be locked up."

"Since you've completed your questioning," Anthony said to the mustached officer, "and the other policeman has located that man, may we return to our hotel? The lady needs her rest."

"Non, monsieur," the officer said. "I request zat you stay until ze inspector returns and ze injured man is brought up."

Deseré tensed. "Must we?" she asked in a small voice.

"Oui, mademoiselle. I apologize, but ze inspector might have furzer questions."

Less than an hour later, the inspector emerged from the catacombs again, this time followed by the attendants who strained under the weight of the stretcher they carried. On it lay a large man who appeared to weigh in excess of two-hundred pounds. The inspector allowed the attendants to pass by him, as they made a great effort to move briskly toward the ambulance. Many people passing by the scene had now stopped to watch.

Still sitting on the bench, Deseré shrank even closer to Anthony, clasping him tightly around the waist with both arms while she watched them. She could feel his heartbeat, then realized it was her own, as its beating caused her entire body to pound softly like a tiny drum.

On the stretcher, the man no longer wore a shirt, but blood stained bandages were wrapped tightly around his flabby white abdomen. As the attendants came closer, heading toward the ambulance, Deseré's stomach churned as she smelled the man's stench of alcohol, urine and filth. She saw that his eyes were closed, yet as the attendants rushed by her, the man's bulging orbs popped open.

Deseré gasped, feeling her heart lodge in her throat, as the man lifted a bulbous bald head, even scarier in the daylight, since it was abnormally large with an irregularly lumpy shape. Upon seeing Deseré, a sinister smile curled thick black lips, caked with dried blood. He appeared completely toothless now because blood covered what decaying teeth he did have. Then the man reached an enormous blood-stained hand toward Deseré. She screamed as his fat fingers futilely lurched toward her. Deseré began crying hysterically, burying her face in Anthony's chest.

"Tu es à moi!" the man croaked, "Tu es à moi!"

Anthony held Deseré tightly. "Is there really any *need* for us to remain here?" he demanded of the inspector and the mustached officer, as Deseré continued to weep against him.

"Non, monsieur," the inspector said, "you may go. If we have furzer questions, we will contact you at your hotel." Then he dispersed the gathering crowd.

****

Deseré did her best to regain her composure as Anthony wiped her tears with a handkerchief. The crazy man was gone now, taken away by the ambulance.

"I'll be right back, darling," Anthony assured her, as he left her side and ran several yards away to hail a cab.

Addie put a comforting arm around her. "You'll be alright, honey."

Deseré nodded, blowing her nose with Anthony's handkerchief.

"You ain't got nothin' to worry 'bout now."

"Perhaps not," Deseré sniffled.

"And after a good rest," Chenault said, "you'll feel much better."

The three of them remained silent for a few seconds until Addie said, "So...I guess this is really goodbye."

Deseré leaned her head on Addie's shoulder for a moment. "I guess so."

"Why'd you have to sneak away in the middle of the night?" Addie asked. Deseré said nothing.

"It wasn't obligation to him," Chenault said. "You aren't a slave anymore, at least as long as you're here."

"I am a slave to love," Deseré said softly, "my love for him."

"Well, he loves you, too" Addie said. "There ain't no doubt 'bout that now, seein' as how determined he was to find you."

"His resolve to break into the catacombs shows a deep concern," Chenault agreed. "However, you must establish that you will *not* be a slave once you return to America. Sinclair must give you a firm guarantee of freedom, although I'm uncertain of how he can do that. He wouldn't be the first white man to go back on his word."

"But he loves her," Addie said. "He'll give her her freedom. Least I think he will. But Deseré, if you feel any doubt in your gut 'bout what he says, you stay here! You ain't got nothin' to be afraid of, startin' all over in a strange place. You done fought off a crazy man to save yourself. You said you wasn't brave, but you are."

"You've seen the strength you have from the ordeal you've endured," Chenault said. "You're worth more than a life in slavery, so don't let Sinclair take you back as a mere possession."

****

Several yards off, Addie saw a cab stop for Masta Anthony. "C'mon, honey, the cab is here." Addie and the doctor each slipped their arms through Deseré's, then the three of them slowly walked to Anthony.

Addie said, "You take care of yourself, honey."

"But remember," Chenault added, "any doubt, you stay here."

"I will, Dr. Chenault," Deseré assured him. Then to Addie she said, "This can't really be goodbye, can it?"

"If you go back to America it is."

"Oh, Addie," tears flooded Deseré's eyes, "I'll miss you."

"I'll miss you too," Addie said, as they approached Masta Anthony and the waiting cab.

Deseré gently pulled her arm from Addie and turned to Dr. Chenault. "Thank you, Dr. Chenault." She gave him a light kiss on the cheek, then squeezed his hand. "Thank you for all you did, and all you were willing to do for me."

Chenault's light brown skin reddened, as he smiled and muttered, "You're welcome."

Then Deseré circled to Addie and embraced her tightly. "Be happy, Addie."

"I already am, chile."

"Then stay happy!"

"I will, long as I'm here...with Vincent."

"Vincent?"

"Dr. Chenault, honey. And I want you to be happy too." Then Addie lowered her voice to a whisper so Masta Anthony couldn't overhear her. "Life won't be the same when you go back. Now you know what freedom is, you gotta make certain you have it, and that Masta Anthony's willin' to give it, you hear?"

Deseré nodded. "I hear," she said quietly.

After Anthony helped Deseré into the cab, he said, "Addie, I wish you a happy life here, but you will surely be missed at Pleasant Wood."

"Thank you, sir," Addie said. "And you were a good masta, but I surely won't be missin' Pleasant Wood. You just take care of Deseré. "

"You have my word." Anthony smiled. Then he extended his hand to Chenault. "And Doctor, thank you for your assistance, and everything you've...helped me to understand."

"My pleasure," Chenault said stiffly, shaking the white man's hand.

Addie and Chenault watched Anthony climb into the cab, then waved as he and Deseré rode away. A moment later, Chenault, sounding rather unconvinced, said, "Well, Addie, you have his word—a *white* man's word." A large dollop of pigeon waste dropped from the sky, splattering a few inches from his feet.

Addie sighed. "Umph... I hope that ain't no sign." Instead, she wished that Deseré would have the happiness she longed for with the man she loved, and not return to America as only his slave.

Chapter 36

Once they were settled in the cab on their way to the Bedford, Anthony put an arm around Deseré. He gazed into her bright blue eyes, then stroked her blond tresses. Despite her bruises and matted hair, Deseré was still the loveliest woman Anthony had ever seen. Even the dank smell of the catacombs clinging to her didn't diminish his ardor.

"If only I'd been there to protect you from that lunatic," he said.

She leaned against him. As the cab's large wooden wheels trounced over the cobblestones, she said quietly, "It's not your fault, I should have waited until the sun was up to make my way back to the Bedford."

Anthony took her hand in his. "Regardless, I'll make everything up to you now."

She pulled away from him and looked deeply into his eyes. "Then you can start by giving me my freedom."

Anthony was taken aback by her forthrightness. He said, "Deseré, I—"

"I wanted to come back last night," she interrupted, her face hard and determined, "because I was afraid of staying here in Paris—afraid of the unknown."

"But, Deseré I—"

"But I've learned, after being trapped underground with that madman," her voice trembled, "that I don't have to be afraid. Like the Bible says, 'I can do all things through Christ which strengtheneth me.' So I've decided I *won't* go back to America with you unless you free me. Will you promise me that?"

"I'll—"

"Of course," she sat taller, again interrupting him, "someone once told me that a white man's promise ain't worth piss—if you'll pardon my language. So I reckon I need something more than a promise—a guarantee of some kind. But I don't know if—"

"I'll give you more than my promise," Anthony said, "more than a guarantee."

"So," Deseré looked at him, uncertain, raising a brow, "what'll that be?"

"I'll give you myself," Anthony said.

Deseré sat wide-eyed, saying nothing.

"I don't want you to be my slave...I want you to be my wife."

"Your...wife?" she blinked, as if not hearing him correctly.

Anthony pulled her close again, then once more grasped her hand and squeezed it. "Was being afraid of the unknown the only reason you wanted to come back to me?"

Her face softened. "Of course not, Anthony, I—I—"

"I love you, Deseré."

"Oh, Anthony...I—I—" She said no more as he covered her mouth with his. For several moments he kissed her, not pulling away until they bounced over a large bump in the road.

"I love you, too," Deseré finally said, breathless. "But why didn't you ever tell me you loved me before?"

"Because I was a fool. I was confused about so many things. I was afraid you hated me because of William; I thought you'd never love me back. But now the only thing

I'm certain of is that I can't live without you." He embraced her tightly, then kissed her again. Moving his lips to her neck, he said, "Deseré, this is the happiest moment of my life—knowing that you love me."

"Anthony..." she pulled away slightly to look at him, "I want to marry you, but we can't." Tears welled in her eyes. "And I can't help but reckon you know that. It's against the law for black and white to marry. Are you toying with me?" Tears slid down her cheeks.

At this, Anthony felt a jagged stab of pain through his heart. Feeling his own eyes well, he said in a shaky voice, "How could you think that after what I just declared? Do you not trust me?"

Deseré sniffed, then swallowed hard. "You're white."

Anthony felt as if the floor had dropped from under him. "Deseré," he said firmly, "I love you! I'll do anything for you, and I *will* prove my word to you!"

Deseré's eyes dropped to her lap for a moment, then meeting his gaze, she said, "The best we could do is live in sin—and I'd be willing to do that, as long as you'd promise—or guarantee me—that you'd never marry another."

"Deseré," he wiped tears from her cheeks with his thumbs, "it's against the law for black and white to marry in South Carolina, but not here in Paris. So will you, Deseré? Will you marry me and be my lawfully wedded wife?"

"Oh, Anthony," she smiled through tear filled eyes, "yes!"

As she embraced him tightly, Anthony felt the soft flow of his tears and hers against his cheek.

****

When they arrived arm and arm at the hotel, Deseré saw Mr. Youngblood sitting in the lobby on a gilded chair as if holding court, while surrounded by three younger gentlemen standing close by. One of the men bore a striking resemblance to Youngblood, as he was tall and thin with a

273

mustache and hooked nose. Probably his son, Deseré thought. One of the other men was as bald as a badger's backside, while the third had brightly colored hair more orange than red. Though the group had been immersed in conversation, with old Youngblood doing most of the talking, upon seeing Deseré with Anthony, they stopped. The four of them looked her up and down as if she were a piece of bruised prime rib on a spit.

Deseré felt herself shrink as she and Anthony walked toward the stairs, which were in the direction of the four men. Anthony nodded silently in greeting to them. Youngblood nodded in return and said, "So Ah see you found that waywud slave." Then he frowned at Deseré's sullied clothes and bruises. "And looks like she got huself in a mess uh trouble."

Deseré bit her lower lip. Anthony slipped his arm around her.

The bald man said to the older Youngblood, "She won't be runnin' away again, will she?"

Deseré felt Anthony's body stiffen. The hair stood at the back of her neck under the scrutiny of these white men who saw her as nothing but chattel.

Then the red haired man said, "Must be good to have huh back so she can start washin' his draw-ahs again."

Deseré trembled. Her eyes filled with hot tears of shame and humiliation, and she lowered them to the ground.

Anthony turned red. He inhaled deeply, ignoring the insults. "Pay them no mind," he said quietly. Deseré met his gaze, revealing her tears. She saw the hurt she felt reflected in his eyes as he said, "Pretend they don't exist, and hold your head high." Too crushed, she only raised her chin a little.

As they passed by the young man resembling Youngblood, Deseré heard him say, "She's a fine lookin' piece of propurty. Must be wurth every penny in the—as they say in Fransay—the boud-wah."

Mortified, Deseré held back her tears, yet she wanted to run away and hide, never to show her face again. But Anthony stopped, pulling his arm from around her. Then walking back to stand directly in front of the man, Anthony said, "What did you say?"

"Ah say-ed, she must be wurth every penny —"

Before he could finish, Anthony socked him in the jaw, knocking the man to the ground. Deseré gasped, putting a hand to her mouth as she watched, wide-eyed, while old Youngblood sat nonplussed observing the spectacle. A collective gasp erupted from all the well-dressed men and ladies in the lobby who turned toward the commotion, followed by snatches on *Mon Dieu*, *Potzblitz*, *Bloody Americans* and the like.

Deseré felt her heart burst as Anthony ignored the stares and comments of surprise he'd created. Instead, he looked down at the man sprawled on the floor like a giant broken peg doll with wiry limbs askew, holding his jaw.

"That's what I thought you said." Anthony glared at him.

"Treachery!" the bald man exclaimed, reaching down to help his fallen companion.

"Nigguh-lovuh!" the red haired man snarled, moving in to throw a punch at Anthony. Yet he was prevented by two hotel employees who rushed over to prohibit any further commotion.

Once the hotel staff restored peace and administered warnings that any further display of uncouth behavior would result in them being asked to leave the Bedford, the employees returned to their posts at the front desk. However, they continued to keep watch on the unruly Americans.

Then Anthony eyed the four men sharply. "How dare you! How dare you insult this lady, the lady I love, my future wife, the soon-to-be Mrs. Anthony Sinclair." He held out his hand to Deseré, who smiled as she walked to him, placing her hand in his. Anthony kissed her fingers. A flood of warmth filled her insides. To the dismay of the four men who looked on horrified, Deseré took a deep breath, and now beaming, raised her chin high. Then Anthony escorted her up the marble staircase.

She looked into his eyes and smiled, the tears now gone. "You make me feel like a queen."

"That's because you are," Anthony said.

****

After Anthony took Deseré upstairs to her room, he returned to the lobby. He stopped by the front desk to ask that the physician be sent to Deseré's room. Then he headed toward her portrait, still on display with the note asking of her whereabouts. Yet before he reached the painting, a firm hand touched his shoulder.

Anthony turned. Upon seeing Edith, he sighed.

"You owe me an explanation." She spoke through clenched teeth, her voice trembling with rage.

Dumbfounded, Anthony asked, "What do you mean I owe you—"

"Step outside with me," she insisted sharply.

"Edith, I'm rather busy, and shouldn't you be getting back to Germany *and* your husband?"

Edith threw back her shoulders. "I'd prefer not to make a scene in here like the one you previously provoked." Anthony pursed his lips, feeling as if he'd been caught in the act of a crime. "I witnessed the entire exchange as I was leaving the dining room," Edith said.

Anthony let out a deep breath, then followed her outside through the large glass doors. Once on the sidewalk, a brisk wind swept over them bringing with it enormous gray clouds and the smell of rain. A clap of thunder exploded in the distance as Edith's brown eyes darkened to black. "That Deseré—she's a—she's a *slave*? *Your* slave? You *own* her? And you say you're going to *marry* her? A *negro*?"

Anthony crossed his arms. "Yes to all of your questions."

"Oh!" Edith gawked, as raindrops began to fall. "And

just what will your mother think when I tell her of your latest endeavor?"

Anthony's eyes narrowed. "I'm not sure, but I am sure she'll be absolutely appalled when I tell her *you* showed up in my hotel room and stripped yourself nearly naked, as if you were nothing better than a *whore*."

Edith's face turned bright red as raindrops clung to the rim of her bonnet. "You wouldn't!"

He looked at her for a long moment. "I wouldn't. I have no reason to, do I?"

Lifting her chin, she said, "Then you're never going to tell her the truth about Deseré, are you?"

"Edith, that's none of your concern. Now, if you'll excuse me, I must tend to Deseré's well-being. Perhaps you should do the same for your husband." Anthony then circled away from her to enter the hotel.

But then Edith struck him with more words. "You, and your abominable life as a slave owner! She'll never really be your wife! When you do find someone *suitable* to marry, will she know about your concubine?"

Anthony turned to look at her one last time. "You're wrong, Edith. I love Deseré and she's the only one I wish to spend my life with. Goodbye." Anthony entered the hotel, leaving Edith alone on the sidewalk.

Chapter 37
Several Days Later

Deseré's eyes widened at the splendor surrounding her as she walked inside Saint-Étienne-du-Mont, one of the most beautiful churches in Paris, tucked behind the Pantheon in the Latin Quarter. It was Saturday, and she held fast to Anthony's arm, as Addie walked alongside her, smiling.

"And we thought we wouldn't see each other again," Addie chuckled. "Little did we know what Masta Anthony had planned."

Dr. Chenault walked ahead of them. "Father Deneuve," he called. This was the doctor's church and he'd spoken to the priest here a couple of days before. Fragrant with incense, the church's interior consisted of ornately carved pillars and elaborate stained-glass windows.

In moments a short white-haired man approached them wearing a long black robe over his stout physique. With a wide smile, he warmly clasped Dr. Chenault's hand. "Bonjour, Vincent and Madame Addie." He spoke with a thick French accent.

"Bong jour, Father Deneuve," Addie smiled.

"Father Deneuve," Chenault said, "allow me introduce

279

my friends, Mr. Anthony Sinclair and Miss Deseré Albright, the Americans I told you about."

After greetings were exchanged, Father Deneuve said, "Docteur Chenault has told me zat ze two of you wish to marry."

"That's right," Anthony said.

"Yet neizer of you are Catolic," Father Deneuve said.

"But as I explained," Chenault said, "their circumstance is rather unique. They won't be able to marry once they return home so a wedding here —"

"Oui, oui" Father Deneuve interrupted. "And I do, as you say, sym-pa-tize. As I promised, I spoke to ze bishop. Zis is a most unusual situation. However, when he considered your generous contribution to ze church on zeir behalf, he granted permission — after much prayer, of course."

Deseré and Anthony looked at Chenault in shock. The man reddened as Anthony said, "You made a contribution for us?"

"For love," Chenault mumbled.

"We certainly can't thank you enough," Anthony said.

Then Father Deneuve cautioned, "Just be aware zat what I perform here today, will be a legal ceremony only, I will in no way be administering a Catolic sacrament."

"But we will be legally married?" Anthony asked.

"Not married as Catolic," Father Deneuve said, "but, oui, you will be legally married here in France."

"That's all that matters to me," Deseré said, squeezing Anthony's arm.

"Mr Sinclair," Chenault said, "as a lawyer, I know you're aware that this ceremony between you and Miss Deseré will be null and void once you're back in South Carolina. However, I take it you won't see it that way, and you'll remain true to your word."

"After all he's been through for her, you gotta ask that?" Addie said incredulously.

Anthony only smiled. "As the Lord is my witness, Dr. Chenault, my word is my bond, and the vow I make as Deseré's husband I make for life."

****

Deseré wore an off the shoulder pale pink dress made of silk. A tier of diaphanous lace covered the bodice, and three additional lace tiers fell from the top, middle and bottom of her skirt. Anthony had told her she was a queen, and today she truly felt like one. And shouldn't she on her wedding day?

Except for the wedding party, the church was empty. As they stood before the altar, Deseré thought that never in her wildest dreams did she envision herself standing in a Catholic church, in Paris of all places, before a priest, of all things, marrying Masta Anthony, a white man she'd despised not that long ago! But here she stood beside him in Saint-Étienne-du-Mont, while Addie and Dr. Chenault, wearing their Sunday best, stood as witnesses to observe the simple ceremony.

Deseré gazed at the two openwork staircases that coiled themselves around large pillars on each side of the altar that led to the choir screen and gallery. The church, like so much of Paris, appeared similar to a royal residence in its extravagance. Then her eyes traveled to her very own king. Anthony, as handsome as ever, stood next to her, wearing a dark suit.

Deseré felt joyfully light-headed thinking about actually being Anthony's wife. It was the same way she'd felt after he'd read her the poem he'd written for her. But soon, Father Deneuve's voice brought Deseré back to the moment, as he said, "Antony, do you take Deseré for your lawful wife, to have and to hold, from zis day forward, for better, for worse, for richer, for poorer, in sickness and in health, until deas do you part?"

"I do," Anthony said.

"Deseré," Father Deneuve continued, "do you take

Antony for your lawful husband, to have and to hold, from zis day forward, for better, for worse, for richer, for poorer, in sickness and in health, until deas do you part?"

"I do," Deseré said.

The exchange of rings followed, and when Anthony slipped the gold band on Deseré's finger, she felt as if a thousand rose blossoms bloomed inside her.

"May ze Lord in his kindness strengzen ze consent you have declared," Father Deneuve said, "and graciously bring to fulfillment his blessings wizin you. What God has joined, let no man put asunder. May ze God of Abraham, ze God of Isaac, ze God of Jacob, ze God who joined togezer our first parents in paradise, strengzen and bless in Christ the consent you have declared, so zat what God joins togezer, no man may put asunder."

****

"Oh, Anthony," Deseré said, "I can't believe we're married!"

"We are," Anthony smiled, opening the door to his hotel room. After dinner and champagne with Addie and Dr. Chenault at the Rocher de Cancale, Anthony and Deseré returned to the Bedford, now needing only one room. "So. Mrs. Sinclair," he said, "are you happy?"

"Happier than I've ever been." She stepped out of her shoes.

"Turn around," Anthony said. As Deseré turned her back to him, he said, "I'd like to make you happier."

"How's that?"

"You'll see," Anthony said, as he slowly unbuttoned the back of her dress, then pulled it from her shoulders. Deseré eased it over her petticoats, then stepped out of it.

Turning to face him, she picked up the dress. "I should hang this up."

Anthony grabbed it from her hands and threw it to a chair. "It can wait." When he pulled her close, she laughed, enjoying the feel of his hard body against hers. Then he reached around her and untied the back of her petticoats. When they dropped to a puddle on the floor, Deseré stepped from them, leaving them where they'd fallen. "I suppose I'll hang them up later," she said.

"Good," Anthony smiled, then helped her remove her camisole. "Now turn around again so I can unlace that ungodly contraption."

Deseré ran her hands over the coutil cloth stiffened with whalebone. "My corset?" As she began to unbutton the front, she turned her back to him, letting him untie the lacing in the back. When he'd finished, she removed it and let him throw it to the chair along with her dress.

Feeling nervous, Deseré trembled as she circled to face him, wearing only her chemise, pantalettes, garters and stockings. When Anthony put his arms around her and kissed her lips, he pulled away seconds later and said, "What's wrong? You're shaking. Do I frighten you?"

"No." Deseré shook her head. "You don't, I mean. I'm — I'm only frightened of what's to come. Mama explained what would be expected on my wedding night when she thought I'd be marrying — well you know. She said it was a wife's duty and that I'd get used to it."

Anthony smiled, then lifting her chin to his face, said, "I promise I won't hurt you." He kissed her again, this time more passionately. Deseré pulled him close, never wanting him to stop, as her body throbbed with heat. When he did stop, leaving her wanting more, he said, "And perhaps you'll come to see what we'll do as more than your duty." He kissed her neck again, heightening her body temperature, "You might even deem it enjoyable."

Deseré's brows rose. "Enjoyable?" Although she thoroughly enjoyed hugging and kissing Anthony, the act itself, as described by her mother, sounded frightful, barbaric, even.

"Why don't you start by undressing me?" he asked.

Deseré gasped, then giggled, covering her mouth.

Anthony removed his shoes and socks. Then his jacket and cravat, throwing them to the chair with the other clothes. "You do the rest."

"Alright," Deseré said, beginning to unbutton his vest. With his help, she slipped it from his shoulders. Then she lowered his suspenders and moved to his shirt, unbuttoning it to mid-way his chest where the buttons ended. Then she pulled the cotton fabric from his trousers. Anthony raised his arms, allowing her to lift the shirt from over his head.

Deseré's eyes widened as she ran her hands over a broad chest that was fair and covered by dark curls. "My," she said, feeling the muscles of his pectorals and shoulders. "I've always wondered what you looked like underneath your clothes."

"I hope you're not disappointed," he said.

"Hardly," she smiled. "I had an idea the day I tailored that vest to fit you, but what I'm seeing now is certainly more than I imagined then.

Anthony cupped her breasts beneath the thin fabric of her chemise and kissed her deeply, causing a volcano to explode within her. "Oh...Anthony," she said as he moved her hands to his trousers and guided them to the buttons. While still kissing him, she unbuttoned the trousers, then pulled them down, over his hips.

Anthony remained only in drawers that came to his knees. Deseré pulled her lips from his and stepped back to admire him. Though still clad in drawers, his body was beautiful like the marble sculptures she'd seen in the gods in the Garden of Tuileries.

Feeling her heart race, Deseré said, "I've—I've never seen a naked man—a real one anyway—aside from all the naked statues I've seen in Paris." Then she remembered the vineyard in Burgundy. "Well—in Burgundy—there were three naked men I saw from a distance crushing grapes, but Addie told me not to look—to keep my eyes innocent."

"You needn't keep your eyes innocent with your

husband," Anthony grinned.

Deseré pulled on his waist band and peeked down into his drawers. "Oh," she said in wonder.

"Perhaps you can remove these," Anthony indicated his drawers, "while I remove the rest of your undergarments."

With eyes wide she said, "Then what?"

"Then I hope to make you even happier than you've ever been."

"But I couldn't be any happier now that I'm your wife."

"Then," Anthony said, "we'll have to see what you think afterwards." Kissing her again, more deeply than before, he slipped his hands underneath her chemise. The feel of his hands against her bare skin made her body tingle intensely as she unbuttoned his drawers. Once her chemise was gone, he moved on to her pantalettes unbuttoning, then sliding them from her body. Lastly, he removed her garters and stockings. Now both were unclothed and still kissing passionately. Anthony carried her to the bed.

"Anthony," Deseré said out of breath, "as long as you keep kissing me, I can't get any happier than I am now."

As he placed her softly on the bed, he replied, "Don't be so sure..."

****

"Happy," he asked, as she lay spent in his arms.

"Happier than I've ever been," she replied groggily.

Chapter 38

Contemplating their return to America, Anthony peered up at a blue cloudless sky as a flock of pigeons flew above. The aroma of fresh baked bread and exquisite Parisian coffee filled the air, while he and Deseré sat at the sidewalk café across from the Bedford having breakfast, as did several Parisians who sat nearby.

Over the rumble of horse-drawn vehicles and the buzz of conversation around them, Deseré said, "Our time in Paris has come to an end."

Anthony squeezed her hand. "We can't stay here forever, can we?"

"Even though it would be so much easier for us."

"Which makes it all the more tempting."

Deseré nodded. "But there's Pleasant Wood."

"Yes..." Anthony sighed wistfully. "Pleasant Wood... And I don't want to return to that life."

Deseré's mouth opened in surprise. "You — you don't want to go back?"

"I want to go back to America," he took a sip of coffee, "but not as a slaveholder. I don't know why I ever thought that even as a benevolent slaveholder, I could make owning people...a good thing."

"So...you want to sell the place?" Deseré asked, while an omnibus pulled by two white horses, clattered to a stop a short distance away.

"I'd like to sell the land," he paused, "but free the people."

Deseré's eyes widened to moons. "But where would they go?"

"I'm not sure. That's why I'm suggesting that once we return to New York, we book passage home through Cincinnati."

"Cincinnati?" Deseré pursed her lips. "Your home."

"Yes, and I'm suggesting we—"

"William's there." Deseré smirked, rolling her eyes.

Anthony smiled at her expression. "That's right."

"When you told me he'd be going there," Deseré laughed, "it was as if you took delight in rubbing salt into my wounds at the prospect of me never seeing him again."

Anthony felt his face blanch at the sting of her words. "Deseré, I'm sorry I—"

"You needn't be." She smiled. "I realize now that it was for my own good."

"But I am sorry for how I handled things; how I took control of your life when I had no right to. It's just that...I wanted you so badly. I...I overstepped my bounds."

"I'm glad you did," she said, "even though I hated you for it back then."

"But...you forgave me?"

Deseré remained silent for a moment. "Although I said I did...I didn't mean it at the time. I wasn't ready, but I felt I had to. You told me as my master to forgive you."

"Deseré, I never meant—"

She put a finger to his lips to quiet him. "But I forgive you now. I love you, Anthony. You made me realize that William never did love me and that I was worth nothing to him."

He grasped her hand in both of his. "But you're worth everything to me and more."

Deseré gazed deeply into his eyes. "I know. You've shown me in countless ways."

As a vendor passed by, Anthony motioned to him and bought three red roses for her.

Deseré smiled, inhaling the scent of the flowers. "Now let's us put talk of William behind us. You were going to tell me why you want to book passage through Cincinnati."

"It's because I have a friend there—"

"Henry Braithwaite?"

Anthony's brows rose as he looked at her strangely. "How did you know?"

Deseré' glanced toward a street vendor selling soaps. Live snakes crawled about him as he politely called out his wares. As if wanting to avoid Anthony's question, she remained fixated on the reptilian clad vendor longer than necessary.

"Deseré," Anthony said, "how did you know of Henry?"

She stayed silent a moment more before meeting his gaze. "I remembered his name; it's distinctive. And he sounded like an abolitionist, at least that's what I thought when I read a letter he sent."

Anthony tilted his head slightly. "You...read a letter he sent me?"

"Well..." Deseré blushed slightly, biting her lower lip, "not the whole thing."

"I see..." Anthony took a deep breath, slightly exasperated once again by her ferreting eyes. "Henry *is* an abolitionist and I believe he can guide me on how to proceed regarding the people of Pleasant Wood. He knows of places in Ohio, as well as Canada, where former slaves can settle."

"Oh?" Deseré said, her inquisitive eyes wide. "Where in Ohio? Where in Canada?"

Anthony paused for a moment. He honestly didn't know. "I'm not exactly sure," he finally said, "but I do believe they would meet the approval of the Pleasant Wood population."

"Are they nice?"

Again, Anthony was silent for a second. "I would reckon that they're not unacceptable."

"Are they safe?"

"Henry wouldn't suggest places that aren't." At least he felt somewhat confident of this.

"But are you certain?"

Anthony hesitated once more. "As certain as I can be."

"How would they survive?"

Anthony had been thinking about this. "I'd give each family money from the Pleasant Wood estate."

"How much?" Deseré asked.

"I don't exactly know yet. I'll have to take into account land, livestock, clothing, seed, lumber and other necessities. Everything needed for them to start their lives anew as free persons of color."

At one time, Anthony had been more concerned with keeping Pleasant Wood afloat with the money his Uncle Jeremy had left him in the estate. Yet now it seemed more important to rid himself of the place and disperse what funds he could to his soon-to-be former slaves.

As Deseré nodded, Anthony found himself waiting for her approval.

"I suppose your answers will satisfy me for now," she said, "but I'd like to speak with your friend, as well, and hear for myself what he has to say."

"I'd prefer that," Anthony said.

Deseré lifted her chin slightly, as if acknowledging the power she held over him that he couldn't deny. "Good," she said. "So, how is...William doing there as a free man?"

Anthony shrugged. "According to the last letter I received from Henry before we left, quite well."

Deseré nodded once more, then as she poured hot milk into her coffee, said, "Is talking with your friend the only reason you want to stop in Cincinnati? What about your kinfolk? You'll want to visit them, won't you?" She watched a well-dressed French woman walk quickly by the café accompanied by a little black poodle with bells on its collar.

"Of course," Anthony said, "because I want my mother to

meet my bride."

Deseré's stunned eyes quickly met his. "You—you want *me* to meet your mother?"

"Yes," Anthony replied calmly. "In one of her letters, she told me that she was praying that I'd find the perfect wife, since there were several southern belles from which to choose."

"But a *slave* wasn't what she had in mind!"

Anthony smiled, ignoring her astonishment. "Mother did suggest, however, that I be cautious in my choice, then quoted from Proverbs, 'Who can find a virtuous woman? For her price is far above rubies.'"

Her lower lip trembled slightly. "What will you tell her about me?"

"The truth," Anthony said simply. "That you're the orphaned daughter of a planter."

Deseré dropped her eyes to her lap, pulling her hand from his. "Whose mother was a slave violated by that planter." He could see that her skin crawled at the thought of her father, Creech. She'd told Anthony she'd never met the man, but only knew what her mother had told her of him.

"I'm sorry," Anthony said, grasping the hand she'd pulled away.

Deseré looked at him for a long moment. "Will you ever tell her I was your slave?"

"All things in due course," Anthony said, "and there's a timing for everything."

"And when would that be?" Her eyes bore deeply into his.

After a few seconds, Anthony said, "Both of us will have to pray about that, won't we?"

"I guess that's all we *can* do," she said quietly.

Anthony thought about his mother's possible reactions, then after several seconds began hesitantly, "Deseré...it is possible...that I could lose my mother, due to our circumstance, but—"

"No, Anthony," Deseré shook her head rapidly, "then never tell her! I couldn't live with myself if—"

"Deseré," he interrupted her, "I can't say I've ever been close to her. So if she chose to cut herself off from me, I'd feel it as no great loss. Besides," he smiled, "as long as I have you, nothing matters."

"But she's your mother," Deseré insisted.

Anthony inhaled deeply, considering an option he'd once thought about. Leaning close to her he said, "I *could* legally declare you as white."

"Declare me as white?" she blinked in question. "It's one thing to pretend...but legally, I'd have to leave behind who I am, turn my back on my people, and live a lie... forever." Her face etched with worry, Deseré lowered her gaze.

Anthony sat back in his chair. His shoulders stiff. Although she didn't appear keen on the idea, he would take on the task if she wanted him to. However, he'd have to lie as well. Only one of her parents was white. Legally stating that Patsy was, would be mere fabrication. While Deseré pondered what he'd suggested, Anthony remained silent hearing the roar and rattle of cabs, carriages and omnibuses that drove over the cobblestones in front of them.

After a short while, Deseré met his gaze, her eyes bleak. "It would be easier... I'll do it...if you want me to."

"The decision is yours," Anthony said.

Deseré sighed. "I—I don't think I want to. I wouldn't like it. I couldn't sleep at night, at least not peacefully."

Anthony's shoulders relaxed. "That's what I suspected. I was only introducing that as an option."

"If I did choose that path," she said, "I'd always be afraid someone would figure out the truth. I may be fair, but not fair enough to some. If I never deny who I am, I have nothing to hide."

He kissed her hand. "I love you as you are. And if my mother should choose not to love you because of your race, then she'll be inflicting a serious disadvantage upon herself. But I think she'll love you, and I won't tell her the truth about you until it's impossible for her not to love you."

Deseré laughed.

"Let's pray for that," Anthony said, "because I'm thinking of moving back to Cincinnati."

Deseré stopped laughing. "For good?"

"For good — once I've handled the Pleasant Wood affairs and helped the people get settled."

"But what if — what if life doesn't work out for us in Cincinnati?"

"It will, but if not, then we'll move somewhere else," Anthony assured her. "I look at moving from the South as a fresh start for both of us."

He'd never fit in as a planter to begin with, nor in his heart had he approved of slavery. Now in the small community of Saint Helena with Deseré as his wife, a woman known as a slave, he'd be a complete outcast living a life he despised. Deseré would be his only reason to go on, but he'd prefer his existence with her to be a worthy one.

"I've discovered that I'm not a planter," Anthony said, "nor a winemaker. I was a lawyer, I can go back to that. Instead of working for success and recognition — I could work for a cause."

"A cause?" Deseré asked.

"While living in a city considered the Gateway to the South, perhaps I can help the enslaved in Kentucky that want to escape."

Deseré's brows rose in surprise. "You mean...you want to be an abolitionist like your friend?"

Anthony sat quietly for a brief moment, a little uncertain of how to answer her. "I hadn't thought of it that way," he said, "but I suppose that's what I'd be."

Deseré smiled. "Then I could help you. I can be negro, or I can pass as white. We could work together."

"We could, couldn't we?" Anthony nodded, seriously

considering what she'd said.

Deseré sat tall, brimming with excitement. "Dr. Chenault and Addie said I could work for the abolitionist cause, but I was afraid. Then I was tested by fire down in those catacombs. I know I can do it now. And perhaps, I can even teach in a colored school."

Anthony smiled. "What greater way is there to help your people than ensuring their freedom and providing them an education?"

"Anthony," Deseré said, the titillation still in her voice, "somebody once told me—well, it was William that told me—all I had to do was sit around looking pretty. That wasn't true when he said it, busy as I was at Pleasant Wood, and now I'm seeing things God wants me to do!"

Anthony laughed at her exuberance, then sobered, thinking of himself. "I've too many shortcomings for God to use me," he said.

"No, Anthony, you want to be an abolitionist! That's doing God's work. You know that. And besides, God can use all of us, despite our shortcomings."

Anthony raised his coffee cup. "Shortcomings and all, here's to His work." Deseré clinked her cup to his. "But," he slowly lowered his cup to the table, "abolitionism is a rather...dangerous undertaking."

This didn't dampen Deseré's spirit. "If God wants you—us—to pursue it," she said, "He'll make a way. He says, 'I will not fail thee, nor forsake thee.' And Mama used to quote Joshua chapter one, verse nine. 'Be strong and of good courage, be not afraid, neither be thou dismayed: for the Lord thy God *is* with thee whithersoever thou goest.'"

****

Anthony stood hand and hand with Deseré on the deck of the ship sailing back to America, while breathing in the slight smell of soot that infused the air. The steamer's powerful engine was at work while a fair wind blew fresh salt air against their faces. Anthony gazed into the ocean.

The sea was dark, beautiful and the deepest blue, its waves appearing sheathed in glass from the sun's shining rays. The water hissed and splashed as the ship sliced through its ridges, while long sheets of bubbling foam ran off the sides of the vessel. Moving his eyes to Deseré's profile, Anthony admired her comeliness and pondered their new life to come. His mind raced, yet he couldn't see past the beauty that had caused him to put appearances and social standing aside. What would his mother think when she did find out the truth about Deseré? What would she think of their work as abolitionists?

Since his younger brother had come along, it had been impossible for Anthony to please his mother. So what did it matter if she liked Deseré or not? And though his mother had ill feelings toward slavery, abolitionists were bad for business for Cincinnati's slave-holding neighbors to the south in Kentucky.

Taking in a deep breath, Anthony tried to calm his mind. Then Deseré turned to face him. Her blue eyes sparkled like sapphires as wind-blown strands of golden curls surrounded her face. She smiled with elation and courage. "A new life awaits you."

Anthony stroked her cheek, appreciating the soothing cadence of her voice that put his mind at ease. "A new life awaits us both."

"And together," she said, "with God's help, we'll conquer its challenges."

Anthony cupped Deseré's face in his hands, then kissed her under the shimmering sunlight above.

CITATIONS

Bible quotations from *The King James Version*

Galignani, A. and W. *Galignani's New Guide of Paris*. Paris: Galignani. 1830.

Watts, Isaac. *Hark! From the Tombs a Doleful Soul*. 1707.

Watts, Isaac. *When I Can Read My Title Clear*. 1707.

Wesley, Charles. *Jesus, Lover of My Soul*. 1738.

ABOUT THE AUTHOR

Maria McKenzie is the author of the Amazon bestsellers *The Governor's Sons*, books one through three of *The Unchained Trilogy: Escape, Masquerade* and *Revelation,* and *From Cad to Cadaver.*

She lives in Cincinnati with her husband and two boys. Before becoming a stay-at-home mom, small business owner and author, she worked in Georgia and North Carolina as a librarian for several years.

To visit or contact Maria, go to www.mariamckenziewrites.com. Find her blog, interviews, reviews, novel excerpts, help for writers, published articles and more!

AUTHOR'S NOTE

When I finished writing my first mystery novel, *From Cad to Cadaver,* in 2015, I debated about what to write next, another mystery or go back to historical fiction. My first love is historical fiction, but I had such fun writing the mystery because it was a comedy and I got to exercise my funny bone! My decision was made, however, when Dr. Alpen Razi of California Polytechnic University contacted me about working with him on a project for his African Survey Class, which I agreed to do. I provided the class with a novel synopsis, and Dr. Razi assigned different categories based on the synopsis for the students to research using slave narratives.

Needless to say, historical fiction won as far as what to write next. The idea for *Deseré* had been floating around in my head for years, so it was rewarding to finally write it. The reports I received from Dr. Razi's class, based on the slave narratives they researched, were quite enthralling and some of them inspired scenes that appear in *Deseré*, such as the prologue showing Deseré as a child, William's backstory, and Careen's past.

In doing research for *Deseré,* I used many sources, including some narratives I discovered through Dr. Razi's students, including *My Life in the South* by Jacob Stroyer and *Life on the Old Plantation in Antebellum Days* by Irving E. Lowery.

To learn about an actual cotton plantation, I used *Tombee: Portrait of a Cotton Planter*, which contains the journal entries of Thomas B. Chaplin, the plantation owner. This source inspired me to place Pleasant Wood on the Sea Islands. *A Social History of the Sea Islands* by Guion Griffis Johnson was extremely useful in doing my research, as was a novel I stumbled upon by Bonnie Stanard entitled *Kedzie: A Saint Helena Island Slave*. Ms. Stanard's work was quite informative, especially since she is a Sea Island native.

A visit to Poplar Grove Plantation in Wilmington, North Carolina helped me in describing the layout of the interior of the Pleasant Wood big house.

In researching travel to Paris in the 1800's, I used *The Greater Journey* by David McCullough and *The Travels of William Wells Brown*. Both were invaluable!

I used many other sources, but those mentioned above were the most helpful.

I apologize and take full responsibility for any and all historical and grammatical errors.

Thank you for reading *Deseré: A Love Story of the American South*, and I hope you enjoyed it! Please stop by and visit me at www.mariamckenziewrites.com. Use the contact page to drop me a line. I'd love to hear from you!

Maria McKenzie

Made in the USA
Lexington, KY
20 July 2019